Must Thee Fight

Cover design by Christo Brock
Cover painting by Dennis Goldsborough
Editors, Derek Stedman, Elizabeth Bunting

Edgmont Publishing
257 Great Valley Parkway,
Malvern, PA 19355

Copyright © 2006 Lynmar Brock
All rights reserved.
ISBN: 1-4196-5968-5
Library of Congress Control Number: 2006903162

To order additional copies, please contact us online.
Amazon.com
Borders.com
Booksurge.com
or
orders@Booksurge.com
1-866-308-6235

Must Thee Fight

A Novel

Lynmar Brock

Lynmar Brock

2006

Must Thee Fight

For Claudie

Chapter One

Thomas Pratt backed the horse towards the carriage and taking the leather traces, attached them to the crosstree. He then brought the reins back and laid them over the front rail. He grabbed a handful of grassy weeds that grew alongside the fence and pulled them up from the drying earth, shaking the loose dirt off. He ran the clean upper ends quickly along the black leather of the carriage's cover, pushing the dust off and spreading what was left in a mottled thin film. The horse flipped its tail to keep the flies moving off its rump and stomped its rear leg as if to add an emphasis.

The day was bright and clear, with white, puffy clouds slowly drifting across the sky, framed by the green of the buttonwood trees, which grew along the creek banks. It was Sixth Day, Saturday, in July of 1776, and Jane Pratt and her daughter were readying themselves to go up and across the narrow dirt road to visit Esther Green at a neighboring farm. There was quilting to be done and others would be there.

Thomas had heard from Annie, one of their daughters, that the Congress meeting in Philadelphia had declared war or something like that against the English. But that was all he knew.

"Father," he asked of Joseph Pratt, "what is this Declaration?"

Joseph kept on working, forking the first cutting of the dried hay into the loft of their small barn. Sweat coursed down in thin spaced out rivets across his face and neck. His shirt was stained and rent where the sleeves had caught stalks of weeds mixed in with the softer grasses of the hay necessary to feed the animals during the cold winter months.

Pausing, Joseph turned to his youngest son standing there with questioning eyes. Thomas had just turned 20, was lithe but strong, shoulders and arms muscular from constant farm work. He was taller than either of his parents. He was even taller than William at 22, who still lived at home not yet having asked the Yarnall girl to marry.

Thomas' hair was light brown growing long, forcing him to keep pushing it aside, away from his face. His deep brown eyes shone out from regular features, angular and handsome, freckles scattered across the bridge of his face. The sun had colored his fair skin with a reddish cast, lighter than the bronze which more clearly marked his father. Muscles of his arms showed as he rested his hands on the rail, still looking at his father.

"Father?" Thomas asked again.

"I don't know," Joseph finally answered. "I'm not sure." He thought for a minute. "We'll inquire a bit at Meeting tomorrow." His face was covered with dried speckles of crushed leaves caught among the grasses as they fell down sticking to his face by the sweat which had not yet run off his brow.

"If it means that the British will come with soldiers like in Boston and New York, what will happen here in Philadelphia?"

Joseph looked at his son with a longing concern. "We farm here. We avoid trouble and we thank our God for the peace and security we have here. Those around us are good people. We farm our hundred and fifty acres and we sell our product in Philadelphia." He waited, and then with a direct emphasis, looked carefully into the eyes of his youngest son, who was now full grown with a yearning, expectant face, full of trust, but ready to break forth from the parental strictures governing their Quaker household. "General Washington is fighting the British around New York. Here in Pennsylvania, it's quiet. We live with our neighbors and can worship as we please. The British are our heritage and the law's fair, the same for everyone. We pay our taxes. We sell our grain and flax and beef to merchants in Philadelphia. They pay us and we buy what we need. Salt, seeds for the next year and cloth we don't weave ourselves. It's enough, and here we can get everything else, shoes from the cordwainer, while the forge at Howellville repairs our iron. We have our own cows with milk, butter, cheese, and meat for ourselves, and our garden is fertile." Joseph was talking faster. He looked away from his son at the small fields that stretched out before him. The wheat was turning a golden color. Leaves in the garden were showing a pale green as vegetables ripened under the summer sun. Blossoms had fertilized under the wide green of the vines, squash and pumpkins were filling in shaping towards maturity. Joseph Pratt was satisfied. There was a certain comfort in his sweat. It showed work, work produced results and helped raise his family, some of who now had children of their own. He turned back to look at Thomas.

"We have a good life here, Thomas. George Fox spoke of peace and it's part of our Quaker testimony, and William Penn made it possible by getting this land from Charles the Second and opening it up to not only Quakers, but Lutherans, Anglicans, Jews, Baptists, even Catholics. He made peace with the Indians, which has been kept ever since. He bought land from them, fairly, even though the king made Penn the sole proprietor. Penn treated with the

Swedes and Finns and Dutch who were here before and gave us peace." Joseph had warmed to his thoughts.

"But father, if we want peace and the English don't, then what are we to do?"

Joseph smiled at his son. "Pray and hold to our faith. Keep the Lord's testimony." Then with emphasis, he said, "And never take up arms to kill another." His lips were firm as he slowed his speaking. His eyes had narrowed and his face hardened. "War begets war. Killing begets killing. People lose reason. Society dissolves."

"But can we stand by and let others decide our future for us? Can't we take a part in our own destiny?" There was a plea within his voice.

Joseph was subdued now. He answered softly. "Yes, by understanding one another and talking and working together, even if it takes a much longer time." He was finished. He moved the pitchfork away from the last pile he had heaved into the mow and turned to gather more of the hay from the wagon to continue his chore.

Thomas was not sure. *Do we have a responsibility to do something?* He realized the conversation was at an end. He slowly moved away from the railing and headed back down towards the pen where the three pigs were kept. He looked over at them, two shifting carefully in the drying mud, delicate as they moved the dirt over their rounded backs and haunches. The other was stepping in the waste corner, moist with the rich pungent odor from their defecations. *Messy pig,* thought Thomas looking over at their big boar who seemed to always make a mess. *Why can't you be like your sisters?* His mind shifted. *But we should do something. Can we just ignore what everyone else thinks? Or does?* He stopped and watched their pigs as each of them pursued a different method of staying comfortable in the burgeoning heat of July.

He was sweating, but not like his father. There was no fat on him. Joseph was a bit more round at the waist, not much to show, but Thomas was flat, slight ripples of muscles over his abdomen. *If only the thunderstorms will not come and wet the hay before we can get it into the barn,* he thought, *dry and sweet with the concentrated smell of the fields, then it will last over the winter, saved under layers of the tangled strands of grass and packed away to nurture our cows and steers and oxen and horses.* He mused on their animals, each playing a function on the farm. The cow provided milk, the sheep wool, the pigs and chickens were slaughtered for meat, the horses and oxen to ride, or draw the wagon, or plow. They were important to the routine of the farm as each year followed another, the months changing from growing to resting in the inevitable sequence. The pattern was the same. The animals knew it and accepted the ongoing routine. It was the way it always was.

Except that this year it was different and Thomas was uneasy. There was an undercurrent in the regularity of their lives that suggested change. Some of their neighbors who were not Quaker talked more openly about the British. Their soldiers had fired on Washington's Continental Army in Massachusetts and New York. *If they did that, is it possible they would come to Philadelphia with soldiers? Would they fire on the people in Philadelphia? Or worse, on some of our neighbors?* Thomas walked slowly back from the creek, staying in the line of the trees and out of the sun towards the house. Questions kept coming into his mind. He wanted to ask his mother with the hope she would ask the women gathered for the quilting what they thought. Most were Quakers, but Esther Green was not. She would have heard from her man what was going on outside Edgmont Township. Quakers tended to keep to themselves and when they went into Philadelphia, they mostly talked with other Quakers, except when business was concerned. Then they spoke directly with anyone, but not much about the war in New England. Thomas was confused. It was only at the Quaker Meeting at Willistown that he could talk openly with the other young men of his age about peace and fighting, and ignoring all the problems, or getting mixed up with those who wanted to use force. He was anxious for the following day, meeting day. It was a challenge to sit quietly for an hour in the silence of the Meeting for worship, to listen to the occasional messages from the older and more weighty members of the Meeting as they shared their inspired thoughts emanating from an unseen force. Sometimes, he felt a certain mystery in the process, but mostly he kept thinking of the war up north, or more and more about Annie Green who lived on the farm close by. She might not be a Quaker, but she had an encouraging smile and a cute toss of her head. *She is a little heavy*, he thought, *but with an obvious warmth in her movements.* But that would be for tomorrow. He headed into their stone farmhouse, new sections added over the years, solid, firm walls from the stones and rocks that had been gathered from the fields and streams and assembled into a dwelling that spoke of a deep foundation of purpose and belief. "Mother," he called. Not waiting for reply, he added, "The cart is ready. The horse has been hitched." His mother and little sister, Abigail, were gathering their sewing chatelaines into their little cloth bags. His mother stopped to put on her large, sugar scoop bonnet. She smiled at her son.

"That's good, Thomas." She took a last look in the small mirror hung by the front door. It was a concession to the Quaker reluctance for self admiration.

"Mother?" Thomas asked again.

"Yes." She stopped, knowing there was more to come.

"Is thee going to talk about this new Declaration of Independence we hear about? At the Greens?" He stood by the door as if almost to block her way out.

"If it comes up," she replied sweetly. "I'm not sure that I want to be the first to ask, because I'm not sure what it means." She thought to herself, *And I don't want to appear such an ill-informed person.*

"Well, will thee tell me what thee finds out?" he continued.

"Yes, dear. I'll let thee know," she said as she climbed up onto the seat. Thomas settled the reins in his mother's hands. The carriage backed onto the path then headed towards the crest of the hill. The crunching of the iron wheel rims hitting the gravel and small rocks faded away as Thomas headed into the pasture to lead their cow back to the undercroft of the barn. It was his job to milk twice a day with an unremitting regularity. It was a comfortable routine.

***

It wasn't until much later that Thomas heard the cart creaking and bouncing along the path to announce the return of his mother and sister. He hurried to the bottom of the slight grade leading towards the barn and wagon shed. His mother had a soft smile on her face. She leaned over towards Thomas to acknowledge his waiting.

"Well, Mother?" he asked.

"We had a fine time," she replied. Thomas helped his mother down off the seat of the carriage. His sister jumped down from the other side. When she alighted onto the ground, she added, "Thank thee, dear."

"Did thee hear anything?" Thomas was impatient. "About the fighting up north and this Declaration?"

"No dear. Not much. We just talked about one another and because the Greens aren't Quakers, we really didn't talk much about our response to the danger of war."

"Did anyone know anything?"

"Not really." She smiled at him. "We'll just have to wait for one of those newspapers to reach out here." She walked slowly towards the house. Thomas stood there, disappointed, slowly unhitching the horse.

Chapter Two

First Day dawned clear with the humidity hanging low against the top of the woods as the trees stretched out surrounding the small open fields. The far ridge began to fade into a misty, blending of the sky, submerged in the heavy heat.

Thomas had put on his best linen shirt and heavy dark trousers of honest wool and linen. The combination was kept for Sundays and special events. Clothes were too precious to have more than one good set. The work day shirts and trousers had been handed down from father to older sons and then finally to Thomas. Thomas didn't mind. It had always been that way. *At least my Sunday shirt is mine alone,* he thought. He liked it. It fit loosely. It allowed for growth.

The rest of the family assembled after the necessary early-morning chores were finished. First Day (as Quakers called it avoiding using the word Sunday with its pagan origin) was for Quaker Meeting, for worship, and visiting. It was God's day.

They climbed into the carriage. Joseph and his wife sat on the front seat. Thomas, his brother, and sister squeezed into the back. They began the three mile ride to Willistown Friends Meeting. It was the same ritual, a break in the routine of work that provided inspiration for the week ahead. For most, there was the barely concealed pleasure of talking with neighbors.

Everyone gathered into the simple building that served during the week as schoolhouse, and for worship on First

Day. From a distance, it was difficult to distinguish one family from another by their clothing. They wore all the same browns, grays, and blacks of the simplest cut, with bonnets shading the features of the women, and dark, broad-rimmed hats on the men. It was by the horses and numbers of children riding behind that identified the families.

The Meeting settled into worship. Thomas couldn't get his mind off the possibility of British soldiers coming into Philadelphia, or even possibly into Chester County where they lived. He barely heard the occasional messages being offered. He looked over where he could see his friends with their parents looking suitably religious. And then, one of them turned slightly towards Thomas. It was obvious he also had thoughts other than those of God. The time seemed to drag until, finally, two of the elders sitting on the facing benches shook hands and the meeting was over. People raised their heads, shook hands one with another, and offered greetings. Soon the meetinghouse was lively with conversation. Thomas eased off the bench and headed outside where he knew his cousins would come. He stood by the side of the rail where the horses were tethered. Soon the other young men sauntered over.

"Hi," Thomas said with a single wave of his hand.

"Morning," replied Benjamin Darlington.

"'day," added Abner Baldwin. They were cousins and of a similar age.

Benjamin Darlington was taller than the other two, straight, with fair skin and a few freckles, and reddish hair that went with his hazel eyes. He parted his fine hair in the center, cut evenly around the edges, which kept it from the collar of his shirt on the back of his neck. His hands were big with calluses from constant work around the farm.

Abner Baldwin was shorter, stocky with hard muscles, dark hair, dark brown eyes, and a complexion clear but slightly browned both by birth and the constant sun. He was good looking even with his pronounced nose and ears that seemed to come out from the side of his head a little too far as if to support the unruly mass of hair that fell off his round head.

It was the one time in the week when they were together. They had all gone to school here, walking in from their various farms, but that had ended three years ago. They knew their letters and their numbers and calculations. They had read from the classics, and they knew their geography, for education was important to the Quakers, boys and girls alike. But now the three of them worked year round on their families' farms which was the greatest education of all, of crops and weather and animals and birth and life and death either by design or merely by the end of life.

"You still watching over Annie Green?" Abner asked. "She's not bad looking."

"But a bit plump," added Benjamin.

"How does thee know?" asked Thomas defensively.

"I see her occasionally at the store at Sugartown," Benjamin said. "But she's got looks," he quickly added with some honesty and to make Thomas feel better. He cocked his head waiting for an answer.

Thomas considered. "Yes. I do see her occasionally. We share some labor on their farm," he continued by word of explanation. "She's hard to miss. I go over to help her father bring in some crops and there she is. And then I go to borrow one of their oxen and she is still there, just kind of waiting." He stopped and frowned. Then smiled. "She's not so bad."

"I bet," agreed Abner.

"And then what?" Benjamin asked. "Anything more?" He dropped his voice, waiting for the confidential answer for only the three of them.

Thomas thought about it. And then with a rush of bravura and success, answered, "Well, we did kiss."

"She let thee?" asked Abner in modest disbelief.

"Well, let's say she came close and worked her lips around and they kept getting in the way. And it was the only way I could get past her."

"Was anybody looking?" Benjamin was interested.

"Not behind the barn away from the house. I could hear her father calling to get the ox ready. Her sisters were at school. She knew all that."

"What was it like?" Benjamin persisted.

Thomas smiled. "Nice. And warm."

"Did she come close?" asked Abner.

"That's the only way to kiss." Thomas looked around to make sure no one else was close enough to listen in. "And then she squeezed a little bit." Thomas was satisfied to share his experience with the others. They had always shared. They learned and questioned and wondered. They knew animals. That was simple, but girls were different. They would or they wouldn't. You never knew, and to get ready for a kiss with your eyes half closed and to be met with an empty space with wide open eyes on the other side of that space was a mortification. But when the warmth of the soft lips met yours and lingered, then that was something else. The animals never knew or understood that. They didn't need to, but girls knew and Thomas and his friends hoped they knew also. But it was always a chance, nice when it worked out and succeeded, and Thomas had succeeded in a satisfying little victory. It was good to share with his two best friends. He knew they would share their dreams with him, especially if they were fulfilled. Fathers might know all this, but you never really asked your father and it was hard to think of your mother having really shared such deep thoughts. They understood something fine must be true between their parents, else, how were they to be born? And little sisters knew nothing, but that was not the problem for the three of them. That was for their mothers to settle.

Thomas shook his head, the thoughts of Annie Green shifting into the background. "What about this Declaration coming out of Philadelphia? Do you know anything about it?" Thomas looked first at Benjamin, then at Abner.

Benjamin shrugged his shoulders. "Only that there was one."

Abner brightened. "Well. Father, who works part of the week at the tavern along the road leading to Philadelphia, overheard the drovers talk about it. He told mother—and me," he quickly added, indicating some increasing importance at the kitchen table. "It's called a Declaration of Independence and that the Continental Congress meeting in Philadelphia determined to be free of Great Britain."

"And then what?" encouraged Thomas. "What will happen now?"

"Well, father said that because we're already fighting, the war would spread. The British don't want us to be free. They want us to stay as colonies so that they can buy our food and lumber and other natural products, and we'll buy their manufactured goods."

"Has there been any reply from the governor?" asked Benjamin.

"Father didn't say. I guess the drovers hadn't heard, but there still hasn't been enough time for an official reply from London."

"With British troops in New York, that's the real answer, regardless what anyone says." Thomas looked out over the burial ground set beside the meeting house where the small, simple grave stones set in rows in an interrupted pattern were an indication of the brevity of life and the finality of death. It was all the natural progression, but to *be killed as a soldier was unnatural, and was it necessary?* Thomas thought to himself and then, out loud as if to continue his mind, he said, "So if there is fighting and the army comes here, should we join and fight?"

Thomas, with a stark clarity, had distilled the question of the new Declaration of Independence to the base reality of its importance to the three of them. The others had not wrestled with the significance of the document in those immediate terms.

"I don't know," Benjamin admitted. "My Father says we, as Quakers, stand for peace. Let others fight."

"My father didn't say," Abner added. "But I know he's not comfortable with all this talk of fighting. Any time mother brings up the question, he becomes silent and doesn't answer." Abner shook his head. "I don't know either."

"Well," Thomas replied, "if there is to be fighting here in Pennsylvania, if the British send an army here to take away our freedom, then I think we have to fight." He said it with a hesitancy working through the implication of his thoughts. His eyes left the burial ground and came back into focus first on Benjamin, then Abner. "I think I would fight," he said, and then with more confidence, he added, "I think we have to fight. If I think others need to fight, then I feel that I would need to join them. It's only right. If I want an outcome, then I have an obligation to help make it possible." His voice became lower with the firmness that suggested a determination.

"Then will thy father allow thee?" asked Benjamin. "Mine wouldn't."

"Maybe he won't, but I'm almost 21 and I can handle a rifle."

"Yes, but killing a deer for food is different than killing a soldier, even if it is to support the Pennsylvania government."

"But with this Declaration, they say it's now for more than this Commonwealth. It's for all the colonies." Thomas became resolute as he continued to explore his reasons. "If the British want to take away our liberties and control us from London, not let us farm here, not be able to sell our produce where we want, and make us do what they want, then we lose our ability to govern ourselves. It's not right for others so far away to make decisions for us."

"And so you'd join the army?" asked Abner.

"Maybe. If there's an army to join."

"Well, Father also heard that Edgmont Township is forming a militia to help the Continental Army of General Washington if it becomes necessary, which some of the men coming out of Philadelphia say it will."

"Then I might join them. It wouldn't be full-time. I'd still work on the farm and be home most of the time. I think father might let me do that." But Thomas was not sure.

"But what about the elders here at Willistown Meeting? They'd never allow it." Benjamin was secure in his analysis of the Meeting. "Thee would probably be read out of Meeting. Thee'd not be a Quaker anymore." He shook his head. "That'd be bad."

"Or maybe not as bad as doing nothing and letting others decide for us, do all the work for us, fight for us. Is that right?"

"Is God first?" Abner was quizzical.

"Will there really be a God if we're not free to worship as we will?" Thomas was intense.

"Yes, if it stays the way it is now."

"But it's not going to stay the way it is now. The British won't let it and now the Congress won't let it."

"But is it that important?" Abner was not sure of the question.

"I think Thomas is going to say that it is." Benjamin was musing and felt Thomas needed some support.

"Yes it is," agreed Thomas. "I think we need the courage to stand up and do what's right and necessary. Else we lose whatever we have now and that would be wrong."

They were silent, each thinking of his own situation. Abner took off his hat and scratched around his ears. Thomas watched, then observed, "Trying to get thy mind to work?"

"Maybe it's working too much," laughed Abner. "If I tickle it, maybe it'll stop thinking."

From the far side of the courtyard, Joseph Pratt called, "Ready there, Thomas?"

"Yes, Father," Thomas said with a bit of resignation and then said louder, "I'll bring the carriage on up." He turned to his friends. "Let me know what more you learn. It's really important."

"Sure," Benjamin said.

"I'll tell thee what I hear," Abner said, and then in a more conspiratorial tone he added, "but thee needs to tell us about Annie."

"Sure. Sure. Everything, if there is anything." Thomas was casual.

"Oh, there'll be," Benjamin said.

"She is interested," Abner said.

Thomas was quiet as he loosened the reins from the rail and turned the horse away towards the meeting house. He had a slight grin on his face. He was afraid his friends might see it, then again, he rather hoped they would.

Chapter Three

"Tomorrow we'll go across and help Abel Green bring in his hay," Joseph said to his family as they sat around the great table for the midday meal. Joseph always sat at the head in the only chair that had arms. His sons were in their normal places, without formal agreement, but always in descending order of age. Abraham, the oldest, had come from his own farm close by to help his father and brothers scythe their hay to let it dry in the sun.

"Why didn't Abel have at least one son?" asked William. "It always seems that we're doing his work for him."

"It's not so wrong to have daughters," his older brother, Abraham, said in defense of his brother.

"Just because you're already married and settled doesn't mean that a farm doesn't need men." William warmed to the subject.

"But then, Thomas here wouldn't have the chance to visit those girls and make it seem natural. After all, even if they're too young for us, at least the oldest is Thomas' age." They both looked at Thomas, William poking him in the ribs with his elbow. Joseph raised his eyebrows in expectation of a reply.

It was their mother who spoke. "Now you two leave Thomas alone. Those girls are nice even if they are not Quaker." She brushed her skirt smooth.

"Less temptation?" quizzed William.

"Maybe more," Abraham said, egging them on.

"A man is fortunate to have children to grow up," their father said, steering the conversation away from the subject in which he felt uncomfortable in front of his own daughter, Abigail, just turning thirteen. "There's a place for boys and a place for girls," he concluded as simply as he could.

"Good thing there're girls around," William said, nodding. "Our Thomas here would be lost in a community of only men."

Thomas blushed.

"Is that why he is always anxious to help the Greens?" Abraham asked. He had been gone from the family farm for two years.

"I never knew a fellow so agreeable to bring in another man's hay," William said.

"He's just doing a neighborly thing," Jane said of her youngest son.

Thomas tossed his head slightly and lowered his eyes, afraid to agree too openly.

"The hay still needs to be brought in," Joseph said, "and daughters can't do it as well or as quickly as we can, especially if there's a chance for a thundershower wetting that hay down on the field." He hoped to put an end to the subject.

Abraham continued. "So Thomas, when was the last time you visited the Greens? It's a fair walk if I remember."

Thomas looked up. The family was all looking him.

"Is that where thee was?" asked Jane of her son.

Thomas looked around and then at his mother. They were all quiet waiting for an answer. There was no way out. "Yes, Mother. I did visit the Greens."

"I'm not sure that's a good thing," his mother said quietly. "Abel Green keeps the tavern at Edgmont and he might not always be at home."

Thomas was silent.

"Maybe Thomas feels that every farm needs a man and

if one is away, then it's a neighbor's duty to fill in," Abraham offered in support.

"I think the Greens can manage quite well when Abel is at the tavern," Jane persisted.

"Tomorrow we'll go," Joseph said. "Abel still needs our help, just as his daughters come here to help your mother in the spinning and weaving of flax. It's share around as we have the ability. It's God's way."

Jane nodded approvingly, especially as she felt the conversation drifting onto a more comfortable subject.

The midday dinner was quickly finished and the brothers were first up and to the door.

"Father, we'll finish cutting the lower field," Abraham said. "Then we can help thee turn the cutting of yesterday in that upper far field." He didn't wait for a response as he led his two younger brothers out, each putting on their broad-brimmed straw hats, and gathering the great, long-bladed scythes. They headed down and across the snake fence towards the field of tall grasses waving in the gentle breezes of August, peaceful and soft, surrounded by woods, the trees tall and close, the green canopy of leaves making the under carpet cool and still.

Thomas hurried to catch up with Abraham and William as they strode side-by-side down from the house. "Why the hurry?" he asked.

"Sooner there, sooner done," Abraham called back, "and I need to be at home tonight to care for my own wife and thy little niece."

"But thee'll come back tomorrow?" Thomas asked.

"I'll go straight to the Greens," Abraham said. "Less time to waste. Quicker, in hopes we can finish by nightfall." He kept up his fast pace, now leading as the path narrowed.

The afternoon sun bore down on the four of them,

Joseph having joined his three sons as they swung the scythes back-and-forth in a regular motion. The grasses lay in an even pattern on the ground, just deep enough to let the heat dry the stalks within a day, avoiding the chance of rain which might mold the hay and make it less appealing to their cattle. Joseph rolled up his sleeves, sweat breaking out on his brow and chest.

"Is easier with you," he called out, standing aside to announce a break in the routine. The others stopped and leaned on their tall handles, the wood of ash worn smooth by the constant rubbing of their hands. "Done by nightfall," he confirmed, surveying the remainder of the field, "and thee'll get home," he said, looking at Abraham. "My thanks for it."

"Thanks enough to have William and Thomas over to help me," said Abraham smiling at his two younger brothers.

"Better we're thy brothers rather than thy sisters," replied Thomas. He straightened up.

"Will of the Lord," Joseph said.

"God was in his right mind," William said.

"Careful," said Joseph. "God acts in His own way."

"I'm still glad to be a man," Thomas said.

"At least it's better for the hay," replied Abraham. "Father's and mine."

Joseph took up the scythe and began a new row. The others followed. They were quiet, working down towards the edge of the field in the final areas.

* * *

The following morning, the household awoke as the dawn started to lighten in the east. Cold water splashed on their faces, hands washed in the same bowl, Jane and her daughter were more careful, using a bit of the coarse soap to wash their hands and behind their ears. The men quickly drew on their shirts and trousers, laced up the boots, and headed down to the kitchen. Thomas went to the barn to milk the cow while William added small wood to the hot embers to encourage the fire to come to flame again for the new day.

"We'll start early, Mother," said Joseph to his wife as she came into the kitchen. "It looks like a clear day. We hope to be done with this cutting and get all the hay in the barn before nightfall." He sat down as the bread and cheese were placed in front of him. They were silent, each thinking their own thoughts.

William finished cutting the day's supply of kindling from the log pile and stacking wood beside the open hearth, easy of access. Abigail sat at the end of the table to start on the hot porridge her mother placed in front of her.

"What's to do today?" asked her father.

"Mother thinks I should do a bit of spinning of the wool. It's ready from the spring fleece and I need to practice."

"And the boys will need some new winter shirts," Jane added, "especially our Thomas. He's grown so in the year."

"I think I am taller than William already," said Thomas quickly.

"Fine for thee," said Joseph warmly, "but just remember, most people with sense measure men from the neck up, not the neck down."

"That's good for them, but it does help to have some muscle in a fight," replied Thomas.

"And thee shouldn't fight," Joseph said.

"Yes," William said, echoing his father. "What would the Meeting say?"

"The elders will not take kindly to any fighting," Joseph said.

"And thee shouldn't fight at all," added his mother. "Thee knows it's against our Quaker doctrine." She looked at him with compassion.

Thomas involuntarily flexed the muscles of his arms. The shirt hid the tightening of the shoulders as he looked around. "If it's necessary, then I think I have to stand up for what's right. I don't want anyone to think they can push us around."

"Beginning one fight begets another, then it becomes worse and one never forgets a fight. There's no end to it." Joseph was serious. "We in Pennsylvania especially, when the Quakers were the responsible majority, kept the peace."

"Yes, Father, but then the French and the Indians came and began to invade. They started to kill those settlers particularly in the western part of the state. We couldn't stand by and let that happen. A defense was necessary."

"And then more suffered. It's not the way to settle differences."

"But maybe it's the only way. The French were driven out and the border became safe again." Thomas was now standing.

"Oh, Thomas," pleaded his father, "the British fought against the French and Indians and now they impose taxes on us to pay for the cost of the army; and now, so many don't want to pay, so the king sends his army to Boston and the colonies send delegates to Philadelphia. The British fight and now we declare our independence. The fighting escalates. Discussions stop. We have no peace and men will be killed. Is this the way?"

"But, Father. Is there any other way?"

"Yes. Work for peace through the absence of war."

Thomas hesitated. Quaker values had been instilled in him over the years. "I know our teachings," he admitted, "from George Fox and especially William Penn, all at First Day school and in meeting for worship, but what can we do now that we, even here in Pennsylvania, are at war with Great Britain? Can we merely step aside and let them come into our communities? Onto our farms? Into our homes? Tax us? Make us slaves to their power?"

"Yes, if that's what becomes necessary to avoid fighting as we seek peaceful means for a peaceful end. We must step aside and remain neutral and take neither one side or the other." Joseph rose slowly to his feet. His voice became lower, the words spoken more slowly. Jane remained at the great open hearth. "Thee's a good son," Joseph said. "We don't want thee in the way of any army."

Thomas raised his head, his eyes glancing at his mother, then looked straight at his father. "I know that we all have a responsibility for our home and our farm. We can't let anyone come here and take it from us. We can't let the British come with an army and remove our freedom. We're Americans, not slaves, subjects of the king perhaps, but only if we can trade freely and set our own laws." He stopped, then continued. "The Committee of Safety is calling for a militia to protect us."

"Is thee thinking of joining?" asked his mother, the first to lay open their concern. "Must thee fight?" The others were quiet now, looking at Thomas as he stood alone, close by the door.

"I think Benjamin will," he responded quietly. He waited, then added, "And I think Abner will also, and I think I should." He stood straighter. "It may be that I must do it if I think we need an army. If I think we need to defend ourselves against the British army, then I can't avoid my responsibility. It'd be the act of a coward to not step forth."

"It may take a greater strength to stand aside in support of our peace testimony." Joseph was firm with a certain sadness. "Many fight. The truly strong work peacefully."

"Is peace possible without force?" asked Thomas.

"Is it really possible with force?" replied his father quickly.

They fell silent.

"Let's go a haying," said William, breaking the tension.

***

Without a further word, they headed out into the summer heat to pick up the path, then the widening cartway that led to the farm of Abel Green. They walked quickly. The tall trees shaded them from the rising sun, still hidden, as they followed the familiar rutted road that led from Edgmont to the great road. The Lenni Lenape Indians had first trod it as they made their way down to the Delaware River. Shortly, the Pratt men turned off and into the cartway to the Green's farm. They saw smoke coming from the chimney, the wagon standing outside the barn, Abel's horse tethered close by ready to be harnessed.

"Hello," called Joseph as they marched toward the house. Abel appeared in the doorway.

"Greetings," he replied, and smiled broadly with his arms outstretched. "Welcome."

"Good day for haying," Joseph said.

"Perfect," Abel agreed. "Come in, have some coffee. We're out of tea," he apologized, "and I suspect, even if we had any left, we'd not serve it as our part to protest."

"Thank thee, neighbor. Coffee will be fine." Joseph

clasped Abel's hand. Behind in the doorway crowded the four daughters. Annie was first to come out followed by the three younger.

"You remember my girls?" Abel asked. "Annie over there, then Mary, Faith, and the little one, Charity."

They stood in a row making short, uncomfortable curtsies.

"Nice family," said Joseph.

"Daughters," agreed Abel. "Not even one son like you, but these are good girls, a real comfort, until haying," he added at the last, recognizing the Pratt boys standing aside.

"Thee knows mine," Joseph said. "Abraham there helps us from his own farm. William's still with us, then Thomas, our youngest." He looked over at Annie. "About the age of thy eldest there." Annie blushed. Joseph hesitated, then continued, "Of course, I forget that Thomas has been here before. She would know him already."

"And a good lad, too," agreed Abel. "Been a help when I needed some strength." He looked over at his eldest daughter. "Remember Thomas?"

Annie blushed again, slightly nodding. Thomas hung back.

"Thomas would be the one to come," nudged William. "He was always the first to volunteer."

Thomas gave a sour look at William but remained silent, afraid to agree.

"Well, there's time for visiting later," Joseph said. "I suspect thee'll want the hay to be turned one more time into the morning sun, get the night's dew off the grasses."

Abel nodded, "You know the field, Joseph. I'll bring the wagon down. It'll be ready to pitch the hay into it just after the sun reaches above the trees."

The Pratts headed down in the same order, Thomas last. He slowed and looked back at the four girls. Annie smiled at him. He gave a quick smile back, hoping no one else would notice, particularly his brothers, but the younger girls saw.

"Annie," they cried out softly, "he remembers you."

***

The day became hot with the sultry humidity pressing down, the sweat showing on them all, as they forked, then pitched the hay on to the rear of the wagon, Abel forking it forward and higher. By noon, half the field was done and Abel called a halt.

"I see some dinner coming," he said, pointing towards the path where Annie Green carried a large basket of food and fruit.

They lay down their pitchforks and stood in the shade of a large walnut tree at the field's edge waiting, wiping their brows from the perspiration that continued to bead, then run down their cheeks. Annie went first to Joseph, then to her father, showing the basket with bread, cheese, some cherries, and a jug of milk to add to the water jar they'd been using.

"Here's for all, Pa," she said simply, giving a sideways glance at Thomas who was looking at her. She turned back to her father.

"I'll be back later. Do you want anything else?"

"No, dear, this is just fine." He sat down on a tree stump and pushed the basket over to Joseph. "Here's for you."

They took a hunk of bread, placed a slice of cheese on it, and chewed away.

***

By mid afternoon, the hay was out of the field. Abel clicked his cheek and started the horse and wagon off to his small barn. For the next hour, all in a line, they stood, forking the hay into the mow. Finally off the wagon, Abel stood aside, wiping his face with his large cotton cloth, looking at the empty wagon.

"It's in. Let it rain now." He breathed out heavily. "I'm grateful Joseph for all your help and that of your boys. I couldn't easily do it myself, what with the tavern I keep up on the great road, this is just too much alone. You're good neighbors." He reached out to shake Joseph's hand.

"Thee is welcome," replied Joseph. "I'll have Thomas stay and get the hay properly set in your mow. We just left some in the middle of the floor up there."

"Nice help, that is for sure. I'd be appreciative. I need to walk on over to the tavern. There's only my woman there and she can't handle both supper and sorting out lodging if we have more than a few staying."

"Thomas, thee'd be willing to stay?" asked Joseph of his son. "It would be a nice help for the Greens."

"Of course, Father," Thomas replied, more quickly than he intended. "I'll take care of what's left. If he wants me to," he added so that he would not seem too anxious.

"Good fellow," confirmed Abel.

"I don't think Thomas objects," William said.

"Let him be," Abraham said.

"With all those girls, it'll not be a chore, I suspect," William muttered to his oldest brother.

"Thee's been known to linger about when thee's had a chance," Abraham replied as quietly.

"I know," William said, "but when I do, there's always someone else around."

"Thy time will come," Abraham said.

"There're chores to be done," Joseph called out to William, noticing his three sons standing aside, talking among themselves. "William, thee and I need to be about our business."

"And I need to be off myself," Abel said. "Hungry and tired travelers are not going to wait for me to make up my mind when I want to show up." He clamped on his hat and turned to go. He thought again and turned to his eldest daughter. "See to Thomas there, Annie. I'll not be back tonight, so you take care of your sisters. Your mother will come back in the morning."

"When thee's done, on home with thee," Joseph said.

"Yes, Father," Thomas agreed. The group dispersed, each heading in opposite directions. The sun cast long shadows over the cartway making the road seem narrower than normal.

Thomas picked up his pitchfork and went into the barn, climbing up the ladder to the upper level. He started to pitch the hay from the floor up to the mow. He worked at it for some minutes until he heard a noise of the ladder creaking. He turned around to see Annie's head appear through the opening of the floor. He leaned on his fork.

"Can I come up?" asked Annie, not stopping as she stepped on to the floor. She adjusted her long skirt and smoothed out her apron, her hands then making sure her cap was probably set, her long hair hanging below the back hem.

Thomas came towards her. "It's nice to see thee again," he said agreeably. "It's been a long time."

"Too long," Annie agreed.

"Thee's grown a bit."

"And so have you," she retorted, "but its suits." She came closer.

"I need to get this hay put away," he said, picking up his fork again to gather the long grasses and heave a pile up onto the layer already in place.

"How high do you have to go?" she asked.

"Almost to the rafters," he answered, not stopping his swing. "That way, it'll be out of the way and thy father then only has to toss it down the chute to the animals below."

"Can I climb up and see?"

"Surely."

"Will you help me up?"

He set the pitchfork aside. "Here, step in my cupped hands."

She came alongside, hiking up her skirt, exposing her ankles. "I'm ready."

"Right. I'll give thee a little boost. Just grab onto some of the hay that's already up there and pull yourself onto the top. It is loose but soft, not too many scratchy stalks."

She stepped into his hands, holding on to Thomas' shoulders as he gave her a boost up. She scrambled the rest of the way up to settle comfortably into the hay, turning around, looking down. Thomas looked up as she arranged her skirt, slowly letting her leg show a bit more, swinging the hem casually until it settled out.

Thomas smiled. "Be careful I don't throw any hay onto thee," he teased.

"Then you'd have to come up here and get it off of me," she replied lightly.

He gathered a large bunch of hay and with a great effort, the muscles of his arms bulging, heaved it up to her side.

"Don't you think you'd be cooler if you took off your shirt?" she encouraged. "It's warm and with all your effort, it would be more comfortable."

Thomas thought for a minute, stepped back, and gazed

up at Annie, her chin resting on her hands. He nodded and unbuttoned his shirt, dropped his suspenders, and pulled the shirt out of his trousers and set it on a hook close by. He pulled the straps of the suspenders back on to shoulders, his chest moist, showing a narrow cluster of hair just starting to be obvious. His stomach showed a further line of soft, faint hair coursing down from his navel into his pants. He ran his hand across his chest to wipe the sweat away and picked up the fork again to continue pitching the hay up in an even layer. Annie watched intently as Thomas worked more quickly, aware of her staring, slightly embarrassed for the audience, but anxious to complete the job. He worked faster, sweat glistening.

"Don't you think you should rest for a bit?" Annie suggested after some minutes.

Thomas pitched another load up, closer to Annie, the level crowding against her. He looked up as she leaned forward, peering down, her mouth open slightly, her tongue showing between her parted teeth.

"Why don't you come up here and shift some of this hay? If not, I don't think there will be room for it all." She shifted to make room. Thomas lay known his fork. He slowly set it against the post and grabbed the crossbeam, and in one quick jerk of his hand, pulled himself up on top of the hay. Annie rolled onto her side as Thomas knelt facing first at her, then at the hay, then back again. She let her skirt ride up on her legs. She made no effort to adjust it, raising up on her one arm to wrap her other around Thomas' neck with a gentle pressure bringing him down into a short, then longer kiss. He was surprised by the suddenness but then moved his legs out to stretch alongside her keeping his lips pressed against hers. He stopped for breath, taking a quick look down to confirm their privacy. It was still, no untoward noise to disturb the insulated space of the barn. She wiggled closer, pressing against him. He pulled away then came close. She fumbled at his suspenders as he carefully began to tug at her skirt to raise the bottom higher. Annie worked her arms around his back, sliding them down to his waist then lower. He inched her skirt up carefully and hesitantly. She suddenly pulled away and quickly raised the skirt, her clear thighs exposed. She came back each hand now on Thomas' pants and pulled them down. He did not resist, his head warm from the blood coursing behind his eyes as he moved his legs up and over, relaxing with an increasing tension. She opened her mouth as he leaned down to a longer kiss with a greater urgency as she shifted under him. She moved her hands down and under, feeling, guiding, leading, then tense as he thrust, his mind swirling, the warmth unexpected and new, soft and hard. Annie moved in a rhythm as Thomas lay closer, muscles stretched, eyes closed, suddenly washed with waves of sweet sensation. Annie jerked, then shuddered, grabbing Thomas by his buttocks, gulping in breaths with a low moan, straining under him until he softened, relaxed, then lay limp in her curves, breasts tight, still against her bodice. She dropped her hands along her side, then brought them up to wipe her forehead, and then to smooth them over Thomas' face. He lay still, surprised at the experience and afraid what might be next. He did not move as she shifted out from underneath him. She looked into his face, eyes still closed.

"Thomas," she whispered softly.

"Yes," he answered non-commitantly.

"The hay is soft."

He waited, and then responded, "Yes."

"Better than straw," she went on.

"Sweeter smelling," he agreed, responding automatically as his mind began to race.

She stroked his face. "Worried, aren't you?"

He lifted his head, a little unsure of what's next.

"Don't worry," she reassured him. "It's all right."

He rolled off her, self consciously pulling his trousers back up, getting his suspenders back in place as if a defense. She lightly and in one motion drew her skirt down.

"There," she added brightly. "Just like before." She turned again putting her chin into her cupped hands looking at him straight. "Your first, wasn't it?"

Thomas nodded once, his mind mixed with guilt and pleasure and ignorance.

"You're fine," she offered encouragement.

He was quiet.

"Have you noticed me before?" she continued.

"Yes." He waited, then added, "Whenever we come to help thy father."

"You like what you see?"

"Thee has grown."

"You didn't answer my question."

"Thee has grown nicely."

"So have you. I kept watching you, every time you came and then you spoke to me. I liked that." She sat up. "You've been nicer than your brothers."

"Well, Abraham is married. And I think William is sweet on a girl that goes to Meeting with us."

"You don't have a girl?"

"I know some," he said defensively.

"But no one special?"

"Not a particular way."

"Anyone like me?"

"No one. The others are shy. They barely look at one. But thee is different, more outgoing, more worldly I'd say."

"Well, I do see a lot, especially when I help my father at the tavern. We have all sorts of men stay with us."

"No women?"

"Generally not. Women don't drive wagons and they rarely go along with their men folk. So we hear stories about Philadelphia and other towns, some as far away as Lancaster and York. We had one who came from New York and he'd sit around after supper and tell stories of that town and what he'd heard about from New England."

"That's more than we hear on the farm of course. When we go to Meeting we hear things, and when someone gets a newspaper, we know."

"But it's not like listening to a person telling a story because he's been there." Annie took Thomas' hand. "You'll see, when your father takes you into Philadelphia. It's different in the city, bigger than the towns close by."

"Father did say that the next time he would take me to Philadelphia."

"You'll like it," said Annie as she swung herself down on to the floor. Thomas easily followed her. "I've got to get back inside. I'm responsible for supper and my sisters will wonder what's keeping me." She laughed. "I'll not tell them of course, but they can guess about you." She twisted her body to let the skirt drop down around her ankles naturally. She dropped carefully down onto the floor, headed for the door, and called back to Thomas. "I hope Father will need you again." She did not wait for an answer before going out and across the yard to the kitchen of the farmhouse.

Thomas started again to pitch the hay up, this time to the spot where they had laid down, his mind a swirl of conflicting emotions. *What is she thinking now? It all happened so quickly. Should I have done it? She was the one who wanted to be in the hay! Was I wrong?* He stopped, suddenly seeing his shirt hanging by the post, and put it back on. The last hay was gathered and lifted in the final heave to the top of the mound. Thomas looked around, then out the barn door towards the kitchen where the lantern cast a soft, yellow glow, showing the Green daughters at the table. The sun was down below the trees and the dusk muted the shadows as the light in the sky paled. He glanced to make sure no one was at the window to see, and putting his pitch fork over his shoulder, quickly headed down the path towards his own farmstead.

Chapter Four

Thomas slowed his horse to a walk as he came to the little cluster of buildings passing first by the blacksmith's shop and along to the Quaker meeting house at Goshen. Two young men his own age left off from the general store and stood in Thomas' path. Thomas recognized the older, the son of a neighboring farmer, not very friendly, Baptist, and strange to his Quaker ways, always distant to Thomas.

The summer heat was heavy over the fields, misting in its sultriness, changing the color of the trees as they receded from the dirt road from green into a pale, gray haze.

"Good day to thee," Thomas carefully offered to Caleb Bishop.

"I want to talk to you," replied Caleb with an ill-concealed anger.

Thomas stayed on his horse, looking down, wary and silent. Caleb came over and grabbed the horse's reins.

"You've been seeing a certain girl, my girl, Annie Green, and I don't like it." His eyes flashed. Caleb's friend, younger, shorter with thick wiry hair and a rough face came to the other side of the horse. He grabbed the other half of the reins as the horse tried to shake free. Joshua looked around to Caleb offering support.

Caleb continued, emboldened by Joshua. "She's mine and you need to stay away from her." He pulled all the reins harder yanking the horse's head around towards him. "Understand?"

Thomas was surprised, his face coloring as his muscles tensed. He looked first at Caleb and over at Joshua looking up, his lips in a thin, defiant smile.

Thomas looked back to Caleb. "What's she to thee?"

"More to me than to you," came back the quick reply.

"Maybe it's not thy decision whose girl she is."

"If I say so, then it is."

"And if Annie doesn't agree?"

"Oh, she agrees all right." Caleb spit it out. He tugged the reins again, tighter as the horse let out a snuffle, then a high pitched whistle trying to shake its head loose. It was more comfortable with the gentle tug and urgings of Thomas than this abrupt handling and sound of the threatening voice.

"You don't like it because our farm is closer to the Greens," said Thomas, more gently in greater contrast to Caleb. "Thee thinks she cares for thee more than me?"

"I know she doesn't take to Quaker ways," replied Caleb.

"And how would thee know? Just because Quakers don't have a preacher, don't like to fight, does that make a big difference?"

"Come down off that horse," said Caleb with a biting, strong voice, "and I'll show you the real difference."

"Yeah," Joshua chimed in, standing short and stocky, urging his friend. "Show him."

"You're pretty confident with somebody to help thee," Thomas replied, not getting off his horse. "Would thee be thus if thee were alone?"

"I can take care of myself," reported Caleb. "You come on down here and I'll show you."

Thomas hesitated. He knew that Caleb was strong, had seen him on market days handling the oxen and heavy barrels of oats and sacks of wheat with ease, and he wasn't sure he could beat him even in a fair fight. He also knew Joshua wasn't to be trusted, always hanging around Caleb as a puppy to a larger dog. Thomas hesitated and relaxed. *Thomas, thee must not fight,* he could hear his mother saying. *It settles nothing, it only encourages more fighting.* Thomas took a deep breath and stared down at Caleb with as benign a look as he could put on in his anxiety. "I'll not fight thee," he said.

"Coward."

"Brave when needs be."

"Afraid," Caleb taunted.

"No mind to follow thee."

"Weak."

"No need."

"Get off that horse and I'll show you." Caleb tugged the reins again, then hit against Thomas' boot.

"Get off me," Thomas snarled.

"Yeah. And who's going to make me?"

Thomas wasn't sure what to do. He wanted to kick at Caleb. *That would make a difference,* he thought, *and then I am in a fight.* He kicked the horse violently in the ribs and the horse shifted its hindquarters around towards Joshua who dropped the reins to get away from the kick of the hooves. Thomas kicked again as Caleb moved away from the head of the horse just in case.

"Ask Annie whom she really likes," taunted Thomas, giving another kick to the horse, which bolted and shook free of both Caleb and Joshua. The horse leapt forward, Thomas leaning down on his neck, urging the horse into a gallop, away from the two.

"You stay away," Caleb called out a last time as Thomas rode a short distance up the road. Thomas heard but didn't turn to acknowledge since he was upset and shaken. *Even if I had fought and lost, at least I wouldn't have been called a coward.* He trembled, pulling the horse to a walk and patted its neck, shuddering involuntarily, a pit in his stomach from the confrontation. "Sorry, old boy," he murmured. The road turned around a cluster of trees and out of sight from the general store and the two of them, still standing there.

Chapter Five

Autumn brought cooler evenings and less humidity across the fields of the farm. The green of the woods paled, looking tired, the bright luster of summer gone with the walnut trees beginning to drop their leaves, the outermost ones high up, browning and curling, ready to drift quietly to the ground. The crops were all harvested. Only the garden still produced with a few beans, greens of the lettuces, squash, and pumpkins swelling from the many blossoms that had been fertilized late in the spring. Carrots, turnips and potatoes were ready to be dug up and placed into the root cellar alongside the kitchen. There was a feeling of plenty as Joseph came out of the house to find his youngest son feeding left over peelings and green tops to the pigs.

"Thomas."

"Yes, Father."

"Those pigs look good. They must like the care thee gives them."

Thomas nodded in appreciation. "They seem content, especially the two sows. It's just that when the big boar sees me come out, he runs over out of his mess, pushing the other two aside to be the first to eat."

"That's fine. If he'll fatten first, he'll be first to be butchered." He turned to Thomas. "That's only fair. Agree?"

"Oh, I do, but I also know thee likes to butcher the male first anyway."

"Well, thee's correct, but then, this seems to give us the right reason." He turned serious. "I think to go to

Philadelphia next week and I would like for thee to come with me to help. We do have a goodly amount of flour from our wheat and we now have an excess of our flax and other crops, and it looks like we'll have an abundant digging of potatoes to sell."

Thomas brightened. He had not been to Philadelphia before, even when the elder Pratts went into the city to attend the yearly meeting of all the Quakers. This was the first time Thomas had been asked by his father to go to Philadelphia to help him in a business way.

"I'd like that," he replied. "I'd like that very much, Father." It was hard for Thomas to restrain his excitement at the prospect.

"And I see that steer standing out there by the fence is good and filled out, ready to be taken with us and sold in the market in Philadelphia. He'll not gain any more weight and we'll not want to feed him over the winter when the pasture grasses give up growing."

As Thomas turned and looked at his father, he tried to be casual in his most mature manner, but his underlying excitement broke through.

"Thanks, Father. That'll be good and I think I can really help thee. It'll be wonderful." He couldn't contain his broad smile. He brushed his hair back off his forehead. "I'll be sure to get all my chores caught up."

"I know thee will and we can depend on thy brother to handle thy responsibilities while we're gone." He tousled his son's hair. "I guess we'll have to get thy mother to give that head a trimming to make sure thee can see out from under all that hair." He pulled his hand away.

"When will we leave?"

"I think on Second Day, in a week. The weather should be clear." He looked up at the sky automatically with an ongoing faith that by doing so the weather would cooperate with his prediction. "We'll stop at Marple, see the Masseys and stay overnight there. They're good people."

"Yes. I remember and they have a girl, Hannah."

"Thee's got a good memory. Yes, it is Hannah, same age as thee. She'll be there." He nodded. "And then it'll be a full day on into Philadelphia. With the big wagon fully loaded we'll need to take our heavy horses. It'll be a lot of work for the team." He was done talking. There was still work to be done. He gave Thomas one more tousle of his hair and left for the house.

Thomas kept on forking the manure out of the stalls on to the pile growing by the side of the barn to weather and become a rich mixture for their garden the next spring. As he kept thinking, his effort gradually lessened. *We can find out what the British are doing, especially about Philadelphia. If they're now in New York, are they going to come down here?* He stuck his pitchfork into the sodden mass, straw binding the dark clods together and, with an easy effort, heaved up and walked outside to add a bit more to the growing mound. He wondered what Philadelphia was like now that the colonies had come together. He walked back in. *Will we get better prices for crops? And for our steer? We should, if there's a danger of fighting.* Thomas moved with a mechanical motion as he repeated the steps clearing out the stall. Finally down to bare earth, he tumbled some straw to start a new layer. *There. Bossy will like that.* He gave a soft snort of realization. *And it's a lot nicer milking on fresh straw than trying to keep away from her dumping.* He looked around with satisfaction. *What would happen if British soldiers come upon our farm and wanted our milk and steer and all our provisions?* He frowned at the thought. *Well, I wouldn't let them.* He headed back to the house to join the rest of the family already gathering at the long table in the kitchen for supper.

"Wash up now Thomas," said Jane, the encouragement from habit. Thomas was already at the trough, scouring his hands and arms up to the elbows with heavy, caustic soap. The table was already set as he became the last to sit down. They bowed their heads and silently in the enveloping stillness each thanked God for their good fortune and bounty. Jane was the first to raise her head as she ladled hot soup from the pot into each bowl.

"I'm taking Thomas with me to Philadelphia," Joseph announced to the family. "I need the help and it will add to his experience." Thomas sat up a little straighter. "And we'll stop at the Masseys."

"That's always nice, dear," Jane agreed.

"That's where Hannah lives," William teased.

"I guess," Thomas agreed with no particular emotion.

"I wonder what she is like now?" William said. "She was always kind of skinny," William added. "Not like Annie Green."

Thomas blushed. He decided to say nothing.

"So I'm going to need help as we get the flour into our barrels," Joseph said to break into the conversation, which he felt was going into a subject he didn't want to discuss around his youngest, Abigail. The thought embarrassed Joseph.

"We're ready to help, Father," agreed the sons in unison.

"I'm sure," Joseph nodded with a smile.

"Abigail and I will pack enough food for the trip." Jane began to think of the baking she needed to prepare.

"We'll buy just a bit when we get to Philadelphia," offered Joseph.

Thomas brightened. He had never had food from a tavern, and the idea of sitting and eating with others with food prepared by a tavern keeper was a new expectation.

"Does thee think there's any danger in going to Philadelphia?" Jane opened her eyes wide as she looked at her husband. "I mean with this Declaration of Independence and the British not accepting it and sending soldiers." She was confident in Joseph's judgment, but there was still a concern in her voice.

"From what I hear, there's no worry there, not yet anyway." He looked around at his sons, still spooning the soup, tearing off pieces of bread to soak in the heavy, hot broth.

"I hear that soldiers formed by the Pennsylvania government are coming into the city," Thomas suggested, "and Abner Baldwin says that Edgmont Township is forming a militia to protect this area. In case trouble comes," he added quickly.

"Abner is always the first to hear," agreed Jane.

"Because his father works as a tavern keeper." Joseph shook his head knowingly, "With some farming."

"It's nice to always have your own food," Jane added. She was not too sure whether it was proper for a Quaker to be a tavern keeper, *and to dispense spirits,* she thought and shuddered at the idea.

"Well, let others form into a militia," Joseph said, hoping to preempt any talk about the wisdom of a local fighting force, especially in an area where there were so many Quakers. "We do hold to the peace testimony," he added for emphasis. "It is wrong to use force of arms, for it is not God's way." He said it with a finality. The table was quiet except for the occasional slurping and infrequent burp, which caused a disapproving eye to the guilty from their mother.

"But shouldn't there be an army?" Thomas persisted, not letting the concern drop. "Don't we think that it's now necessary for General Washington to defend our rights and against the British?"

"But we are British, dear," said his mother.

"Aren't we Pennsylvanians first and aren't we really Americans above all?" Thomas said quietly, his feet shuffling under the bench on which he was sitting, "even if we came from England?"

"But we're still English." She said it sweetly but firmly.

"And the British crown protects us." Joseph was secure in the thought.

"By fighting against us?" Thomas continued.

"But they let us have our own government and laws." Joseph offered it in a kindly tone.

"Then what about the Stamp Act and the taxes they impose on us? Is it fair if we don't have a say?"

"But that's such a little thing," Jane said, "and it does not affect us."

"But Mother, what would happen if we had to pay the tax to sell our wool and flax and flour in Philadelphia, or if the merchants had to pay the tax instead? Then we would get less money." He looked around for support. His older brother was content for Thomas to carry the discussion for them.

"But do we need to go to war to settle our disagreements with the government in London?" Joseph felt it was necessary to continue with his point of view even if there was some confusion in the sequence of events. He was not sure of the logic of the actions taken by the Congress.

"If we've tried peace and it doesn't work, then what?"

Thomas stared at his father. "Do we just let the British walk all over us? What happens if they come down here to Pennsylvania to fight, like in Massachusetts and New York?"

"We have to trust in God." Joseph stared back at his younger son. "Thee needs to have faith. We need have faith." His voice became stronger. "Fighting is not the solution. Killing is not the answer. There might be immediate pain in seeking a peaceful solution. But in the end, it will be of greater benefit to us, for all. The Meeting is firm in this."

"Not everyone agrees, Father." Thomas was troubled. "I know that Abner wonders about the army and there are some I've heard about from other meetings that are unsure."

"Where did thee hear that?" Jane asked in some alarm.

"When we go to Quarterly Meeting, I've heard them talking." Thomas shrugged his shoulders. "It seems like some are unsure?" He looked over at his father.

"I'm sure," he replied with confidence. "It's the only way. I thought about it in Meeting, week after week. I've talked with others of the Meeting, the elders and visiting friends as they come to be among us, especially those out of the city where they hear all the news and are privy to the sense of the populace. Some there are strongly for fighting, others are not yet declared, and many think it wrong to antagonize the country which defends us." Joseph leaned against the back of his chair. He laid his hands on the table on either side of his plate. He sighed. "I'm afraid that events are getting out of hand, that maybe it's becoming too late to settle these issues without rancor, but I do know that we must continue to work for peaceful solutions." He relaxed the muscles of his face. His faith was secure. He was comfortable with himself and confident in his beliefs.

Thomas was silent. The confusion kept swirling in his mind. His questions kept overlapping one another in an illogical sequence, coming and going, never resting at a single point, jumping from one idea to another. He gave up trying, but remained troubled. He was not satisfied with the determination of his father.

Chapter Six

William helped Thomas roll the great barrels of flour out of the shed and with a great effort, the two of them, muscles straining, heaved them up and into the body of the wagon.

Jane placed Thomas' best shirt and trousers with his good suspenders in a cloth sack along with spare socks. He would use his father's razor when they got to the city. "It's important that thee looks well," she had admonished. "People take thee more seriously if thee makes a clean appearance." Thomas was excited with the prospect of this weeklong expedition to Philadelphia.

The wagon was stacked with the last of the oats and wool from their small flock of sheep. Placing the bentwood hoops into place on the wagon and stretching the heavy canvas cover over all to protect the cargo, Joseph was satisfied as his sons worked quickly.

Second Day arrived. The horses sensed the adventure, shuddering in their harness. The steer was led behind the wagon and tied with a line just long enough to keep it from wandering too far to one side or the other. Thomas adjusted the leather straps in place, patting the neck of each horse, and turned, stroking again the sleek hair and mane he had combed out early that morning. The legs and hocks had been washed and brushed so that they also shown clean in the slanting shafts of the sun as it beamed down through the shifting branches of the trees overhead. The leaves hung loosely, flapping back-and-forth in the drying progress of the cooler weather. Thomas held the heads of the horses as his father grasped the reins in his heavy hands. Jane came out and handed up to her husband a pack of food and a little pot of honey especially for the Masseys. She came around to Thomas.

"Keep thee well," she smiled and came close to give him a hug. He looked around to see if his brother or sister were looking. They were not. He put his arms round his mother and kept on tight for just a bit longer than usual. She leaned out and gave him a kiss on the cheek. She smiled and Thomas was pleased, for he had always felt a certain comfort in the warm constancy of her presence.

"Well. Are we going today?" Joseph called over. It was a kindly question. He knew of a particular affection his wife had for their youngest son. It was an unspoken pleasure to see.

"Coming Father," he replied. He took his hands away and taking the little package she had made especially for him, climbed quickly up onto the seat alongside his father, adjusting the brim of his work hat, and gave a slight wave to his older brother standing aside the barn, watching the slow departure. He raised one hand with no wave but acknowledged with a nod of the head. It was his young sister who waved her hand back and forth, a bright smile across her face.

"Tell me all about it," she cried out.

"I will," Thomas called back.

"And everything else," echoed William with another meaning.

"We'll see," Thomas laughed. "We'll see."

Joseph grunted and then with a short command and a flick of the reins, started the horses as they struggled to pull the heavily laden wagon up the slight incline and over towards the road that led down past the local tavern at Edgmont and then towards the crossroads designated as William Penn's Newtown Square. It was a lively day, comfortable, dry, and full of a peaceful serenity as it had been over the years. The wagon creaked and groaned as they carefully made their way down the Philadelphia Road, past other farms, neatly tended with fences snaking along the road and back against the woods, the crops now harvested. The fields were brown and sparse leaving little enough for the cows and cattle to feed upon, only the few sheep content to bite off the thin stalks left from the sizing and cutting from the end of the warm weather. As they came to Crum Creek, Joseph slowed the wagon, letting the horses ease down the muddy slope with the brake on until the horses stood in the smoothly flowing water. The front wagon wheels became braced at the creek's edge, just wet but secure from rolling further forward. Joseph let the horses drop their heads and drink with long, sucking sounds from the cool water. Joseph knew from his years of experience just when to yank on the reins to bring their heads back up, not fully satisfied, but filled with enough water to restore their energy without bloating. Joseph clicked his tongue, snapped the reins, and urged the horses on to the other side of the creek and up the slope on the far side, which was rutted and ground into a pasty mass from previous travelers and wagons. The sun flickered through the trees overhead, and when the fields came close to the road, the road had dried and became slightly dusty out from the dark and damp of the shade. They proceeded at a steady pace, Joseph quiet in his thoughts, Thomas curious with the new sights, occasionally turning around to see their steer ambling along behind.

Coming close to the Newtown Road, they spotted another wagon and team coming towards them. They kept on steadily until it was obvious that both wagons could not pass each other easily. The other wagon was mostly empty. Joseph recognized the farmer from out past Westtown and raised his hand in greeting. The other eased his wagon on to the edge of the field giving a little space and waited for Joseph to come on up.

"Greetings, friend," Joseph called out to the Quaker from Birmingham Meeting, coming to a stop alongside. "Is thee coming out from Philadelphia?"

"Yes. I've been there with our produce. Sold it all yesterday and now I'm headed home."

"Is the road firm?"

"Mostly. Little rain, so the way is solid. Even the creeks are down so fording them is no problem."

"And what of the market? Are the prices fair?"

"Thee'll not find a problem. The city merchants know it's time to lay in food against the coming of winter when it'll be hard to gain other provisions."

Joseph nodded. "Same as last year?" he asked further.

"Mostly," the other nodded. "Even a bit better. With the fighting in New England and now maybe in New York, some are willing to pay more. Many are not sure if the fighting might not come into Pennsylvania and disrupt their supplies, like from us." The other looked over at Joseph's wagon and with a knowledgeable and appreciative tone concluded, "It looks like thee has a good load. They'll be happy to see thee in Philadelphia."

Joseph smiled at the compliment. "Thank thee," he replied, giving a click for the horses to move on. As they moved out of hearing, Thomas turned to his father.

"Thee didn't ask about the fighting?" Thomas kept looking at his father who didn't turn around. He pursed his lips closer.

Finally, he replied. "It is not a subject I want to discuss with another Quaker. I realize he probably knows much from just listening to others in the markets, but I don't want him to think I have too great a curiosity about war or fighting, knowing that we keep to a peaceful life." He turned to his son. "We will hear much of the country's problems when we get to Philadelphia. People will tell us, even if we don't ask. They'll offer their opinions, particularly those who are not Quaker. They are the ones who would resist and fight and bring British soldiers down here without an ongoing effort to bridge whatever differences there might be between these colonies and Great Britain. It's a sad business and if it goes on, many are going to lose their possessions and some their lives. It will tear neighbor from neighbor, friend from friend, even families apart. As Quakers, we need to stand aside from that approach. We have renounced war as a means of settling differences. Our peace testimony remains the only real path to live in harmony with one another." Joseph kept his face forward. He was uncomfortable with his son. "Does thee not see?" he asked.

"Yes, Father," replied Thomas. "Thee has always made good judgments for us. For all of us." He hesitated, and then went on. "But what if the British come down here to Pennsylvania, to Philadelphia, even to our own farms? Are we to stand by and let them do what they want? Maybe to take our pigs, our wheat, maybe even our horses? What do we do then?" Thomas' voice was a plea.

Joseph sighed and slowly answered. "Then we must hope that they'll pay for what they take and leave us alone to live our lives in peace."

They lapsed into silence. Thomas was not satisfied

but was unwilling to pursue further his own thoughts out loud.

***

"We're just about there," Joseph said brightly, approaching Marple. "Thee will like the Masseys," he announced confidently, sure of this Quaker family who had lived and farmed for years at their homestead. Thomas sat up straighter and a little forward on the seat of the wagon as he searched for a roofline among the trees that would show the farm. He waited anxiously. "Around this near bend," Joseph said, anticipating his son's question, "thee will see the buildings in a minute." He jostled the reins to encourage the horses on, now sensing a stop for the night. The barn came in sight first, and then beyond, the house, built years before with its leaded casement windows, different from any that Thomas had seen before. The jingling of the harness brought Phineas Massey out of the barn with a broad smile on recognizing Joseph Pratt.

"Welcome," he called out, waving as the wagon came closer. "What a pleasure," he added as Joseph pulled the horses to a stop. "Good to see thee."

"Does thee mind if we stop here?" Joseph asked with a grin.

"Thee does every year," replied Phineas, "and I expect this year is no different and we're happy for that." He turned his eyes on Thomas. "And who is that young fellow? Thy youngest son I trust?" Phineas Massey was already walking over to the wagon, his hand outstretched to greet Thomas.

"Yes, this is Thomas. It's his first time to help me in to Philadelphia. I need him and I think he'll find the experience important."

They both climbed down off the wagon, Thomas almost into the burly outstretched arms of Phineas.

"Thee is a mighty fortunate son to have a father like Joseph," said Phineas. He was stocky and round of face, ruddy and expansive. "I've heard about thee."

"From my brothers or my father?" Thomas asked quickly.

"Certainly, always from thy father."

"Good."

"Certainly good," replied Phineas.

"And my brothers?"

"They described thee more fully." Phineas laughed. "Thee should not worry. They admire thee even if thee is the last son, which is not always bad. Thy older brothers can blaze the trail for thee, convince thy father that what was improper when they were young is not so now. Yes, I think thee has good fortune in both thy father and thy brothers. So welcome. Let us go into the house. I'm done here with the animals, now down for the night." He winked at Joseph. "Thee doesn't need Thomas' help to unhitch those horses does thee?" he asked as a rhetorical question. "If so, I'll return him shortly, after he's met my womenfolk."

"You mean, Hannah?" replied Joseph, "the light of thy eye," he added.

"Well, I don't want to hide her if that's what thee means," answered Phineas.

"Then, Thomas," said his father, "see for thyself, then thee can come back here and finish putting up our horses." He smiled. "She is a likely young lass," he offered in confirmation of her father's own opinion.

They headed towards the house, smoke curling up out of the far chimney over the kitchen. Phineas stomped his feet on the big stone step, loosening the dust and dirt from his boots and, stepping up, pushed open the broad, wooden door and went into the faint interior. Thomas followed, imitating his example. Coming out of the fading sunlight, his eyes slowly adjusted as the figures setting by the great table in front of the large open hearth became more distinct. Phineas shut the door behind them and came forward, his arm around Thomas, urging him on, until they stood by the small fire shedding a circle of heat from the brick backing of the stone hearth. Suzanne Massey stood up and came forward to greet this stranger.

"It's Thomas, Joseph Pratt's youngest," Phineas said to his wife. "They stopped on their way to Philadelphia."

Thomas nodded to the older woman becoming more distinct as the room lightened as he waited for any reaction.

"Then thee's welcome," said Suzanne Massey. "I've heard of thy existence and it's a joy to meet the last of the Pratt sons." She offered her hand out from under a plain, white, linen shawl. Her cotton cloth cap kept her tightly pinned hair in place and free from most of the dust that constantly floated around, settling wherever there was little movement in the air. Her plain face, lined from years of constant work, spoke of an inner peace and satisfaction from a comfortably full life. She squeezed Thomas' hand. "Come closer, here," she encouraged, moving in the direction of Phineas, standing alongside his daughter. Hannah Massey stood up, brushing her long skirt free of the shavings of the carrot she was preparing for their evening meal. She adjusted her apron and self-consciously put her hands to the sides of her soft white cap to ensure that any strands of hair had not escaped. She stood taller than her mother, her face now distinct to Thomas, was clear with light brown eyebrows, lashes slightly darker which surrounded eyes of the clearest green. Thomas stood transfixed at the vision.

"This is Hannah," announced Phineas with a bit too much pride as his wife held out Hannah's hand to Thomas to encourage the formal greeting. She came forward with only a hint of a curtsey, then in keeping with her Quaker upbringing of equality, took his hand.

"Thee is certainly welcome," she confirmed with an enthusiasm she instantly regretted. Thomas stood before her, looking at her tall, lithe figure, transfixed with the image before him. He realized he hadn't said anything.

"It is nice to meet thee. And thy parents," he quickly added. "It's been a long day on the road and it is good to stop. Father did say his plans for this journey but since this is my first time in Philadelphia, I don't know what to expect." His face warmed and he hoped she would not see the flushing.

"Yes Thomas, thy father always stops here, so we know him well and thy brothers when they come. We're full familiar with the Pratt family, by friendship and thee by thy reputation."

"Good, I hope," Thomas said anxiously.

"Fine, indeed," answered Hannah, "even thy brothers as they teased a bit, confirmed that thee is a good brother to them."

"That's nice," Thomas replied, taking a half step closer to look into her eyes, and shaking his head. "I said I'd go back and help Father with the horses. I need to do that," he explained softly, still filled with a warm exhilaration at this first meeting.

"Of course," confirmed Hannah, "and we'll still be here."

Thomas walked back outside and headed to the small

barn where his father was busy with the harness removed from the backs of the horses.

"Thee met the womenfolk?" he asked.

"Yes. Suzanne Massey seems happy to see us."

"Always," replied Joseph, "and Hannah?" he quizzed, gently tugging the information from his son.

"She seemed pleased also," he answered as naturally as he could, but then opening up his feelings gradually, asked, "how old does thee think she is?"

"I figure she's but a year younger than thee," responded Joseph, having already thought of the suitability of the young girl for either of his unmarried sons.

Thomas was silent as he took up the heavy comb to brush the legs of the horses standing quietly, munching the hay tossed down from the wagon. They expected the care Thomas was now giving. He stopped and turned back to his father. "Does thee think she has any promises to keep?" he asked somewhat apprehensively. The lead horse stomped as if to call attention to the interruption of the grooming. Thomas resumed the stroking of the comb waiting for an answer. Slowly it came.

"Not that I know, at least not when I saw Phineas at Quarterly Meeting last. Hannah was there but stayed with her mother." He smiled. "No, I didn't see any particular young man hanging on to her every word." Thomas didn't reply as he finished one horse, then worked on the other. It was not long before both horses were watered and fed, tied loosely into the stall, silent and content. Joseph led his son as they headed for the house, pushed open the door and walked in.

"There thee is," jumped up Suzanne to give a warm greeting. "And thee remembers Hannah?" she said playfully.

"Of course. How is thee?" he asked kindly. "Still thy father's favorite?" he continued.

Hannah blushed, this time obvious to Thomas who watched the interchange with increasing interest.

"I'm fine," Hannah responded, "and father makes too much of a daughter." She lowered her head.

"Ah, but he's right," Joseph said. "Thee does bring a flicker into his life, I know. He is fortunate in thee." Phineas nodded in agreement. Hannah sat back down onto the bench, picking up the wooden bowl again and continued to work the beans, the finished carrots now standing aside.

***

The supper was lively, simple, and hearty, the men involved with the weather, the crops, their families, and finally the unsettled politics. Thomas listened as Joseph and Phineas held forth, the women constantly rising to adjust the big pot over the fire, adding wood and ladling a bit more soup into their bowls.

"I worry about what Friends might do if the armies come down into Pennsylvania," Joseph said. "It might be too big a temptation for some to join General Washington's Army. Why even Edgmont is forming its own militia."

"And what if it does?" quizzed Phineas. "Will many join?"

"The township will be required to raise a certain number of troops and I think it'll be too great a pressure for some in our local meetings to resist the call for soldiers."

"And what will Willistown Meeting do if a member should join the army?"

"I don't know. Some in Meeting would read a person out, remove them from membership. Others would say, 'let us work to have them see the light through our testimonies of peace, that it is easier to convince those who remain a Quaker in meeting than a removed Friend over whom we have lost any chance to convince of the truth.'" Thomas was lost in his thoughts.

"And what does thee think?" asked Phineas. Thomas suddenly realized the question was for him.

"What do I think?" he repeated, stalling for time.

"Yes, what are thy thoughts about fighting?"

"I don't know really," Thomas replied. "I think we ought to be free to sell our produce where we are able and to pay taxes to our Pennsylvania authorities. I'm not sure what we owe to England." He warmed to the subject. "We've made this country what it is. I see the effort of ourselves and of our neighbors working for our well being. I don't think it is fair for any government to take that away from us if we have not elected them into the power to do so." He glanced at Hannah, embarrassed to be caught staring at Thomas.

"Yes, but what of thy Edgmont militia?" persisted Phineas.

"I think about that," confirmed Thomas without giving a further answer.

"He's a good boy," said Joseph in support, "and I'm sure he'll do the right thing."

"If we only know what the right thing is," added Phineas. "If any of us really knows what that is."

"Only that its right to abhor fighting," Joseph insisted.

"We agree on that," said Phineas.

Thomas didn't comment.

***

The following morning, the household arose before dawn. Phineas was already in the barn milking their single cow. Suzanne Massey came first into the kitchen and carefully placed a few small sticks onto the banked embers from the previous night to encourage the fire to life. She brought out bread, butter, cheese, and preserves. Shoes thumping announced others, still sleepy with tousled hair. Hannah hurried to be in the kitchen before Thomas. She'd taken special care to brush her hair, plaited into a single tail down her back, her cap set aside for now.

"Morning," Joseph said, coming down.

"Did thee sleep well?" Suzanne asked.

"Always here," he responded. "Thee does make a snug bed and Thomas didn't move about, so I was quick to sleep."

"And thee Thomas?" asked Suzanne as he appeared.

"Good and sound," he said. "Father didn't jostle about," he laughed, "so I was able to sleep in a hurry."

"We did just add new feathers," Hannah said.

"Felt soft," Thomas replied, happy for the chance to offer a direct comment.

"And now, have some of the bread we made but two days ago. It's good and firm from our own wheat. You'll both like it, we're sure."

Hannah cut it and set it in front of Thomas. She hesitated, then realizing she had not cut a slice for his father, quickly cut another and placed it self consciously on the table in front of Joseph. The others of her own family were quiet as they spread a little honey on the rich, dark bread, and chewed with the necessary vigor to settle the growing hunger pangs.

"It's good to eat one's own bounty," said Phineas between bites, and a lingering swallow, washed down with a little fresh milk he had just brought in from the barn. "Always seems to taste better when we've done it ourselves."

Suzanne Massey merely nodded in agreement.

Breakfast finished, Thomas sat back on the bench, stealing an occasional glance at Hannah, hoping not to be noticed. He had an off-center laugh that escaped from an embarrassed cough as she caught him looking at her.

"Thee has a long day ahead," she offered reassuringly, putting him at ease.

"Thee's been to Philadelphia?" he asked, now that it seemed safe to speak to her.

"Oh, yes. When we go to Yearly Meeting, it is the full family. Father has taken us there several times. There are so many people, and what sights there are, and we see friends that only come in from their own farms once a year."

Thomas was silent. He didn't want to seem ignorant about all the things Hannah was ready to share with him. He was reluctant to ask too many obvious questions that she would think him a country simpleton. He had mixed feelings of regret and relief as his father called him out to feed the horses. "I hope we will stop on the way back from Philadelphia," he finally said as he got up and stepped out doors.

The sun was barely up when they hitched the wagon, climbed aboard and with a wave, and headed down the short path to the road leading towards Philadelphia.

Chapter Seven

Joseph let Thomas handle the reins of the two large horses as they clambered off the middle ferry. They dug their hooves into the churned dirt and struggled up the incline away from the Schuylkill River onto the level road towards the city of Philadelphia. Other wagons passed by, empty of the product of their farms, carrying back into the country lighter stores of salt and cloth, pans, China ware, and occasional chairs and tables made in the city. There were light carriages and chaises with prosperous families, nicely seated, headed out of the city to their country houses high on the bluffs overlooking the river. Wagons came from other paths and roads to join the increasing traffic converging towards the city.

"I'll let thee drive," commented Joseph to his son quietly. "The experience will do thee fine."

"I've handled the team with this wagon before," replied Thomas, stiffening, his pride deflated.

"Yes, but only at Middletown or Goshen or at the Square, never with so many as we'll find in Philadelphia, and with many more people walking about, the streets are more congested."

"I'll do it," said Thomas with determination, even as his heart pumped faster.

"I know thee will," Joseph offered with encouragement. "Thee is a good fellow and thee knows our team. It'll be fine as long as we anticipate what others might do and look out for another that might not have full control of their own team. Then there are the city dandies who think they know everything about horses. When they have grooms to take care of them they don't even know how to properly hitch a single horse to their carriage. It's all done for them. No. You've been brought up on a farm and horses are second nature. We ask far more from our team than city folks do. Ours have to plow and harvest and pull our carriage and cart, then this wagon, loaded, know how to work alone or as a team. Yes. That's our life, our experience, and we know better than many of the city dwellers who work in a shop or counting houses or by the docks." Joseph kept glancing ahead, watching several wagons in front as they moved in and out of the ruts on the well-traveled road, now wider. Fields opened on either side, steeples piercing the skyline, buildings becoming more frequent until finally houses crowded closer together and the city of Philadelphia spread out before them.

Thomas pulled the team to the side and stopped. It was his first view of the largest city in the colonies. He lay the reins down and stood to get a better view. He had heard about Philadelphia all his life, of ships that came into the port bringing goods from England, taking away the wheat and flour of Pennsylvania to the islands to return with sugar and rum. But with the Continental Congress having convened and adopting a Declaration proclaiming independence from the mother country, it was changing. Thomas was inwardly pleased that men from all the other English colonies had come to Pennsylvania to protest English taxes, to sit in a congress to raise an army to fight against the forces of Great Britain. It was here in Philadelphia where these decisions were being made. His breathing quickened as he gazed out over the streets bordered by houses and shops with the mass of Christ Church steeple jutting up above the skyline of brick buildings, other steeples proclaiming their church buildings below. The sun was high overhead. Puffs of clouds drifted across the blue of the horizon, the humidity of summer gone with the crispness of an exuberant fall day.

"It's quite a sight, it is not?" Joseph said to his son. "I never but thrill to see the city. It's big, vibrant, colorful, and bustling," he nodded, agreeing with himself, "but if we don't get a move on, it'll be too late to get our flour to the shed of our merchant." Thomas sat down, and gathering the reins with a quick snap, the horses picked up their heads, ears curved forward, and pushing against the great leather collars worked the wagon back onto the roadway. He clicked his tongue and the horses picked up the pace to fall into a rhythm heading towards the High Street market sheds then the storehouses just beyond down by the banks of the Delaware River. The noises of the city became louder, people calling, wagons creaking, occasional soldiers marching in cadence towards an unseen encampment. Street sellers were calling out their wares for sale, teamsters shouting, guiding their wagons and carts in and among the other traffic, people milling about, gathering in small groups all too often in the path of horses. Thomas slowed their team to a steady walk, gripping the leather of the reins more tightly. He made ready to pull aside or slow the horses further, watching not so much the buildings, but the people and other wagons working in and out from the activity of the commerce of the city. Here in Philadelphia, the streets were straight, corners precise, traffic regular, following a certain, understood logic. The great sheds of High Street marked the center of activity for the citizens, a place to shop for daily necessities. Even past the noon hour, the stalls were busy, men and women walking with purpose in and out of the columns, many followed by servants carrying the day's purchases, young boys, English, Scottish, African, marching close by their mistresses. Thomas let the horses pick their own pace as they worked their way down towards the river, past the last of the market sheds, past the London Coffee House on Front Street, down to Water Street. There the wharves and warehouses stood, their physical presence a testimony to the importance of the port to Philadelphia. It lay central to the English colonies.

"Stop at the bottom," Joseph said to his son. "I need to find Friend John Pemberton."

"Who is he?" Thomas asked.

"The merchant I normally seek out when we come to town. He is known to us. He's fair and a prominent member of the High Street Meeting. Important in the Yearly Meeting."

Thomas was happy to apply the brakes to the wagon. It gave him the chance to gaze out over the river at the ships lying at anchor, waiting for the tide to slacken so they could come about and slip alongside one of the many wharves. The masts of other ships punctuated the sky alongside the warehouses, some canted away from perpendicular as the cargo was brought ashore. Little rowboats darted in and out bringing messages and people and fresh foods back-and-forth across the water. Small sailboats carried people over to New Jersey or carried along with the tide up towards Pennsbury Manor and Burlington in New Jersey or down towards Chester and Upland.

"Watch thy way!" admonished Joseph to his son, as the wagon veered toward the curb line and buildings alongside the street.

Thomas jerked the reins to straighten out the horses.

"I know thee's seeing all this for the first time, but thee

must wait to gawk until we find a place for our products, then settle our horses in the stable and find our lodgings."

Thomas took his eyes off the shipping and headed the team for an open spot along Water Street. It would be out from other wagons and barrows, people and carts, all jostling back-and-forth obvious evidence to the importance of the port. He pulled the horses aside and stopped, dropping down off the wagon, and went to adjust the bit in their mouths to ease the pressure. The horses shook their heads. He loosened the harness, giving the team freedom to lower their heads, looking for something to eat on the bare, dirt ground.

Joseph slipped down off the seat. "Stay here. I'll seek out Friend John." He dodged an oncoming wagon and headed into the closest warehouse. Thomas stood by the horses, flinging a lead line over a hitching post. He took in the view before him. Stepping farther out into the street, he was transfixed by the immensity of the sights before him. Looking at a group of sailors walking away from the near wharf, he noticed a young girl come in the opposite direction headed for the office of the warehouse next door to John Pemberton's. She was lithe, with soft brown hair flowing out from underneath her lace bordered cap. The flare of her skirt was more pronounced than the simpler lines of Quaker women, and her shawl, wrapped around her shoulders, displayed an understated but elegant print. She walked steadily and purposefully, carefully around the horse droppings, but in a direct line to the office. She mounted the steps and without knocking opened the heavy door and pushed inside. Thomas kept his eye on the warehouse, hoping the girl would come out so he could see her face. He stared for a moment to will her to return, but he became distracted when two wagons crossing on a turn got their wheels caught against one another. Shouting became louder. Several men stopped. A small crowd of children gathered. Thomas could hear the curses hurled back and forth. As the teamsters were arguing, two bystanders grabbed the team on the lead wagon and urged the horses to a tight turn and away from the other entangled wagon and just as suddenly as it started, the furor quieted. The wagons went on their way and the little crowd dispersed. Thomas looked up and down Water Street until suddenly he saw the girl again crossing from the office in his direction. As she got closer, he could see her soft face, her clear blue eyes under darker eyelashes, with an angular nose without prominence, above full lips, lovely but determined. He watched as she came closer, involuntarily stepping a pace away from the lead horse to stand slightly closer to her path. The girl watched her step until suddenly she looked up at Thomas, his outline framed by the upgrade of High Street behind him. She looked at his dusty, plain country clothes. Thomas took off his broad-brimmed hat as much as to do something rather than stand rooted to the spot, his face flushed, embarrassed for his staring. He ran his fingers across his head to loosen his hair. He stood straighter. She looked directly at Thomas, not flinching. He gave a faint smile with a slight nod of his head. She smiled more broadly without hesitation, keeping her steady pace. Thomas kept looking, changed his gaze, then came back hoping he could look again without being noticed. She passed, turning her head towards Thomas. He couldn't help but stare, swept up with her cosmopolitan beauty and carriage, watching her go on past and noting how she straightened her head beginning the gentle climb up to Front Street. He was afraid to keep looking but worried he would lose sight of her as she walked in and amongst others. Thomas followed her progression as she continued on with determination. At the last minute, before becoming hidden at the top of the street, she turned back to look.

Thomas smiled, first to himself and then broadly across his face.

"What's this?" quizzed Joseph coming upon his son.

Thomas focused out of his reverie. "Just looking," he answered. "Just looking," he said again as if to convince his father.

"It must have been a sight," replied Joseph with the benefit of years. "Thee doesn't normally keep staring at something with your mouth open."

"Did thee find thy agent?" asked Thomas trying to change the subject.

Joseph nodded, unwilling to pursue Thomas' lack of notice to their own horses and wagon. "Yes. Friend Pemberton will give us the latest rate for our flour and other grain. Bring the wagon over to the big door of the far warehouse. That's his and we'll set our load inside."

***

As Joseph settled with the Pemberton agent, Thomas slipped around to another cubicle where a clerk sat on a stool recording figures in the great ledger before him.

"Whose wharf is that just by? The next one up river?" he said it softly, nervous that his father might hear.

"You mean Smith's dock and office?"

"If that's the one next to here, then yes."

"Old man Smith is one of the big merchants of the city. Plantations in the south. Property in the Indies. Farm in Delaware. I hear even property in Bermuda."

"Does he have children?"

"You mean, does he have a daughter?"

"Well, yes. I mean, how old is she?"

"Old enough to be the fairest girl in town. A delight to see, comely, but with a strong demeanor. Takes no nonsense. Takes after her father."

"Does she often come to his warehouse next door?"

"Regular like. She's got an interest in his affairs. Mostly she stays at their big house on Second Street below Walnut. But don't get ideas. She's Anglican. They're big at Christ Church. They don't associate with Quakers."

"Not even in business?"

"Well, that's different. Pemberton will work with anyone if they're reliable and if there's a profit to be made."

"And Smith?"

"William T. Smith. Sure. He'll work with anyone. The same. They're all in it for the money."

Thomas stood back, glancing over to see his father still deep in conversation. He took a deep breath, turning back to the clerk.

"So. What's her name?"

"Smith's daughter?"

"Yes, if that's the girl who walks into the office next door without knocking."

"That's the one. Well, her name's Elizabeth, pleasant enough. She comes here on occasion, but I've never really talked to her. Just listened in." He smiled with the memory. "Nice." He leaned back and looked up at Thomas. "But still Anglican and surrounded by a number of interested suitors."

"Serious?"

"They think so but I'm not so sure she agrees."

"Thanks for the information."

"Sure, and say, you've just come in from the country. Why are you interested?"

"Curious, that's all." Thomas was uncomfortable with any further conversation. He turned and headed back to the front where his father straightened up and with a handshake, confirmed their business.

"Now to the stable and our lodging, then thee can walk about," he motioned to Thomas, pushing open the door.

***

Settled in, early supper finished, Joseph suggested to Thomas, "If thee has an interest, thee can see some of the sights of Philadelphia. Thee might like to see the great meeting house on Third Street, perhaps go to the State House beyond Fifth Street, then past Benjamin Franklin's house and shop. There's much to see."

"Thank thee, Father. I'd like that." Thomas brushed off his clothes, trying to look as though the city was an ordinary occasion, even if his shirt and jacket were plain and country like, the black hat now slightly faded, dusty on the brim. He stepped out into the street still full of activity even as the sun reached lower to the west casting long shadows from the variety of roofs against the houses and buildings opposite. As he came to Second Street, he hesitated, looking down the row of brick houses to see a large mansion, taller than the rest, wider and more imposing. He hesitated, then looking about as if to make sure nobody would notice, walked down towards the Smith residence. He adjusted his hat, resetting it in exactly the same position as he made his way slowly down the street. He looked at each house in turn, with neat, tidy, scrubbed marble steps, the brick walk in front swept, the brass polished and the windows shiny, reflecting the light from the uneven streaking of the glass. Coming to the largest house, *a mansion to be sure,* thought Thomas, he stopped and looked up, marveling at the craftsmanship of the front door with a fine carving surrounding the entrance. He stood quietly, his plain country dress, Quaker and distinctive even from the other city Quakers walking about, was more so from the greater number of non-Quakers in all manner of dress without the strictures of plainness.

A door opened and Elizabeth Smith appeared coming down the broad steps followed by a younger Negro girl carrying a large-handled straw basket. She noticed Thomas standing across the street, now slightly embarrassed to be seen looking. She smiled at him and waited. His heart sped up, blood racing through his chest. In slow motion, drawn by a curious energy, he walked across, lifting his hat to her, realizing too late that Quakers didn't raise their hats to any other. Elizabeth Smith stood her ground with a faint smile as she looked at Thomas coming closer. The servant girl waited behind her. Words raced through Thomas' mind but none seemed quite right as he grappled with an appropriate opening.

Elizabeth broke the tension with a confident familiarity. "You're new in Philadelphia?"

Thomas hesitated, trying to figure out what to say to the obvious. "Yes," he finally said simply. Picking up his courage, seeing that Elizabeth Smith was waiting for something further, he added, "We've just come in from outside Philadelphia, Edgmont, bringing our grain and flour to sell."

"I figured, seeing you down by the docks with your wagon. You obviously aren't from the city." She said it not unkindly, only as a matter of fact.

"Thee was born here?" asked Thomas regaining his presence.

"No," she answered, "in St. Kitts, but I've been back to the islands with my father," she added.

"But not to the Pennsylvania countryside?"

"That too. Father has a farm in Delaware that we visit at least once a year." She tossed her head slightly aside. It was a sympathetic response.

"So. What does thee do here, in between times? I mean, if thee has everything, what is there to fill thy time?" Thomas felt emboldened.

She looked him straight in the eye, hesitated, then answered, "I help Father with his affairs, manage the house, and I write letters for him." She lowered her voice feeling she had answered too much.

"Is that why thee was at the docks earlier?" Thomas asked openly.

"Of course. I don't go there for social visits. It's a rougher part of the city." She came closer. "And what are you doing here, on Second Street, standing outside our house?" she asked in a sharper tone. He realized he was now suspect. He could think of no good reason not to answer as he felt.

"Thee looks different. From others. From everyone else."

"How so?" Elizabeth asked, now increasingly interested.

"The way thee walks, with a bold stride and purpose." Thomas spread his hands. "Thee doesn't seem to need any man to escort thee, to keep thee from trouble."

"How silly," she tossed her head looking up and down the street. "It's safe here." She laughed. "If it were not, would I be talking with you?"

"I guess not," admitted Thomas.

"And what else?" she probed.

"Well, thee is right presentable," answered Thomas with a bit more candor then he would have wished.

"At least you're honest."

"I've been raised to always be truthful."

"Never a little untruth?"

"Never." He lowered his head. "If I don't want to answer, pushed to say an untruth, then I don't answer at all."

"Is that what Quakers are taught?"

"It's our habit and when we converse with one another, then we don't have to figure out if what we hear is the truth or not."

"Well," Elizabeth exclaimed, "that's a change. I do know that Father prefers to deal with Quakers, like your John Pemberton, and he's said when I overheard him that he doesn't have to wonder whether he should believe what he has been told when dealing with Quakers." She moved back toward the front of the house, away from the street, no longer so obvious, particularly to anyone who might be looking out a window of the great house. "It is good to tell the truth."

"Then people don't have to guess," agreed Thomas.

"Do you think I'm presentable?" she smoothed her skirt shifting slightly.

Thomas was silent.

"You're not going to answer? Does that mean you don't think so?"

"Contrary. I don't know whether it's proper to tell thee that I think thee is beautiful, that thee has style and presence and that thee commands attention." Thomas looked into her eyes with an intensity he had not felt before.

"Well, you're direct, that I'll say for it."

"Thee asked."

"Yes, and I guess I knew that if I didn't want an answer,

not to ask." Then she burst out with a sprightly laugh. "But I like the answer so I'm happy I asked, and knowing you will only tell the truth, it makes it so much more to be appreciated." She came closer and took his hand. "And now that I have your opinion, I need to know your name. Just in case," she added as an afterthought.

"Thomas Pratt," he replied, firmly drawing himself up.

"Thomas. That's a nice name. And Pratt. Quaker?"

"From the first who came to Pennsylvania with William Penn."

"That long ago?"

"Yes."

"Do you want to know mine?"

"Elizabeth Smith. It is thine?"

"Yes. Of course. How did you know?"

"I asked at Pemberton's. Thee seems to have a following and are well known."

"So why did you come down Second Street?" She was serious again.

"To see where thee lives," he answered slowly.

"And?"

"And maybe to catch a glimpse of thee again." He felt emboldened.

"I did notice you looking at me earlier."

"Which means thee was looking at me." Thomas smiled.

"I keep my eyes open. It always amazes me what I see," she continued as a soft defense. "Besides, if I had not, I would not be here talking to you for the first time. Perhaps thinking you're strange, or impolite, too forward even."

"And now?"

"Now, I know about you, that you are not strange. You

are someone who is willing to talk his own mind, straight, truthful, presentable, even if from the country, still a little dusty." She flicked a stem from his coat, brushing the arm free of the dirt smudge.

Thomas felt a surge in his throat. "Thee, uh, thee had an errand?"

"As you can see," tossing her head towards the servant waiting patiently just out of hearing.

"Knowing that thee then will not be alone, may I escort thee on thy mission?"

"You are a bold one!" Her face became severe, but then softened. "Well, it is still daylight and I do have a chaperone here, and heaven knows all the others can't speak their minds clearly."

"Others?"

"Friends. I don't mean Quakers of course, real friends."

"But I'm a real Friend," said Thomas quickly.

"Yes, I know, but I mean persons that call on me, not business, just social visits. You know, friends."

"Sure, it's just that most of my friends are Friends. You know, Religious Society of Friends."

"Very well," she relented. "Come with me. I was just going to pick up some sewing for a new dress. You can come. People will talk, but I don't care. With all I do particularly down at Father's wharf and onto his ships, people always talk, but not so much anymore. So come, it'll be fun." She waved at her servant to follow as she stepped away from the front steps and walked purposefully back towards Chestnut Street.

Thomas felt elated, in the great city, talking with a lovely girl who did not make fun of him for his plain dress and simple manners. Elizabeth Smith walked with the same strong strides he had witnessed before. It was simple to keep up, more like those he knew in Edgmont.

"This is your first visit here?" Elizabeth finally asked knowing Thomas' company was her responsibility.

"Yes. Father said it was my time to come." He glanced sideways at her, taken by her profile now more beautiful than when trying to make conversation.

"It's a big city, the more so now with the Congress coming and going and the Continental Army under General Washington fighting. People are worried that the fighting will come here." She looked at him. "I'm worried."

He returned the look. In Edgmont, the armies seemed far away.

"Then there's the Royal Navy. Father has ships. He trades with British possessions in the West Indies and with England, and now that we're at war, he is worried for the safety of his men and the ships and the cargo and what might happen. He's always been friendly with the English. He trades with them." Elizabeth lowered her head, her eyelashes flickering up and down.

"Is he a Tory?"

"No, unless to trade with the English makes one a Tory, but then he also trades with the other colonies. Does that make him a rebel?" Elizabeth lowered her voice. "Father wants to stay out of the way, continue to trade, respect everyone."

"But that may not be possible. We as Quakers are against fighting. We want to live our lives, free, but not join in the fighting."

"And what about you? Do you agree that you should stand aside, do nothing, pretend nothing is going to happen?" She stopped and looked at him directly.

He turned his head away. She waited. He hesitated, then finally turned back and with deep, questioning eyes slowly answered.

"I know the fighting is wrong. It's wrong to kill another person."

She wanted to interrupt but thought better of it. She waited quietly.

"But I don't think I can stand by and do nothing. We're fighting now to be free. I don't know all the troubles, but if so many from the English colonies see their way clear to declare for independence and are willing to take a stand for it, with an army, then I think I want to help. I have an obligation to do what I can." He was breathing more quickly. The words came faster. "I think we are no longer English colonies. I think we are really States of America, united, wanting to be free." He stopped.

"Have you said that to anyone else?" Elizabeth asked.

"No, never, but I've been thinking all the way into Philadelphia and I've seen the ships and warehouses and all these buildings and thy grand house."

"Will you?"

"Say anything?"

"Yes."

"Maybe, but not yet. I would not know how. Not to my father, who is opposed to supporting any army and particularly not to the Meeting where there is a firm testimony against fighting as a means to settle disputes." His voice softened. "What about thy father? Will he trade with the British? Will he maintain his contacts in England? What happens if the fighting comes to Pennsylvania? What will he do?"

Elizabeth Smith now looked away in her turn. She didn't look at Thomas. "I don't know. Father talks about it all the time, but it's with other merchants. I know the Congress wants to buy his supplies, but they only want to pay with a Continental currency, paper, nothing to back it up. Father is worried."

She started to walk. Thomas followed. She headed out on Chestnut Street. They'd gone two blocks when she spoke.

"You've never seen the State House, have you, where the Declaration of Independence was signed?"

"No."

"Well, we're almost there. You should see it. It really is central to what's going on."

"Is it out of thy way?"

"Yes, but no matter. You can't go back to Edgmont without knowing this. Maybe it'll help you make up your mind." She picked up the pace until suddenly Thomas could see the tower and then the long brick facade, large windows set regularly facing the street, the largest building in Philadelphia. They came up in front, Thomas staring at the building and then at the guard posted at the front door. Men were passing in and out, the bustle and activity intensifying with the increased fighting up north.

"Well, there it is," Elizabeth said, motioning toward the building.

Thomas stood transfixed.

"I can leave you here," she said.

"No, I'd rather walk with thee."

"Well, fine. We'll go around the other side and then to my seamstress."

As they arrived back on Second Street, Thomas could see a man dressed in all of his finery standing outside the Smith house. As they got closer, he drew away from the person at the doorway and started up the street towards them.

"Where have you been?" he called out to Elizabeth.

"To the seamstress!"

"With another?" he pointed to Thomas.

"Yes. Of course." She was slightly defensive. "Are you worried?"

"No, but your father was."

"I should be sorry that you weren't worried," she teased.

"Oh, well, of course I was. Your father said you only had to go to a shop not far away."

"Yes, but then I decided to show the State House to Thomas Pratt here."

"Oh, so that's who he is," the other fellow suggested with an air of superiority, the lace showing around his neck and hanging below the cuffs of this finely tailored coat waving with every motion.

"Thomas, this is Jeremy Oliver, a friend of father's."

"And yours also, I hope," Jeremy added quickly.

"Of course," Elizabeth said gently.

Jeremy was tall, with clean hair tied at the back with a purple bow accentuating his angular face, which showed a few lines at the eyes, perhaps a witness to his thirty years.

Thomas was feeling uncomfortable in the presence of the other. "I need to get back," he said, and left with a nod of the head to Elizabeth.

Chapter Eight

The following morning, Joseph spoke to his son. "We need to pick up some supplies to take back home. My friend, Phineas, has asked that we bring him back six dishes in a blue pattern as a surprise for his wife and thy mother would have a teapot."

"Where will we find them?" asked Thomas.

"We'll ask Friend Pemberton. He'll know. Then we'll go to get our salt and a bit of sugar." He looked at Thomas with a bright smile. "Thee knows how thy mother likes to bake a sweet cake."

"And how thee likes to eat it," laughed Thomas.

"I don't deny. I also observe," he responded in as serious a tone as he could muster, "that thee also asks for another piece of cake." He looked at his son in admiration. "Thee's done well Thomas. Has it been a good experience?" His tone was kindly.

"Yes, Father." Thomas looked over as Joseph pushed his son's rumpled hair back into place after the night's rest in the Quaker boarding house. "It's a big city, so many people, crowded, alive, with the ships from so far away." He waited for his father to lead the way down the narrow steps into the common room. A small fire was whispering quietly in the fireplace, warming a copper pot hung over the little flame, spirals of vapor escaping from the curved neck of the spout.

"Here they are," called out the woman of the house coming in from the pantry just behind. "We have hot biscuits ready and even a little coffee if thee wants, Joseph."

Her familiarity was a comfort. "And for thy son? Maybe tea, still a little left, that which they didn't throw into Boston Harbor." She chortled at her own joke. "And some bacon and some fresh eggs, enough to get you going and back to the country." She bustled around the room, picking up the porringer and mug from the other table.

"Thank thee kindly, Bertha," Joseph replied. "Thee always has a way."

"Now, thee does go on," she teased, her ample girth jumping up and down behind her apron, with a series of chuckles in appreciation.

"We have errands to get done before the sun gets too far up over New Jersey."

"No worry. You'll be out before the grand folks make it to the windows of their bedchambers." She turned on her heel calling back, "You have read Ben Franklin's advice?" She stopped. Joseph shook his head. "Early to bed. Early to rise. Makes a man healthy, wealthy, and wise."

"Well, I'm certainly healthy. Wise? Thee'll have to answer. Wealthy? Only because of my family."

"With thy son, Thomas, I can see. Yes, Ben's got it and so does thee." She scuttled to the back room, singing to herself.

"Do we go down to the wharves?" asked Thomas.

"Yes. To Friend Pemberton's."

"And for the salt and sugar?"

Joseph looked at his son, then answered, "And to have another visit with Elizabeth Smith?"

Thomas colored.

Joseph continued. "She is a right comely lass, that's for sure, but thee needs to understand she is a city girl, well-to-do, and Anglican. William Smith is fair to deal with, a man of his word, but their lives are far different from ours. Business, yes. Otherwise, no."

Thomas lowered his eyes.

"She may not even be there when we stop." Joseph tried to soften his advice. He put his arm around his son and added brightly, "But if she's there, we'll offer a pleasantry."

Thomas didn't say anything. Joseph thought about it, opened his mouth for a further comment then thought better of it and closed his mouth.

Thomas walked out into the freshness of the morning, carts just beginning to rumble by, tradesmen opening their storefronts, vendors calling out their fresh fish, chickens, and vegetables. Philadelphia was awakening. He stood there watching the activity, drawn to the confusing mystery of Elizabeth Smith and the seemingly impossible gulf that separated them. He adjusted his black hat, shifting it higher into as close a fashion as he had seen on the dandies who met up with Elizabeth. He tilted it a bit to the left to add more of a city look. He didn't hear his father come up behind him.

"Ready?" his father asked. Thomas startled, quickly adjusted his broad-brimmed hat lower on his forehead, and turned to follow his father to the stables. They were quiet, walking first on the brick pavement then stepping into the dirt of the street to let a lady pass. Coming to the stable, they moved to the head of their horses, gave them a rub around the ears, and worked them out into the center of the small building, placing the harness over them.

"We'll make for the waterfront first," announced Joseph.

Thomas did not let his disappointment show. He was sure Elizabeth Smith was one of those who rose late, when the morning sun finally streamed into her room and across her bed.

The horses knew the routine as they easily followed

around to where the wagon had been left. Joseph backed them up as Thomas stepped behind and attached the leather straps to the crosstrees, laying reins up and over the seat of the wagon, now empty.

"Is thee the one to take us down to Pemberton's?" Joseph asked. He didn't wait for an answer as he climbed up onto the near side of the wagon. Thomas got up onto the off side, grabbed the reins, and with a snap and double click, moved the team out on to the road and headed down towards the waterfront.

The streets were becoming crowded. Thomas, with the experience of a country fair and gathering of wagons at the meeting house, the confidence of his youth, worked the team in and out with no more than a gentle tug, a pull or loosening of the reins, an occasional "hoo," and "yoh," as they made their way to the waterfront. The ships lay still, sails on some hanging limply to air and dry. Sailors called back and forth, working the rigging, while laborers hoisted barrels of wheat onto the ships' decks. Others were offloading casks of rum, cones of sugar, bags of salt onto the docks and into the adjacent warehouses. Thomas pulled the team to a stop in front of Pemberton's.

"Wait here," Joseph said. "I'll see where we can find thy mother's request." He hopped down and through the door, standing ajar with noises inside.

Thomas watched then looked over towards Smith's. There was a lamp in the window, someone already at the accounts. He kept staring. It wasn't until Elizabeth Smith was at the door that he noticed her. She turned and waved at him, a faint smile as she slid inside, leaving the door open. He sat up straight and leaned forward to shorten the distance, his face flushed in the early morning light. He looked into Pemberton's, wishing for his father to come out and say they needed to go to Smith's. Thomas became impatient, then worried that Elizabeth would finish her business and leave before he could get there. He was ready to tie the horses to the hitching post when his father came out, a paper in his hand, a look of satisfaction about him.

"We've done fine," he exclaimed to his son. "Better than I thought." He climbed up. Ignoring Thomas' nervousness, he said, "Now for Smith's." Thomas jerked the reins and the team lurched forward, more quickly than Thomas hoped was noticed, faster than Joseph would ever start the team. They crossed the intervening space as Thomas drew up to another hitching post, jumping down and throwing the reins in a loose loop to keep the team settled. Joseph, bemused by the hurry, got down and, glancing at his son, headed for the entrance. He looked in and seeing Elizabeth Smith talking to one of the clerks, he understood. He hesitated, with Thomas standing close behind. He felt committed and so with an uncertainty, stepped inside.

"Mistress Smith," he acknowledged with a careful courtesy. "Lawrence," he nodded to the clerk, familiar from before. Thomas came in and stepped from behind his father to look with apprehension and appreciation at Elizabeth.

She looked up and smiled with what was the most glorious smile Thomas had ever seen. It coursed through his body.

"What can I help you with?" she said to Joseph but looking at Thomas.

Joseph turned aside, and realizing the question was for him answered. "I understand thee has a new shipment of sugar and salt, perhaps molasses." He looked at Elizabeth closely for the first time.

"We have a goodly supply," she answered. Joseph was impressed. Beauty was one thing, but with a quick mind, much the more to be admired. Thomas edged closer.

"Oh, this is your son?" she asked.

"This is Thomas, my third," answered Joseph with an unseemly pride.

"I know his name," answered Elizabeth.

"Oh?"

"Yes, we met previously. I showed him the State House," she said lightly. "It's such a pleasure to lead another to the center of government and the home of the Continental Congress, at least for the first time," she added quickly, reluctant to be too forward. Joseph turned to look at his son.

Thomas nodded. "We did take a walk," he admitted. "I saw a bit of Philadelphia."

"And the first time is always the most exciting," Elizabeth added. "I can't remember when I first saw the city. I was born in the West Indies and was very young when I was brought here, but as I grew up, I have found the city wonderful, bustling, vibrant, full of life." She stepped towards Joseph. "It was a pleasure to show your son some of the sights." She was confident as she said it. Joseph said nothing, his mind racing from the situation he had never faced before. Elizabeth turned to Thomas.

"Do you like Philadelphia?" she smiled and waited. Both were silent. Then Thomas spoke.

"Very much."

"I'm sure he's much obliged," interrupted Joseph, gaining his wits about him.

"Don't worry," said Elizabeth, "I'm not out to turn a Quaker into an Anglican. Habits are too deep in both of us. Nevertheless, I enjoyed the company of your son." She stepped over to Thomas. "Did you enjoy my company?" She nodded with expectation.

"Oh, yes," Thomas replied, regaining his bearings.

"Nothing unseemly," she confirmed to Joseph. "When you're walking in a public street, there's hardly any privacy, nor any need." She laughed. "I realize that my father thinks I'm too wild, too much of a free spirit, but without a mother, I have no good example to follow other than the men folk who seem to have all the best time of it. Isn't that so?" she asked of the clerk, sitting at his desk trying to stay busy while containing a smile which was difficult to keep within his innocuous demeanor.

"Yes, miss," he replied dutifully, "as thee says."

"There, you see, just as I say." She turned serious. "But you are here on business and so we should attend to our affairs."

"We've come to purchase some of thy salt and sugar and molasses. They said at Pemberton's that thy father's ship docked this week."

"That's so and it may be the last for some time." Elizabeth Smith spoke with a certain wistfulness. "The captain reported that with the fighting it was a close run thing to ship the cargo, then run before the Royal Navy could stop him. Yes, we have salt and sugar, but it's become precious, so buy what you need. See the clerk there, but take care, it may have to last until the end of fighting."

"You mean until General Washington sends the English back across the ocean," said Thomas.

"Or perhaps until Britain brings a proper sense of belonging and restores order to the colonies." Elizabeth looked at one then another. "We are loyal subjects. We only seek to trade within the British frame of government and its possessions, including Pennsylvania. That is just and right." She spoke with a quiet conviction raising and lowering the front of her foot for emphasis.

"Come Thomas," Joseph said to his son. "Let us conclude our affairs here." He went to the clerk and made the arrangements, lesser amounts than originally anticipated with the increased prices. He stepped back and without a bow or lifting of his hat, said, "We'll take our leave now." The voice was neutral, Joseph's Quaker stance expressed with a subtle conviction.

Thomas hesitated, then added, "We'll be going." He didn't know what to say further.

Elizabeth Smith brightened. "We'll be here. Our ships will continue to sail in between the armies." She had a broad smile on an open face. "So when you return, see what we have then." She put out her hand. Joseph hesitated, then took it, releasing the grasp quickly, embarrassed by the unseemly nature of the gesture. Thomas watched, then put his own hand out, waiting for Elizabeth to take it. Joseph looked askance as she took it with a firm, warm curling of her fingers around his, saying with a bright cheerfulness, "Come back, there's more to see in Philadelphia." Thomas released the grip, not sure what he should do next. Joseph settled it by turning to the clerk. "We'll draw the wagon out back and ship our goods and be on our way." Thomas took one last look at Elizabeth, standing there confident, serene, and lovely in the early morning light.

They said nothing further as the warehouse man helped load the barrels and sacks onto the wagon. Joseph climbed purposefully onto the driver's seat and with a snap of the reins, guided the horses out into the morning traffic and away from the waterfront. He was anxious to leave the area, feeling his neutrality was in danger of compromise.

Thomas wasn't sure. *Surely, someone so bright and confident couldn't be against the new nation,* he contemplated. He said nothing to his father.

The morning activity was increasing. Peddlers hawked their wares down the residential streets, while large wagons slowly moved along the commercial streets, teamsters calling out to make way. Occasional carriages with the privileged and wealthy threaded their path carefully through the throng of people. The congestion increased as horses or an infrequent cow or steer was guided to a stable or slaughterhouse. Joseph knew the way but the Philadelphia crowd made him uneasy.

"We'll stop on High Street. There is a member of the Quaker meeting there that has fine china."

"For long?" asked Thomas, sorry to leave the experience of the colony's largest city. Soldiers in uniform, a small detachment, marched by on Second Street, the sergeant setting the pace. The uniforms were plain, green pants, buckled at the knee, stockings pulled up tight with boots burnished brown, dusty in the dried, dirt street, but brown jackets with brass buttons and white stocks around their necks creating a fine sense of confidence. Their tri-cornered hats were set at just the right angle, straight on in contrast to the tilt of their long rifles on their shoulders as they kept a steady pace.

"Is that part of Washington's Army?" asked Thomas of his father.

"I think not," replied Joseph. "The Continental Army is blue over bluff. I suspect that group is part of the Pennsylvania Militia, less fancy, but they do seem in good order," admitted Joseph.

"I hear that Edgmont is forming our militia," Thomas ventured.

"Thee means, their militia," retorted Joseph quickly.

"Well, it will be from our township."

"Yes, but we'll not be party to it." He looked over at his son. "It's not our way and the Yearly Meeting has reaffirmed our testimony for peace." Joseph snapped the reins for emphasis.

Thomas watched the soldiers turn on Walnut Street and out of sight. He waited, then asked, "Does thee think there'll be fighting in Pennsylvania?"

Joseph pondered, then finally spoke. "I fear that the British will force an advance on Philadelphia. It is the seat of the Congress and from what I heard last night, the Pennsylvania Assembly and executives are preparing for a defense, although how our Pennsylvania boys could stand against a regular British Army advancing, I don't know. I suspect that is why we saw that detachment just now." He worked the horses towards the sidewalk in front of a line of stores, each displaying the goods in the windows, confirming the painting of their signs.

Before he could climb down on to the street, Thomas spoke. "Does thee think it wrong for Pennsylvania to order up its own militia?"

"Thomas," replied his father in a direct tone. "Thee knows I deplore fighting, the use of force, the act of war, that the Executive Council has ordered men into the army is a judgment made in error. It can come to no good. To fight means men will die. Our concerns need to be settled by peaceful resolution, with an ongoing dialogue. War is wrong." He softened his voice. "I know the Congress has created an army and ordered Washington to be its Commander-in-Chief. I fear the direction we're headed with the fighting up north which I worry will come here to Pennsylvania, to Philadelphia. I dread to think it may come close. I worry." He shook his head. "No, I do not approve of calling out the militia. Our peace testimony speaks of God's way."

Thomas was quiet. He didn't look at his father as he slid off the seat, jumping down into the street. Joseph watched as his son took the reins and tied them against the hitching post. He debated in his own mind whether to ask Thomas for his thoughts, but Thomas was already looking into the shop window, the passion of the subject having passed. *I guess he thinks no more about it,* thought Joseph.

***

Joseph selected the teapot after a careful look at the small display. The blue pattern on the china was simple, in modest taste but lovely to look at.

"And it'll hold a right nice mix of tea," encouraged the shopkeeper.

"Does thee think thy Mother will like it?" asked Joseph.

"It is good-looking and I think that any choice thee makes for Mother she'll like, because thee chose it."

The shopkeeper smiled, handing it over to Joseph. "Thy son is a good judge," encouraged the merchant, "and I can tell thee Friend, it'll be awhile before we get many more of these. The British are restricting our trade and I'm afraid with the conflict going on, we'll feel the effects." He shook his head. "Bad business," he determined.

"I do try to bring a surprise back to the farm and I know my Jane has thought of a fine teapot for some time."

"It does always taste better coming from a proper spout. There's nice decoration on the pot itself and this is the finest china we can get." The shopkeeper was encouraging.

"What say thee, Thomas?"

"We should do it," he answered.

"Fine then," Joseph said, "and make it into a pretty package, if thee will, so we can get it home safely."

"Going far?" inquired the keeper.

"I plan for Marple this night, then on to Edgmont tomorrow." He nodded to Thomas. "Another good meal at the Masseys, I suspect," he laughed, "but we need now to make our way."

"But a moment," replied the shopkeeper, taking the coin from Joseph. "No paper," he said appreciatively.

"I keep to real value," said Joseph. "Both offering and receiving."

"Rightly so," was the response, "keeps the trade fair."

"Thank thee, Friend," Joseph said, shaking hands with a fellow Quaker. "I'm pleased."

***

The sun came bright into the sky drying the few puddles left from the latest rain. Dust rose, kicked up by the horses' hooves as they kept a steady pace, leaving the city behind them, now on the road west to Chester County.

Thomas liked the strong air, the wind blowing into his face from the west, the freedom of space after the confines of Philadelphia. "At this pace, we'll be to the Massey's before nightfall," offered Joseph. Thomas was silent. "They're a good family," encouraged Joseph, "and thy mother and I are right fond of them." He waited, then continued. "We're sorry they belong to another Quarterly Meeting, else we'd see them more frequently." He leaned back, the horses keeping a steady pace, reins loose on their backs. "And their Hannah is a fine girl." Joseph was reluctant to use a warmer description. He waited, then asked, "Didn't thee think she was a nice person?"

I don't even know her, thought Thomas. *She didn't really say anything when we visited before.* Thomas nodded. "I guess so," he answered, "but a little shy."

"In front of her parents and myself thee would not expect anything more from a well brought up girl."

"But Elizabeth Smith is well brought up," countered Thomas.

"Yes, but she is a city girl and an Anglican, and from what I observe, in trade, with, or for, or because of her father."

"She was nice to me."

"There's more to a woman than a quick smile and a ready wit," observed Joseph. Thomas was silent as the horses kept their pace, the wagon moving around the larger rocks, clicking on the scattered stones, bouncing over the occasional hole.

***

They rounded the familiar lane and came in sight of the Massey homestead. Thomas was a little apprehensive to see Hannah again. The first time was simple, but this time his father offered encouragement. They pulled the wagon to a stop. Phineas was in the far field but waved as he saw them come into view. It was Hannah coming out of the chicken coop who offered the first greeting.

"Good afternoon, Friend Joseph," she said cheerfully. "And to thee also," she repeated to Thomas with a slightly more hopeful smile.

"And thank thee Hannah," said Joseph, jumping down and shaking her hand. "I see thy father. Is thy mother about?"

"Inside. She'll be happy to see thee, I know," she replied.

"Thomas, thee can take care of the team?" He didn't

wait for a response but headed towards the house, leaving the two of them there.

"I can help," offered Hannah hopefully.

Thomas was annoyed with the intrusion. "If thee wishes," he finally responded.

Hannah was hesitant as she held the reins as Thomas unhitched the horses.

"Here," he said, "take the one. I'll follow where thee has room for them."

She quickly clicked her tongue and led the off-side horse into the barn. Thomas was taken by surprise but followed. "They'll be best here," she said leading the horse into the stall.

Thomas watched as she took the bit from the horse's mouth and with several deft motions had the harness hung up and the horse comfortable and munching the loose hay. She was light in her movements. Her hair danced out from underneath her simple cloth cap, the ties hanging loosely down the side of her tanned face. In the dusky light of the stables, her eyes looked out with a green intensity that belied her gentle personality. She stood back waiting for Thomas to finish the same with the other horse. He didn't like being watched, unsettled as with a test given by another, younger, and a girl. He moved swiftly and stood back against the door, straight, a barely perceptible challenge to Hannah for the next move. She tossed her head lightly looking directly at Thomas.

"I have a few more chores to finish," she said in a matter of fact tone.

Thomas, not taking his eyes off hers replied evenly, "I'll help if thee wants."

"Surely. It's the sheep and goats that need tending, down by the croft, close to the creek."

"Lead the way," Thomas said, at least happy to have something to do to avoid conversation.

Hannah strode off, her hips a little too tight against the long gray skirt coming down to her ankles swinging her backside a bit more than normal. Thomas followed, without enthusiasm, his mind a blank, his eye on the back of her neck, her hair flouncing back and forth. His gaze lowered bit by bit, stopping at her buttocks, firm, sensuous, energetic, propelling her forward. He tripped on the edge of a rock sticking up in the path and took a two-step, bringing himself closer to her. He maintained the shortened distance, her warmth in the still air noticeable. She stopped suddenly and turned. He almost bumped up against her.

"If thee will chase those goats over to the shed, we'll be able to bed them all for the night." She didn't wait for agreement but left Thomas to do as she instructed. The baaing of sheep mixed with the chattering of the goats amused Thomas as the animals followed the path to the croft. *It was easy,* Thomas thought to himself. *She probably does this alone. I'm merely an excuse.* He pushed the goats ahead of him as they danced among one another into the little shelter.

Hannah was waiting for him by the door. She smiled as she bolted the door behind the goats.

"Thanks," she said in a soft tone.

Thomas couldn't help himself. "Easy," he said casually, and then with a bit more enthusiasm, "happy to do it."

"Let's go to the house. The others will be waiting." She walked slowly, keeping to one side of the well-worn path. Thomas was two steps behind but then felt it would be no harm to come alongside.

"Was Philadelphia exciting?" she asked.

"Interesting," he replied, not wishing to admit that it had been exciting.

"I was fascinated when Father took me and the whole family into Yearly Meeting for the first time. There's so much to see, different than out here in the country." She looked at him in a cheerful mood, remembering.

He couldn't help but return the look and laughed in spite of himself. "Yes, I found it so new and big and crowded, and to see the ships by the waterfront was for me the best part." He did not add that Elizabeth Smith might have been an even greater allure.

"But I wouldn't want to live there," admitted Hannah. "I like the open spaces, even the smell of goats and sheep," as she wrinkled her nose, "as long as I don't smell like them." She was suddenly embarrassed, blushing.

"Well, thee doesn't," said Thomas quickly. He felt it was a silly, stupid reply, not very sophisticated as he tried to impress her with his new-found stature from the experience in Philadelphia. "We all smell of the freshness of the farm," he added by way of mitigation, for talking about how people smelled was a topic not going anywhere but into trouble. He tried to figure out how to change the subject. Phineas Massey called from the door of the house saving him the challenge.

"Here we are," he boomed out. "I bet thee is tired and not a little hungry," he called out.

"Well, I was happy to get off that wagon," Thomas admitted to Hannah. "It gets hard on my back just sitting for a piece."

"And when was it thee last ate?" asked Hannah.

"Mostly breakfast," he admitted, "a little bread and

cheese midday. We didn't stop so we could get here in good time."

"Well, I know Mother will set a full table," Hannah said.

Thomas suddenly became hungry as they stepped up into the house. The greetings were simple and heartfelt.

"Sit here young Thomas," Suzanne Massey instructed, "and we'll put Hannah by thee, to make thee have what thee needs," she chortled good-naturedly.

Thomas was pleased in spite of himself. The food appeared and Thomas looked at it during the customary period of silence to thank the Lord for their continuing good fortune of all the bounty before them. He started to eat as Hannah laid the various dishes before him. He felt strangely comfortable in their company.

Thomas listened to the conversation but didn't hear, feeling Hannah's warmth alongside him, afraid to look and be obvious in his surprising curiosity as she offered simple replies to her parents' comments. Joseph was conscious of Thomas' reluctant reserve as his son took a quick look at Hannah then back to the food in front of him. Thomas offered the platter to Hannah keeping his eyes down, looking at her hands, unlined in spite of the constant chores to be done. Her hands were clean with long, full fingers, the nails short but clean. He looked up along the length of her arms to find Hannah gazing at him. He was embarrassed to be noticed but couldn't take his eyes from hers, the intensity mesmerizing with his growing interest. He moved a bowl back and forth to capture her attention. She slowly took it, passing it on as the others stopped talking, bemused.

***

They left early the following morning as mist rose from the hollows by the creek and the early sun filtered through the trees. There was a country freshness around them. "It smells good out here," Thomas said to his father, "and it's free of most else, unlike Philadelphia with the bustling of so many people and the dust and dirt always kicking up."

Joseph nodded. He had watched his son exude a growing spirit of optimism and enthusiasm for his life, enhanced by the trip to Philadelphia. Thomas whistled a little ditty then went on to make up a melody with the birds chirping their morning songs as if to accompany him. The locusts had not yet dried to become taut enough in the morning sun to vibrate with their energetic rattle.

"I think thee's had a good trip," concluded Joseph.

"Yes, Father," Thomas agreed. "Now I know what Friends mean when they talk about gathering for Yearly Meeting in the city."

"And the different attitudes from those not Friends?"

"Which don't seem to be so very different from the Quakers we know."

"Except Anglicans and Presbyterians and all the others who want to make war." Joseph was serious. The horses knew the way as he let the reins rest easy. He turned to Thomas. "Thee does know of the energy for fighting, the rush to kill."

"Yes, Father, but thee will admit that we respect the rights of all to have a different opinion, a different approach, even from Anglicans."

"Peace is the only permanent approach to the future."

"Maybe we need an army to defend ourselves, to make sure the new Declaration of Independence means just that." Thomas was soft as he chose his words carefully, working out his thinking as he spoke.

"And what does Hannah Massey think of all this?" Joseph asked, trying a new approach. "Does she think fighting is good?"

"Not good," replied Thomas, "but perhaps necessary, especially if the British army comes into Pennsylvania, to Chester county, over to our farms."

"She's a nice girl," Joseph said, finding his new approach not having the desired affect.

"Yes, Father," Thomas answered, looking far into the surrounding woods, not seeing the trees.

Chapter Nine

With the arrival of spring of 1777, the Continental Army marched south into Pennsylvania from New Jersey. The British under General Sir William Howe were rumored to be sending their troops from the comfort of their winter quarters in New York to capture Philadelphia.

What happens if the armies come to Philadelphia to fight? mused Thomas. *What happens if they actually come into Chester County, trample over our fields, destroying our crops, taking our horses, killing our pigs and sheep? What would happen if a British soldier stood at our front door? Would he shoot? What might he do to my mother, or worse, my little sister? Or even myself?* Thomas gave an involuntary shudder as the thoughts raced through his mind. He sat quietly in meeting for worship at Willistown on First Day, surrounded by his family and neighbors. They filled the plain, wooden benches ranged in order facing the front of the room, outlined with a wainscot of walnut paneling accenting the regularity of the space with its high ceiling. The older and weightier Quaker elders sat on facing benches as they looked over the gathering with a dour and serious demeanor devoid of outward emotion as they privately waited upon God for His word and inspiration.

Thomas kept his eyes closed as he wondered whether he should join the militia of Edgmont Township to defend the family if need be by force of arms. He was afraid to open his eyes just yet for fear that the thought of taking up arms might escape and be noticed by the elders looking down at him. Closed, they could not know what his thoughts were. He knew that his mother would never agree that he join the army. Thomas didn't know about his father. Joseph Pratt was quiet, and solemn, but strong physically and emotionally, sure of his place in the Meeting and within his circle of friends and neighbors. *What would Father say if I took up arms?* wondered Thomas. He worked to change his thoughts, now to Annie Green. *What about her? She said she wanted to see me. Again. Soon. Why? It is nice being with her. Nothing serious of course,* he continued in his mind. *She's a Baptist. It wouldn't do to become serious with a non-Quaker. But this is a meeting for worship. I shouldn't be thinking of girls in meeting. I ought to be thinking of God, or least wait for God to give me a message. Tell me what to do. Whether to be a pacifist or a neutral. Let the Continental Army and the British Army fight it out. Or as the Yearly Meeting has determined, keep talking. Resolve our differences peacefully. Is God going to speak to me?*

Thomas opened his eyes slowly, as if to let the bright light of this clear spring morning stream into the meeting house. He quickly looked to see if any of the elders noticed him. They hadn't. Then he glanced around the benches to those he could see by not turning his head. No one was moving. All was in order, peaceful, searching for that moment when God might offer inspiration, which would encourage one of the Meeting to stand up and speak. Thomas relaxed. *No one has noticed my thoughts.* He felt relieved. His mind cleared. He gazed up through the windows to see the slight swaying of the branches on the trees outside. The light green buds were just showing from the force of the sap rising up the trunk of the ash, a new cycle of rebirth coming into the Pennsylvania countryside. He tried to assume the demeanor that would suggest to any who might notice that he was gazing towards heaven where God resided. *Then what about the call from the Pennsylvania Supreme Council to strengthen the militia?* Thomas couldn't concentrate if the British were to invade Philadelphia. *Even Annie Green would have to wait,* Thomas smiled to himself.

Finally, there was a wrestling and movement on the facing benches as the elders started to shake hands, one with another. His mother turned to shake his sister's hand, then leaning across shook his and his brother's. His father turned to the man sitting by and shook hands. Meeting for worship was over. Little conversations started as some stood, pushing open the door to the outside while others lapsed into a time of sociability.

Thomas stood and slipped out the side door and around to the wagon sheds. His cousins, Benjamin Darlington and Abner Baldwin joined him, all laughing quietly not to disturb their parents on the Lord's Day. They began to share the week's experiences.

"I hear Annie Green is asking about thee," chimed in Benjamin, his best friend.

Thomas reddened. "Who says so?" he asked.

"I heard it down by the crossroads. Someone stopped their wagon and talked to Caleb Bishop. He's sweet on her, doesn't like anyone interfering, getting in the way."

"Like me?"

"Like thee." Benjamin turned serious. "Caleb's trouble. He's always throwing his weight around, thinks he's important, thinks we Quakers are weak, no backbone, that we're not willing to stand for what we believe, that we're not willing to fight."

"He's trouble," agreed Abner, "constantly talking tough."

"So what am I to do?" asked Thomas. "I like Annie, not seriously, but she's nice to be with."

"That's the problem," answered Benjamin. "She likes

thee more than Caleb. It makes him angry because thee is her neighbor. Thee doesn't really care, but she cares for thee and she doesn't care much for Caleb."

Thomas looked away, then down at his boot as he scraped a path in the dirt. The others were silent. They knew Thomas, quiet, thoughtful, determined, intense. Thomas looked up at each of them in turn, first Benjamin, then Abner, then back to Benjamin. "And that's the problem." Thomas spoke deliberately. "We're raised as Quakers, we go to Meeting, we're not supposed to fight. We have to listen to someone like Caleb saying I'm a coward, that we're all cowards, that we can't fight, that we're too weak." He paused. "I've been thinking," he added.

"About joining the militia?" asked Benjamin.

"Maybe."

"Maybe yes," replied Benjamin with a slight smile. "I am thy best friend and I think I know thee."

"And thee is my cousin," he smiled, "and yes, I am thinking about joining the militia." He waited for a response from Benjamin.

Benjamin nodded. "I'm thinking we should both join the militia."

"What about me?" asked Abner.

"What about thee?" responded Thomas.

"Well, if you two are going to enlist, then I will too."

"Serious?" asked Benjamin.

"I'm not going to be left behind," answered Abner. "We've always hung together. Might as well be criticized for joining the army to support you two as for staying home as if nothing is really happening. I know people will talk and all the elders will say it was right to stay behind, but I know the others, like us, they'll say, 'Well, he stuck together with his friends.'"

"And thy father?" asked Thomas.

"Same as thy father. He will be upset, will argue against joining the army."

"Will he talk thee out of it?" Benjamin asked.

"Not if the two of you have already joined." Abner looked first at one then the other, and back to the meeting house to make sure no one could overhear.

"Well. I've made my mind up," continued Thomas. "The Supreme Pennsylvania Council says the army needs new men, that the British are going to come into this area, into Philadelphia, and they need to be stopped, that General Washington needs support and the Edgmont militia is looking for recruits." Thomas clenched his jaw, the muscles in his face working.

"Do they think the British will come here to Chester County?" asked Abner, worried.

"If the British invade Philadelphia, they'll need food, guns, and other supplies," Benjamin replied evenly, having already analyzed the situation.

"Washington will fight," Thomas announced with a certainty. "This is the center of the colonies, home of the Congress. We're right in the way and I'm not willing to stand aside and let others protect me. If I believe that we should have independence, that Washington's Continental Army is right and necessary, then I need to support his army. I need to join it." Thomas stood straighter.

"I'm coming with thee," Benjamin affirmed slowly.

"Me too," Abner added.

The three stood there for an instant, then laughing, slapped one another on the back.

"Looks like you all have agreed on something," William called to his younger brother. He came striding down from the meeting house towards them. "You all look like a bunch of conspirators, like a cat that's just eaten the pet bird."

"We agreed," Abner confirmed, happy to be the first to admit their conversation.

"Agreed to what?" William asked more seriously.

"Nothing yet," Benjamin offered.

"Later," Thomas said, looking at Abner with piercing eyes.

"Later, what?" William persisted. "Does it involve me or the family?" William stepped close to his brother. "What's going on?"

Thomas stared back. "I'll tell thee later, after I've talked to Father." His voice was soft.

"I wonder," William said, looking at the other two. "You're all talking about joining the army, aren't you?" He waited. There was no response from the three of them. William opened his mouth to talk then shut it not sure what to say. He opened it again and said, "Yes. That's it. You all want to enlist in the army. Here you've just been to Meeting and you're thinking of fighting." He waited. His black, broad-brimmed hat sat squarely on his head, brown hair sticking out from underneath, spreading away from his neck.

Finally Thomas spoke. "I don't want thee to speak to Father. I'll do that, but I want thee to know that I've been thinking about this for some time, ever since they started the fight up in Massachusetts. I know Quakers are not supposed to fight. Maybe it takes more courage to say that I believe in peace, that I won't fight and keep on talking even when the British send over their army and start to shoot at Americans. Do we just stand there and let them? I don't think so. If I believe that we need an army to defend ourselves and that force has to be met with force, then I cannot let others do the work, to shoulder all the responsibility. It's my obligation to join and help where necessary, to do my part." Thomas looked at his older brother with a steady gaze. "I'm going to join the militia to defend Pennsylvania, to defend our farm."

"I don't think thee is right," countered William. "Force is better met by peaceful means. It's wrong when God has given life to take upon thyself to take that life. A life lived in the light of God has far greater meaning than one lived by the gun. Besides, we are all English, from the same heritage, believing in the same things, in the same God, no matter the differences in style of worship. We have our freedom here. Yes, we pay taxes. So does everyone, English, German, Scots-Irish, wherever we've come from, but all under the mother country of England." He spread his arms wide. "That is why we have all this. Just look at the fields, trees, our laws and an ability to worship in our own way, seeking God, searching for that of God in everyone, and we can do that now and here and thee can't do that if thee's out to shoot someone else, trying to kill him." William stopped.

"Just don't tell Father," Thomas repeated quietly.

"I'll not," William replied. "Thee needs to," he said with finality.

Chapter Ten

Thomas picked up his rifle and balanced it against his shoulder. His feet were together as he stood at attention. He was hidden around the corner of the barn, imagining himself already in the Pennsylvania Militia as part of the contingent from Edgmont Township.

"Already playing soldier," William said, coming unnoticed from the lower field. Thomas was startled, then relaxed, bringing his rifle down and laying it across his arms. "I didn't see thee coming," he replied with a touch of embarrassment.

"If thee didn't hear me, then it's a bad sign." William was serious. "If thee is set on going away and joining the army, then I want thee to come back. Safely." He said it in a more sympathetic tone. "Thee is a farmer, not a soldier. I understand thy feelings. I don't agree. I don't think it's right, but I do support thy right to make thy own decision, at least thee and I agree on that. I'm not so sure about Father." He came and put his arm around his younger brother. "Thee will always be a farmer first, but if thee must, be a good soldier." He gave a slight squeeze on Thomas' back.

"I know thee thinks ill of me for joining, that I betray the family and the Meeting."

"Yes, but thee has character and courage to go with it, so go on back to the house and get the goodbye over with." William left him, going ahead. Thomas shifted the gun, adjusting the pouch with powder and bullets and followed William into the farmhouse.

"Is thee heading out?" asked his sister.

"Yes," Thomas responded, setting the rifle down and leaning over to pick up Abigail into his arms. She gave him a kiss on the cheek and leaned her head on his shoulder. "We'll miss thee," she whispered, tears forming, moistening his neck.

"And I'll miss thee," he answered, setting her carefully down. His mother came away from the hearth, the small fire warming and cooking at the same time. "Here, Thomas, some biscuits and meat and cheese to keep thee fed."

Thomas took the package adding it to the sack filled with an extra shirt and stockings. He turned back to his mother. "Thank thee." He looked at her with longing. She took a step forward. Thomas moved quickly to his mother and gave a strong, lingering hug.

"Thee take care," she offered as much a hope as an instruction.

"Yes, Mother, I'll take care." He felt younger than his 21 years.

"Return when thee can," Joseph said coming into the kitchen, "as soon as thee is able. Stay with the militia as ordered and then come back when thy duties are over. This is thy home," he added for emphasis.

"Thank thee, Father," Thomas said, shaking hands. "I need to go now," he said, breaking the emotion swirling about. "I told Benjamin and Abner that we'd meet at Middletown and head to Chester where the militia is mustering to drill to receive our orders." He picked up his sack and strapped it over his shoulder, the rifle trailing in one hand as Abigail grabbed the other.

"Let me walk with thee," she said.

"To the fence line, then thee must let me go," Thomas said softly as the two of them walked out.

Reaching the end of the near field, Thomas stopped

and, releasing Abigail's hand, he leaned over and gave her a quick kiss then a quick wave at his parents and brother still standing in the doorway. He turned and strode off down the path to the Edgmont Great Road leading to Middletown.

***

Coming up to Middletown Meeting, he could see Benjamin and Abner already there, backs to the stone wall surrounding the burial ground. Two others were facing them. Thomas got closer and recognized Caleb and Joshua. His heart pounded faster, perspiration forming under his arms. He slowed his pace suddenly aware that now he would have to confront them, this time not on his horse. *At least Benjamin and Abner are here,* he thought.

Caleb was raising his hand to make a point. Thomas could hear the talking, but couldn't make out the words. Suddenly, Caleb stopped. He turned around and stepped away from Benjamin. Joshua followed. They came towards Thomas. He kept his pace, dreading the confrontation. Caleb came to a halt and with his rifle cradled in his arms, stood astride the path, feet apart, and waited for Thomas to come up.

"So you finally did come to your senses? You're going to join up, ready to be part of the real army?" Caleb had a smirk on his face. As usual, Joshua stood behind him, imitating Caleb. Thomas walked up to Caleb, keeping a distance but stretching his head forward towards the older fellow, shorter but heftier.

"I'm doing what I think is right and necessary." Thomas spoke as evenly as he could.

"Yeah, that's what your cousins said. You're all going to join the army. The Quakers are finally realizing what they ought to do."

Joshua chortled in agreement.

"I'm willing to make up my own mind," replied Thomas. "Quakers think there's a better way and they're strong to take that position."

"So that means you're weak to join and fight?"

"Of a different mind, perhaps, but as strong of conviction."

"Well, at least you have some ability to make up your own mind. Maybe not as much of a coward as I thought," Caleb smirked.

"I'm not a coward," Thomas said with as much bite as he could develop.

"But then your brother is," retorted Joshua, trying to get into the conversation.

"He is not!" Thomas exclaimed in a higher voice than he would have preferred. "He's as brave as any, stronger of conviction than most. It takes a real faith to keep to what you believe deep down is right."

Benjamin and Abner picked up their rifles and knapsacks and came alongside Thomas for support. Thomas breathed heavily.

"So are the three of you going to be tossed out of your Meeting now that you're going to fight?"

"That's for the Meeting to decide," Thomas answered. "Quakers are strong for nonviolence, but they are also greatly respectful of the rights of others." Thomas paused and then added, "It takes more than physical strength to be strong. Thee has muscles, thee can fight, especially when thee has someone like Joshua standing by thy side like a puppy," Thomas said with a biting sarcasm.

"You put that rifle down and I'll show you," Joshua taunted with a sneer. "I'm nobody's puppy." He glowered at Thomas.

"That's what I mean," Thomas replied, looking not at Joshua but at Caleb, "always willing to bully someone, unable to talk about differences."

"I don't need Joshua to stand up for me," Caleb answered, quickly putting his arm out to keep Joshua back. "Besides, I see you have your cousins alongside, against the two of us. Pretty fancy to talk big when you yourself have help." He snorted in derision. Caleb shook his head at Thomas. "When we get to Chester and begin to assemble as a real fighting force, then we'll all see what you're made of." He picked up his own knapsack and placed his rifle on the shoulder. "It'll be different. You'll find out, then all your brave talk will not stand for anything but words." He turned to go then wheeled around again and put his face into Thomas'. "I just hope I'm there to see how you react when there's a British soldier trying to shoot you, or coming after you with a great, sharp bayonet pointed right at your gut. That'll be something to see." He gave a short laugh. He grabbed Joshua by the arm. "Come on, let's get going. Chester's a fair walk. Let these talkers come as they may." Caleb strode away from Thomas leaving the three of them standing there silently watching Joshua running to catch up with his friend.

Finally Benjamin spoke. "He's a bad one."

"Yes," Thomas agreed, "and I'm not sure I'd want to be in a fight with him even though there's a lot more talk and bluster in him than even he knows."

"We need to keep our distance," Abner chimed in. "I wouldn't trust him around me, even less Joshua, stupid lap dog." Abner chortled at his own humor.

"Yes, and an uneducated dog can be dangerous," Thomas added. "They can be unpredictable, never know what they're going to do."

"At least we know about Caleb," Benjamin agreed. "He's totally predictable, always the same approach, fight."

"I guess he is pretty upset that Annie Green is my neighbor." Thomas smiled at the thought.

"She is still sweet on thee, isn't she?" Benjamin asked.

"Well, we see one another and I think she'd like to see me more, but it's hard to get the time, there's so much to do. Then I'm not sure that her father always wants me hanging around."

"So, is she nice?" Abner asked, pushing his curiosity forward.

Thomas looked at him, then over to Benjamin. "She's warm."

"How warm?" Abner persisted.

"Pretty warm," Thomas replied carefully. He thought for a moment. "Nice and warm."

"At her place?" Benjamin asked.

"The Greens have a full hay mow," Thomas answered, "and Annie Green likes me better in that hay mow than she does Caleb Bishop."

"Thee sure?" Benjamin persisted.

"Well, I don't think that it was the first time for Annie." Thomas gave the nod of his head to his friends.

"Thee went that far?" Abner asked.

"She didn't want me to stop," Thomas answered.

"But she's a Baptist," Abner said, with worry in his voice.

"Girls are all built alike," Benjamin agreed.

"There are differences," Abner said.

"But not in the basics," Thomas said.

"No wonder Caleb is angry at thee," Benjamin said. "He's a Baptist, thinks that a Quaker boy shouldn't have any claim over a Baptist girl, even if she does live closer."

He looked around to make sure that Caleb and Joshua had not returned. "Thomas, thee does need to be careful. Caleb can be a mean one, particularly with his sidekick."

"Well, it's Annie's decision who she wants to be with, me or Caleb."

"Could be both," Benjamin answered in his most thoughtful, Quaker approach.

"Yes, and I could see other girls, like I saw in Philadelphia."

"When thee was there?" Abner asked in surprise.

"Go on," Benjamin said.

"Well, I saw this girl, all dressed up, city like, not fancy, but stylish, head up high, walking with purpose, in command of herself. She was coming towards the warehouses down along by the river and I couldn't keep my eyes off her. As she turned her head, there was the most beautiful girl I've ever seen."

"Was she Quaker?" Abner asked.

"No. I confirmed that. No. She's Anglican, and not only that but her father's rich. He owns a big house on Second Street, overlooking the waterfront."

"Did thee talk to her?" Benjamin had never met a city girl. "What was she like? Would she even speak to a country Quaker?"

"Yes. By chance, I met her. I admit, I was hoping, but then I wasn't sure what to say. She was so beautiful, but firm and confident, not mousy like we think city girls might be, and she did talk to me."

"Nicely?" Abner asked hopefully.

"Yes, and we walked together. She showed me the Pennsylvania State House where the Continental Congress has been meeting."

"And then?" Abner said.

"And then she met up with her city friend all decked out in finery that we'd never see on a Quaker man and that was the end of it." Thomas breathed out with the memory still sharp and colorful in his mind.

"Thee'd better start dreaming about Quaker girls," Benjamin admonished. "There are enough around."

"For us all?" Abner asked, hopefully.

"For us all," Thomas said, "even if they don't belong to Willistown Meeting."

"They're all taken," Benjamin moaned, "or they're related to us, or they're too young and not interested."

"Other meetings have girls," Thomas said.

"Hard to find. Harder to meet," Benjamin added.

"Yes, but when we go to Quarterly Meeting or even to Yearly Meeting in Philadelphia, there's a good chance some will be there."

"I'll never find a girl," Abner said. "They don't come into the tavern where Father works and they're certainly not out in the fields where we work."

"I know, but Father stays with a family in Marple on the way to Philadelphia. They go to Springfield Meeting and they have a daughter and she was nice. A bit shy, but when she got up she was right presentable."

"Could she talk?" Benjamin asked with a smile.

"Yes, and not only that, she had a nice way about her, soft and easy manners."

"Eligible?" Abner asked finally.

"I'm sure that's what Father had in mind," Thomas said. "I think Father's worried I might take up with the Baptists. Between joining the militia and keeping company with Annie, he's not sure where I'm headed." Thomas was serious.

"Well, if we don't get headed to Chester, we're going to

be late for muster with no place to sleep. We'd better get moving."

"Thee's right," Thomas agreed, "and by this time, Caleb and Joshua are far enough ahead we'll not have to walk with them."

They adjusted their rifles and sacks and marched onto the Edgmont Great Road that led to Chester.

***

Coming over the slight crest above Chester, they saw well laid out fields of wheat and corn, the corners marked by piles of fieldstones surrounded by hedgerows of young ash, poplar and walnut trees, left after the large trees had been cut for timber. Pastures were enclosed by snake fences, chestnut rails laid horizontally alternating with the rails of the next span working back and forth, held in place by two upright posts at the angle keeping the split lengths in place. The greening of the fields provided the frame for the clustered stone and timbered houses of Chester at the far side. The main road from Philadelphia ran through the town on its way south to Wilmington. The Delaware River sparkled at the town's edge, the sun playing off the wind whipped ripples of the water as the river coursed slowly towards the bay and Atlantic Ocean beyond. Ships lay at anchor waiting for the surge of the incoming tide to carry them further upstream to the wharves in Philadelphia, the greatest port in the largest city of the newly united States of America. It was the first time Thomas, Benjamin, and Abner had been to Chester. They lingered to take in the spectacle. The saw the gathering of the militia on the field close by the courthouse, the stonework of the walls, well laid with the round cupola showing its prominence above the roof lines of the surrounding houses. The weather vane on top twisted to the wind as if to seek out the truth in the shifting breezes of a new revolution against an old order.

"Come on," called Thomas as he led the others down the slope and into the town, striding with purpose towards the table at which a captain and two sergeants sat. Others were coming in, distinguished by their rifles or shorter muskets. A group of men were already lined up, sergeants barking out commands to instill the basics of military discipline.

Men gathered around to sign on to regular duty with the various militia companies in support of George Washington's Continental Army. Thomas braced himself straight to show full confidence, but with an inner queasiness that gnawed at the edges of his bravado.

Caleb had just finished the formalities. "Finally got here, I see. Didn't change your mind yet?" he smirked. "Not too late to walk away," he said more loudly. "Quakers," he announced to the young men standing around. Caleb sauntered away. Joshua took a last look at the three of them and quickly followed after Caleb.

"Pay them no mind," Thomas said softly to Benjamin and Abner. "Ignore them. They'll fall by their own weight."

"Next!" the soldier at the close end of the table commanded, obviously addressing Thomas. "Step up here, lively now."

Thomas stood in front of the sergeant.

"Name?"

"Thomas Pratt."

"Township?"

"Edgmont."

"Militia?"

"Yes. Since spring. We've been drilling."

"Yes, I'm sure, but this will be more than just drilling." He checked the list before him. "Right." He turned a sheet of paper around and pointed to a spot on the form, "Here. Sign. That'll make it official." He handed Thomas a quill pen, motioning towards the inkwell and tapping the official muster roll.

"You others?"

"I'm Benjamin Darlington."

"And I'm Abner Baldwin."

"Same thing then."

They signed. Satisfied, the sergeant stood and shook their hands. "You're part of us now. Good. Now go over there with the other men. Officers are inside the courthouse getting a briefing. They'll be out shortly, and then you will know what to do. Until then, stay together so we don't have to scratch about town to gather you all back." He started to talk to the other sergeant. The captain sat there quietly, the only one in any uniform, blue and bluff of the Continental line. He continued to look over the militia, evaluating from a distance the character of the new soldiers.

***

As the days wore on, the sun rose high in the sky, the weather became hot and the green grass trampled underfoot turned brown. The monotony of the routine was only broken by orders to the Chester County militia to join those from Philadelphia to help work on the defenses along the river. There was fear that General Howe planned for the Royal Navy to sail up the Delaware with the British Army to capture Philadelphia. The militia sweated, shoveled dirt onto simple redoubts, placed wooden stakes along the mounded earth, and hauled timbers to secure the gun emplacements.

Back at their camp, there was the daily inspection of their tents and whatever clothing they had, care of firearms, powder and shot, cleanliness of mess kits, just a wooden dish and spoon and a deep-sided handled pot.

Sergeants bellowed out orders to individual companies. The drilling was incessant. "Left face. Right face. By the column. Forward march. Halt. Skirmish line. Space out. Kneel in front. Load. Don't fire yet. Save your powder. We'll do that soon enough. Reload. I know you all hunt and you think you know about your quarry, but remember, animals don't shoot back, British soldiers do. You need take care, with a steady aim, to fire, then reload again."

The days were hot, standing in the dusty fields, other men marching the same, wheeling, kneeling, halting, and turning.

Groups of small boys would occasionally appear, more often than not with wood staves to act as guns as they imitated the actions of the militia. The people of Chester showed a curiosity at first, mixing in the late afternoon with some of the recruits occasionally to share honeyed biscuits or newly ripened fruit from the abundant crop in scattered orchards. But as the fear of fighting increased, most stayed within their houses or small farm plots securing for themselves provisions against marching armies.

* * *

"Alright. Fall out. Have a little water." Thomas moved into the shade of a tree, leaning his rifle against the trunk and wiped his face with a stained and dirty cloth, mottled with ragged edges.

"Did we do the right thing?" Benjamin asked coming up alongside.

"No choice now," Thomas replied.

"Could still walk away."

"Yes, but then we're deserters with no place to walk to.

They'd find us, call us cowards. Besides, I'll not give Caleb Bishop the satisfaction. No way."

"Does thee think we'll actually fight?" Benjamin continued.

"The rumors are that the British have headed out from New York. Their ships were going to come up the Delaware, but now they're saying they've been sighted in the Chesapeake Bay, coming up from the south."

Rumors kept passing back and forth. Men grumbled about the constant drilling. "To what purpose?" one would ask.

"To make sure you point that rifle at the enemy and not at us," replied an older soldier, at 35, senior in age.

"Line up by twos," ordered the sergeant. "Come on now. Lively. Right where you are. Get in line." The sergeant, a little older than most, with service in the Pennsylvania Militia from the previous year, imposed training with an inexperienced hand.

Caleb ended up alongside Thomas. Joshua had not been quick enough to get up forward. "So now I have to march beside you," Caleb jibbed.

"Only if thee can keep up," replied Thomas.

"I can keep up with you any day," Caleb sneered. "Just because you think you're so good," he growled under his breath in a snarl.

"Keep it quiet back there," the sergeant ordered.

Caleb looked at Thomas out of the corner of his eye, suddenly swinging the butt of his rifle around, catching Thomas on the thigh with a heavy thunk.

"Damn thee," he muttered to Caleb, a little too loud.

"I ordered silence," the sergeant called out. "Who spoke?" he ordered.

Thomas hesitated.

"The Quaker boy here," Caleb said before Thomas had taken a full breath.

"Pratt," snapped the sergeant coming back along the line, stopping in front of Thomas. "When I give an order, I expect it to be obeyed. Is that clear?"

"Yes," Thomas replied.

"Yes, what?"

"Yes, Sergeant," Thomas said.

"I don't care who's Quaker and who is not. I really don't care what you are. All I care about is for you to follow orders and shoot straight. Your life is going to depend on it and more importantly, my life is going to depend on it. If you don't like someone, keep it to yourself. Remember, we're fighting the British, not our neighbors. Is that clear, Pratt?"

"Yes, Sergeant," Thomas replied reddening.

The sergeant turned away. Caleb smiled with satisfaction from his little triumph. The sergeant got back to the head of the column, now feeling a bit uncomfortable with his newly installed discipline. "Forward march!" he called out as they moved towards the river bank. Thomas took a half step as the muscle in his thigh cramped, the deep pain searing down his leg. He tried to hide the suffering, particularly from Caleb who marched with a light, brisk step, satisfied with the blow. Thomas gritted his teeth, forcing his leg forward in cadence with the company. They reached a clearing and halted.

"We're going to fire with actual powder," the sergeant announced. "By files. The first file on command will kneel to fire in front, the second file to fire on command over their heads, between the men kneeling in front. Understood?"

"Hey Sarge," Caleb called out. "I want to change places with this Quaker. The way it is now, he's behind and above me and I'm not sure his aim is that good." Caleb Bishop waited for an answer. He didn't care, he got in another jibe.

"You know how to shoot, Pratt?" asked the sergeant coming back down the line.

"I know my rifle," he replied.

"Well enough to show us?" he asked.

"Point out the target," Thomas answered.

"See that oak tree over there?" the sergeant asked.

"With a branch out either side at man's height?"

"Yes. Can you hit it? The trunk?"

"Yes. Easy. But which branch does thee want me to select? Right one?" Thomas stood his rifle butt on the ground spreading his feet.

"Right branch if you can do it. Company stand back." Caleb had already moved away, over to where Joshua was standing. Thomas carefully measured black powder into the pan, closed the frizzen, then emptied the rest into the barrel of his rifle. He took out a lead bullet, applied the patch and forced it down on top of the powder with the ramrod, tamping hard to get a good seat. He stood at an angle towards the tree. He wiped off the end of the barrel and brought up the rifle to his shoulder and pulled back the flintlock. Sighting his rifle, he closed one eye to stare at the branch. He offset the aim a touch to the left to compensate for the wind from the river. He squeezed the trigger slowly. The hammer came down, the new flint sparking against the metal of the frizzen. The rifle fired and white smoke surrounded the pan. There was a crack as the bullet lodged fairly in the right branch. Thomas lowered the rifle, steady, without any outward emotion.

"Huzzah," came from several of the men. "Well done,"

said another. There were laughs of relief as the tension subsided.

"Good shot," offered the sergeant with a neutral voice. "Bishop. You want to try?" the sergeant nodded towards him.

Caleb hesitated, looked around at the others all staring back at him. "Why not," he answered, feeling no way out.

"Then see how close you can come to where Pratt has placed his shot." Caleb moved over to the spot as Thomas shifted towards where Benjamin and Abner were standing. Caleb repeated the drill and lifting the rifle, sighted, shifting the barrel, then back a little, drawing a deep breath, waited, then fired, closing both eyes at the same time in an involuntary motion. There was a crack and flare of smoke. The shot plunged into the left branch. There was silence.

"Right tree. Wrong branch," announced the sergeant sensing a growing problem.

"Thee all right?" Benjamin asked Thomas.

"My leg feels that blow," said Thomas quietly, looking Benjamin in the eye. "But the rest of me is just fine," he said a little louder, looking back at the tree.

"Thee did right well," Benjamin said.

"It was good," Abner agreed. "Showed that bully what's for."

"I don't think it's going to help my relationship with Caleb," Thomas sniffed.

"Who cares?" Benjamin said. "He gets what he deserves."

***

"Well lads," the sergeant said as Thomas' company mustered for quarters in late August of 1777. "We've news and orders. I'll give you the news. The captain will give out the orders."

"We're finally going to do something useful?" one of the young privates asked.

"Yes boys, I think our time has come. We hear the British have landed at the head of the Elk on the Chesapeake and they want to march up here and take Philadelphia."

"But not if we're in the way," Caleb replied with bravado.

"Let's get them," Joshua joined in, always predictable.

"How many?" another asked.

"A whole army, I expect," an older man said from the rear rank.

"Well, it's General Howe's Army, if that's what you mean," the sergeant replied. "Attention!" he called with a gathered authority as the company captain came out of the courthouse with the other officers. The sun was bright in the hazy sky, the humidity hanging low along the Delaware River. The men of the Edgmont militia stood upright, then heads turned slightly to see their captain. The sergeant saluted. The corporals followed suit. The captain was tense, the blue of his uniform standing out 'midst the array of homespun shirts, breeches of leather or wool or linsey-woolsey cotton, sometimes in a variety of muted colors.

"At ease, men," the captain ordered. "We've been here for a while I know, but it's been for a purpose," he added. "We've been ordered to join the main Continental Army. They'll pass by here tomorrow and we're to fall in and follow, so get your packs ready. Double check your rifles. Rations will be passed out tonight. Powder. Shot."

Benjamin nudged Thomas. "Finally."

"Hard to believe."

"I'm a little nervous," Abner admitted, "to be with a real army, I mean."

"We knew it would come," Thomas said. "It's what they've all been saying. Can't realize though it's really going to happen."

Chapter Eleven

"So where are we headed?" Thomas asked to the back of the sergeant marching on ahead.

"Who cares," Caleb called back, "as long as were going to get a chance to fight."

The column of the Pennsylvania Militia, with the Edgmont company, moved steadily, strung out along a line three abreast following the dust of the Continental Army ahead. Thomas ignored Caleb.

"If we get too close to a real fight, you're going to march another way," Caleb taunted, hoping for a response. "Quaker boy," Caleb said, now talking to Joshua, but for everyone's benefit.

"Keep down the chatter there," ordered the sergeant finally. "There'll be time enough to prove yourselves. All of you," he added, more loudly.

Thomas adjusted the rifle on his shoulder and kept step as they moved farther out from Chester along the road towards Concordville and the area beyond surrounding the Brandywine Creek.

"Is it true Sarge," Benjamin asked abreast the company sergeant, "that the British have landed from the Chesapeake?"

"That's so lad," he responded, "and General Washington is taking his army and us down towards Wilmington to meet him. Give him a welcome in this part of the country." He said it not unkindly.

"What if we don't stop them by the Brandywine?" Thomas asked from behind. "Will they be able to come into Philadelphia?"

"It'll be a lot harder to stop them," replied the sergeant.

"Thomas doesn't think we'll succeed," Caleb said from several ranks ahead.

"General Washington won't give up, you'll see. He'll keep this army together, keep finding places to fight."

"So Thomas will have more than one chance to see what he's made of," Caleb said, derisively.

"Is there any other place to do battle?" Thomas continued. "I've been to the Brandywine. It's got hills on either side, but I've never been beyond."

The sergeant kept pace and thought. *Maybe south a bit, but the Brandywine's the only real creek of any size between here and the Schuylkill River.* He thought some more. *No. That's where we have the best chance.* He wiped his brow as the sun bore down through the humidity. He slackened his pace, drifting back alongside the ragged column, keeping his eye out for the captain marching smartly at the head.

"Hey, Sarge," Thomas asked quietly. "Have you ever been in a battle before?" He lowered his voice still more. "I mean, have you ever fired a rifle at someone, you know, to hurt someone or even kill?"

The sergeant gave a faint smile. He looked at Thomas, keeping pace, making sure that the road was even. "No." He shook his head. "Like you, I've done plenty of hunting. I know my rifle and I've been in the militia as long as anyone. My pa was in the British Army so I know some things, not everything of course. I've heard enough stories about being shot at, particularly by Indians when they were allied with the French against us. Funny. Now the French are our allies fighting with us against the English." He was silent. Thomas kept pace. The little talking in the ranks had died down, each man lost in his own thoughts. They marched past farms with the family standing alongside their fields as the army moved on. Little clusters of houses at crossroads pressed the column together. Local taverns, prominent with their signs hanging above the main door, gave a sense of cohesion and ease to the small communities straddling the route towards Chad's Ford and Kennett beyond.

Late in the afternoon the columns ahead stopped. The Edgmont militia in its turn came to a halt. Thomas could see an officer on horseback moving down along the line of soldiers, talking to various company officers then moving on again. He watched as their captain received his orders. The colonel, in the full uniform of an officer of the Continental Army, then cantered on by towards the end of the militia companies and the supply wagons in the rear.

"Fall out!" came the order from the sergeant. Thomas headed towards the shade of a tree. Benjamin and Abner soon joined him.

"What's happening?" Abner asked.

"I bet that's all the marching for today," Thomas answered. "See, here come the supply wagons for the regular army, with all their tents and provisions."

"I hope we have a wagon," Benjamin mused. "I'm so hungry, I'll eat anything."

"If I understand the Army, it'll be anything, nothing we might recognize on our own tables back home, but enough to keep our bellies filled."

"I'd guess we'll appreciate our mother's cooking all the more," Benjamin added.

"All right," the sergeant called out. "You men. Prepare to line up your tents over there, next to the Willistown militia. Keep it neat. In a row. Our wagon is coming up. You there," he pointed to Thomas and the others. "Leave your rifle with Caleb. Go out and collect wood for our fire.

And Joshua, get some buckets and gather water out of that creek over there." The sergeant was brusque. He snapped out the instructions in rapid succession. Soon what had been a marching column turned into a large, temporary gathering like a revival meeting, but without the women.

"You trust me with your rifles?" Caleb jibbed.

"Sure. Knowing that my rifle might be the one to save you," Thomas replied.

"Fat chance," Caleb sneered in return.

"You hope," Thomas said.

"I have Joshua by my side."

"But thee has two sides!" Thomas quipped. "Unless thee's counting on a tree for the other side. Of course, trees don't fire rifles. They might offer protection as long as the enemy doesn't advance, but then, they lose their usefulness." Thomas thumbed at his cousins. "I'd rather have someone I trust on either side." He didn't wait for a reply but headed out to gather the firewood.

The assembled militia settled into an uncertain routine, wondering what advantages the Continental Army had that they didn't. They were aware that they were in their own, familiar countryside. Night fell, pickets were set out, fires kept a soft glow as the men lay down, the night noises less amongst the sleeping militia.

***

"Up and about!" the corporal called out, striding along the line of tents. The sky was still dark with only a streak of pink across the horizon to the east. "Look lively now." His voice trailed away as he headed on by. Thomas could hear other officers calling out. There was mumbling as the camp roused itself. The fires were stoked. Corn mush was heated and hard bread passed around.

"What's the word?" Benjamin asked as their sergeant came around from the backside of the line of tents. "Where're we going?"

The little chattering ceased as all within hearing waited for an answer.

"Orders will come out shortly. All I know is that we're to be up, organized, packs on, ready to move out." The sergeant stood, feet apart, and called out, "Get those tents folded! Stack them over there by the wagon! And get your bellies full! You may not get a hot meal for some time. Those pots. Clean them up! Smartly now, men!"

Thomas pulled on his shirt and adjusted his braces. "This may be it," he said to Benjamin and Abner, organized and standing along side.

"Washington's got something in mind," Benjamin agreed.

"Going with a real army is dangerous," Abner mused. "I feel different."

"At least the real army has real officers," Thomas said, "not that our own captain doesn't know what to do. It's just that none of us have had any experience in battle and the Continental Army has."

"Yeah," Abner agreed. "Too bad Caleb and Joshua don't recognize their own inexperience."

"I got more experience than the three of you," Caleb spit out coming from behind, surprising them. "Think you're so good! Well, I'll take Joshua any day. Experience or no, he's got desire and he's fearless."

"I've got a dog just like that," Benjamin retorted.

"That's a good partner," Thomas said. "Need one. Good to have." Thomas didn't define between Joshua or a dog.

"So now you appreciate a fighter?" Caleb came closer.

"As long as at they're fighting someone else and not me."

Thomas walked away, tired of the arguing and apprehension of the coming day. He turned and said quietly to Benjamin, "I think after this week we're all going to have more experience than we care to admit." He turned again and continued on to the wagon.

The column headed off, the sky lightening, the men subdued as each thought about the reality of the British Army, now no longer an illusion in another state, but close by here, coming towards them in their own Pennsylvania.

At midday, they halted, close by a slowly running creek bordered by trees. Men ahead had already dropped their packs and were lying down in the soft green grasses to wash water across the sweat of their faces cupping water into their mouths.

The captain was called into conference, clustering around several Continental Army officers having dismounted from their horses.

"I figure we'll find out soon," Thomas mused to no one in particular.

"Can't be too soon for me," Abner answered impatiently. "It's been too long not really knowing what our orders are."

"Soon enough," Benjamin said.

"We're all just as anxious," Thomas added. "Look around, not much talking is there? Everyone is thinking the same. We're not the only ones wondering what we're going to do next." He gave a deep breath.

The captain left the dispersing conference.

"Fall in!" their sergeant shouted. The Edgmont militia responded. Other companies up and down the line fell into position, ranks became more formal than before, during the weeks of training, the thought of a professional army coming up against them.

"All right men," the captain began. They were quiet. "General Washington is going to defend at the Brandywine. We've been ordered to go above Dilworthtown to Birmingham Meeting House. While the main army will stretch along the Brandywine northwards, we're just to back them up." He looked over the various companies, men and boys, older and younger, most untested in any fighting. "The Continental line will take on the British and we'll be behind them and act as reserves, fit in where they need us under the command of a colonel."

A captain walked up and down, inspecting the ranks of the Edgmont militia. Satisfied, he turned to the sergeant. "Form the men into line. Move out!"

At Concord, columns split, the greater number headed out the Baltimore Road, others marched towards Dilworthtown.

"First time we see the regular army ahead," Thomas commented to Benjamin marching by his side. "They keep a steady pace."

"Obviously under orders," Benjamin said. "They know there's action ahead."

"I'm relieved we're only back up. Reserves," Thomas admitted to Benjamin.

"Is thee scared?" Benjamin asked under his breath.

Thomas was silent. Finally, he replied as quietly so that no one else could hear. He glanced sideways at Benjamin. "Yes, a little."

"I am too," Benjamin admitted. "My stomach's all tight."

"So's mine," Thomas agreed, now more open, comforted that he was not the only one to be apprehensive. "Does thee think the rest are?"

"Yeah, they'll not admit it, especially Caleb. He'll talk

big, never let you know what he really feels, never admit anything to anyone."

"Funny. I thought about this ever since I went in to Philadelphia and saw where the Continental Congress met, saw where they signed the Declaration of Independence. When thee sees the place, close-up, then it begins to sink in. It's really happening. Then I wondered, should I do something to work for independence or let others settle the matter?" He became silent. Benjamin said nothing. He knew there was more Thomas wanted to say. Best friends sense that. They kept a steady pace and at each rise in the road, they saw the army ahead, horses dragging the carriages with the cannon.

"I knew deep down looking in the windows of the State House, watching men go in and out, that I had to do something." He laughed nervously. "So here we are, rifle in hand, marching off to give battle." He turned his head slightly to Benjamin, "and now I'm nervous, but can't change my mind. I can't stop. We're here and I wonder what's going to happen." His voice was low to keep anyone else from hearing.

Benjamin nodded. "Thee's the real reason I'm here. I know thee figured it all out and I wasn't going to let thee go without me. And just think. We'll have things to tell when this is all settled, our families, maybe even children someday. I don't want to be in a position to say, 'well, Thomas went, I didn't.' I want to be able to hold my head up, even if I'm read out of Meeting for joining the militia."

Abner could hear the last comment. "Well, if they read thee out of Meeting, then all three of us are gone and I don't think they're quite ready to do that yet."

"Willistown and Goshen are more liberal than Chester or Philadelphia. City Quakers are conservative, country

Quakers are willing to listen to reason." Thomas was speaking louder. "We're not the only ones who left to fight. Others have too."

"The meetings are getting nervous with the war coming close," Benjamin said. "I think they have more on their minds now, wondering about gathering their crops in."

"Yeah," Abner added. " My pa kept hearing all sorts of rumors and opinions, how to protect the family and the cattle and the horses."

"Well, my father keeps saying God will protect, sit silently in the spirit, wait for guidance, but others rise with a passion for physical force." Thomas was speaking louder.

"Yeah, and let others do his work for him," Caleb retorted, overhearing the conversation.

"But we're here," Thomas replied with enforced calm, his jaw muscles working.

"Keep it down!" the sergeant ordered, dropping back alongside the column, marching with irregular spacing. "You're all loud enough for the redcoats to hear." He marched alongside Thomas for a bit then said, "Don't let anyone bother you, look out for the real enemy. Remember," he said in an undertone, "a lot of men talk loud, but I like to see how they act. That speaks louder to me." He dropped back towards the rear, watching the full company as they marched with a steady pace, keeping within sight of the cannon ahead.

***

The army marched along the crowded road. It was dank and moist in spots, shadowed by great trees, dusty in the sun. The fields along the road were browning, wheat already cut, corn losing the bright green of summer, pumpkins and squash patches showing their colorful growth under green leaves and vines. Thomas wiped his brow with his arm, holding his broad-brimmed hat in his free hand, looking towards the next patch of shade to dampen the sweat on his neck and face.

As the road curved around, he could see Brandywine Meeting up ahead.

"Company, halt!" the sergeant ordered. They stopped and stood waiting. Thomas watched as two of the cannons ahead were directed off the road to the left beyond the meeting house. The army dispersed by command into the woods, then along the open fields facing down the slope in front. The Edgmont captain came back and stood off to the side under a clump of trees, gathering the company sergeants together, the men keeping their ranks but turning to watch the quick conference. Their sergeant returned.

"All right men, here's what we've been ordered to do. We'll head by companies to the meeting house. Our company will head off to the east a hundred or so yards and move in behind the regular army."

"Think that'll give us a chance to fight?" Caleb called out.

"You're so anxious to shoot someone?" replied the sergeant.

"If they get in my sights," Caleb answered with a broad snicker.

"They'll be in your sights I expect, but remember, if a lobster back is in your sights, you may well be in his sights."

"That's all right, Sarge, I plan to have a tree between him and me."

"It's pretty hard to shoot through a tree," Abner taunted.

"It's fine," Thomas soothed. "I think it's no more than what we'll be doing."

"I may even go for a stone wall," Benjamin added.

"If there's one to be found," Thomas said. "Let's just hope that the regulars can hold on without us."

The sergeant joined in. "Lads, Washington figures that the main attack will come across the Brandywine at Chad's Ford. We're all up here to protect the right flank of his army in case some redcoats try coming this way. It's a good possibility we'll not see any fighting up here."

"Particularly around a Quaker meeting house, right Sarge?" Caleb Bishop inserted sarcastically. "Peaceful place? Too bad for us," he ended with a sneer.

"You better hope that it remains peaceful," the sergeant replied.

"Washington must think there's some good chance of fighting," Thomas said, "else, he wouldn't have those cannons set up there." He pointed towards the stone farmhouse set across the road from the meeting.

"Prepared, that's what he is," Benjamin agreed, but was looking at Caleb.

The sergeant put an end to the discussion. "March! Follow the Willistown militia ahead!" There was a tingling in Thomas' chest as they picked up the pace. The simple fieldstone structure of Birmingham Meeting stood beside the road, sheltered by large trees. The space beyond was open with simple, low headstones of the cemetery, indicating by their presence a life to be recognized, the only physical testimony of a life after death, marking lives well spent, some too short, now in the eternal hereafter. Those who passed on were now in another world. They were acknowledged with a certainty by most of the Quaker Meeting, secure in the knowledge of that great Force, called God by George Fox and William Penn in their writings, Jesus Christ by more conservative members in Philadelphia, but all recognizing the power of the Bible and the teachings divinely received and shared with an immovable faith and trust. Thomas had never been to Birmingham Meeting but knew well of the strong belief and confidence in a divine guidance reflected in the solid and plain stone rectangle of the building. The sergeant led them past the two front doors set evenly apart under the roof of the porch, between the carriage sheds and alongside the burial ground bordering the fields, past the tree line separating property and farms.

"Company, halt!" the sergeant called out to the Edgmont militia who had already slowed down into loosened ranks. The men ducked under branches, avoiding brambles, keeping an unconscious vigil to their left as they watched the Continental Army organize itself along the ridge of the modest rise.

A regular army major came out of the clearing ahead. "You there!" he called to their captain, "take your positions along this tree line. Spread out, stand back of us, evenly spaced, but close, and then do like we're doing. Set up your defenses, something to hide behind, to shield yourselves, like the divisions over there." He pointed to men dragging fallen branches and logs into place, forming a barrier from which to fight.

Thomas watched a cannon being wheeled into place, high on a mound jutting out from the far edge of the field. Others were placed by piles of fieldstone clumped together by the farmers who had cleared their fields of rocks over the years. The light played softly on the deepening green of the mature corn stalks, the silk brown from exhaustion, the rows of yellow kernels in the fat ears, plump from the summer, ready to dry and for the harvest. But with the soldiers tramping over the plantings, stalks fell to be ground into the dirt of the field.

The sergeant issued no orders. The major had spoken clearly enough. Thomas motioned to Benjamin and Abner.

"Come on, I see a good spot over there, a little depression. We can get some of those branches and build up in front." He started over.

"Where're you going?" Caleb called out.

Thomas ignored him, setting out.

"Not where I have in mind," Caleb continued. He was closer and nudged Joshua. "C'mon," and the two of them headed quickly to the spot identified by Thomas. Thomas stopped. Benjamin and Abner came up and stood alongside.

"I thought thee wanted a tree," teased Benjamin. He turned to Thomas seething with anger. "Come on, let them have it."

"Yeah, we'll go for rocks," agreed Abner. They headed for a little pile of dumped stones by the worm fence line, exposed but close to the woods behind.

"Don't pay them any mind," Benjamin continued. "We'll do better over here." He thumped Thomas on the shoulder as he had done over the years growing up together.

"Thee's right," Thomas said. "They'll never change, and wherever we are, we're better off together, the three of us."

Abner had already gotten to the new location a few yards away from where Caleb and Joshua were setting up their wood barricade. Abner started to pull the rocks apart from the mound, setting them into a rough wall. Benjamin laid his rifle down, resting on a chestnut rail of the old fence and started to help. Thomas stood apart, looking up and down the line, others making do dragging larger, fallen tree trunks out of the woods, piling up brush and branches for better concealment. The sergeant walked about, the two corporals helping here and there as the militia improvised with whatever was at hand. Several with small camp shovels dug sod and soil up against fallen rails, pulled together to support earthen breast works.

"There will only be a little fire tonight lads," the sergeant spoke to each group. "We don't want to give those redcoats any knowledge of where we are. Let the Continentals know we're as tough as they. Not cold tonight anyway."

"How far away are the redcoats, does thee think?" Benjamin heaved a rock on top of the pile and stood up.

Thomas stepped back to look at their newly formed defenses. "I don't know for sure," he answered, "but if Washington is putting the army and some cannons in place here, he must know something."

"Figure he'll let us know?" Abner asked standing by the others.

"I expect when we hear some firing, then we'll know," Thomas mused.

"Today?" Abner asked.

"No," Thomas answered. "It's too late. Sun's going lower. Not enough time to make a real fight."

"Tomorrow then?" Benjamin asked.

"Probably," Thomas said.

"We'll stay together, won't we?" Benjamin asked. It was both a hope and a question.

"Always together," Thomas said. "We're cousins and you two are my best friends."

"We have done everything together," Abner said. "Even

when we all went hunting together, alone, for the first time."

"Yeah, and we were pretty excited about bringing back a couple of squirrels." Thomas smiled. "Then Benjamin shot at a squirrel and got himself a bird."

"I would have got that squirrel if the bird hadn't gotten in the way," Benjamin flushed with the memory.

"Well, it wasn't much for the pot but it was a good day." Thomas gave a sensitive look at his closest friend. "The first time hunting together is always the best."

"When this war is over, we'll go again," Abner said.

"Well, we're hunting again and together," Thomas added. "This time, it's for real."

"I hope I don't have to fire at someone," Benjamin said. "I know that's what fighting is all about, but I'm not sure I want to aim at another person, pull the trigger, and hope to see him fall." He shuddered involuntarily.

"When that man has his gun aimed at thee, then I think thee'll be encouraged to shoot." Thomas put his arm around Benjamin. He glanced around to see if anyone else was looking, particularly Caleb, then gave a slight tug. "None of us really want to kill another and we all hope we'll not be needed if the regulars ahead of us can do the job, but we've got to be ready." He released his hold. Benjamin stood up straighter.

"Thee's right of course, but it's just that when we signed up, it was hard to imagine we'd face British troops. Then it seemed far away and we'd just offer encouragement and support, relieve regular troops for the real fighting, that we'd pick jobs away from the killing." Benjamin looked at Thomas. "If something happens thee'll take care of me?"

"Nothing's going to happen," Thomas said with a wistful smile, watching Benjamin's smooth face creased with a growing anxiety, "and sure, the three of us will take care of each other. We always have."

"Like when Thomas let the oxen get into the pigs' pen and they scattered out into the garden and then the oxen got into the wheat field. It took the three of us and Thomas' brother to straighten it all out." Abner was laughing.

"Father was really upset," Thomas remembered.

"But we said part of the fault was ours," Benjamin said, laughing. "If we hadn't been there and helped get thee out of trouble, I'm not sure what would have happened."

"Father was really angry," Thomas agreed, "but he couldn't get too mad because you were there. And after, he calmed down." He looked at the two of them in turn. "Mother wasn't happy with her vegetables all trampled and eaten. Took me some extra work to repair the garden. Good you stood by me."

They stood silently, thinking of simpler times, trying to release their built up tension which knotted their insides.

Chapter Twelve

The supply wagons came up with the tents as Thomas hurried over. He came back to their spot. "Got ours before they did," he said with satisfaction.

"And none too soon," observed Benjamin. "Here comes Joshua with theirs. Caleb's just waiting for us to do something so he can do something different, and in his mind, better."

"Best take care of ourselves," Thomas said in the softer voice to Benjamin and Abner. "There's no answer to Caleb. It's very tiring." Thomas turned his back to Caleb who stood there in some frustration at being ignored by the three cousins as they unfolded the tent, staking the corners and raising it up.

The Continental Army soldiers forward organized quickly. In short order they had small fires going and soup heating in their pots.

"We better get ours going," Thomas said. "Else, we're going to search a good distance to find wood." He nudged Benjamin. "Let's go before we're completely set up, before Caleb figures it out."

Benjamin smiled. "Abner and the others can handle things here. Let's go." Saying nothing further, they headed out.

Shortly, they returned with arms full of sticks and branches.

"Here we are Abner," Thomas said as he dropped his load in front of the tent, "enough for a while."

"Seems so," Abner agreed. "Good thing. When Caleb

saw you were missing, he took a fit, ran off with Joshua. I guess he figured you were going to take all the best wood.

"Well, at least the closest," Thomas confirmed. "I see he's not back." Benjamin chuckled.

***

The camp had quieted, only broken by an infrequent scream from an animal that found itself in the clutches of a fox.

"I need to rest," Benjamin finally said. "Maybe that'll keep me from worrying about tomorrow."

"We all worry," replied Thomas, "but now we all need our rest."

"I'm headed for out tent," mumbled Abner in agreement.

They stacked their rifles, ready for the following day and crawled into the crowded tent, finding spaces among the other sleeping soldiers.

Sentries had been posted, fires were now covered, and locusts were chirping the last clicks of summer. Thomas lay on the ground, his blanket the only softening on the packed earth. Restless and awake, his mind racing, he raised up, quietly moved out of the tent and sat on a log nearby. The stars across the sky were nothing more than pinpricks in a black covering with light shining from behind. *The sergeant said the redcoats were really coming. Reports from the couriers had fighting below Wilmington. Men were killed. So it won't be tomorrow. Day after? And then shooting? Down by Chad's Ford. Probably not up here by Birmingham Meeting. Possibly. What if? What if someone of the Edgmont militia gets wounded? Caleb? That would solve a problem. Shouldn't wish that. What about Benjamin? It can't be. Why am I here? Is it right? Do we have to fight? I guess so. If they want to fight. Then we have to. But is it fair? Am I in danger? No. But possible. No matter. I'll just stay out of the way. But is that fighting? Maybe. But if I only fire from behind cover. Then they'll not see me. Safer.*

There was a rustling behind him. Benjamin sat down alongside him in the soft dark.

"Couldn't sleep?" Thomas asked.

"Couldn't thee?" Benjamin asked.

"I was thinking and then I tried not to and the more I tried, the more I thought, so I figured I might as well get up, maybe dredge my mind of all the thinking and then get some sleep.

"Same here." Benjamin was almost too quiet to hear. He was silent for a moment. "I'm worried. We've never done this before. What if I get scared and start to run away?"

"I guess we all wonder that," Thomas replied. He waited, then added, "Here we are, a bunch of farm boys. We know pigs and sheep and horses, we raise wheat and corn and flax, we even go into the woods and hunt, shoot birds and animals. Now we're expected to shoot at men and try to kill them. I think when we try to figure it out we can't, and then I think we're all scared. I mean the Hessians are professional soldiers. They fight for a living. And the British. They have a trained army. That's all they do. I bet they're not scared, but we aren't that way and I wonder what will happen." He hugged his knees. Benjamin sat, then got up and walked away from Thomas. He stood apart, close by the tree line in the faint shadow of the woods. Thomas sat there, rocking slowly back and forth. He stopped and got up and went over to Benjamin.

"I think we're all scared. We were not raised to do this, but we did what we thought was right, what we had to do." He put his hand on Benjamin's arm and pulled him around to face him. "We'll be fine, we'll do what we have to do to keep others from taking our land, our farms."

"I'm going to lie down again," Benjamin said, "if I can just stop thinking."

"Don't stop thinking, just stop worrying."

"Like thee?"

"Like I'm trying to do," Thomas admitted.

Benjamin smiled in the dark throwing a gentle punch at Thomas' arm.

***

"Get up! Everyone! Up! Up!" the sergeant called out, calling across the line of tents. "Day's coming. Much to do. Look lively now."

There was grumbling and rustling in the tents, men pushing out into the morning mist, stumbling about, heading for the edge of the field to pick out a private tree. Some poked the ashes, trying to raise a flame, here and there a scowl as the first man out found a dead fire, black and cold, with no twigs to get the fire from another. Noises grew louder as other companies were rousted out. The Continental Army was quiet but busy, quickly following the familiar daybreak routine. Talking was a hindrance.

Thomas nudged Benjamin. "Did thee get some sleep?"

"Not much. Kept thinking and even when I fell asleep, I kept dreaming of the British coming after us, running towards us, and in my dream, I couldn't move, and as much as I tried my legs wouldn't move and they kept coming closer and closer, running faster and faster, with their bayonets sparkling in the sunlight."

"And then what?" Abner asked, leaning in closer. Only the three of them were now left in the tent. "I mean, did thee start to run?"

"No," Benjamin answered. "I just looked around for thee and Thomas, but you were not to be seen." He dropped his head. Thomas and Abner stayed still. "Then all I could see were the backs of our militia disappearing into the woods followed by the regular army." His head came up and he looked first at Thomas, then Abner. "I was alone and I felt warm and comfortable and it became light, then everything faded away," he smiled, "and my dream was over and I woke up."

"Because the sergeant was making such a racket?" Abner pulled the tent flap apart and nodded towards the outside.

"No, I was awake when he started to bellow."

"Like my older brothers," Thomas offered.

"Like my father when we had a full day ahead of us," Benjamin agreed.

"Well, I think the sergeant has a full day planned for us," Thomas said, smiling.

"We better get going," Abner said, slipping his suspenders over his shoulders and scuttling out into the morning gloom.

An officer from the regular army rode along the line towards the militia.

"Something's up," Thomas observed. "When we get a real officer on horseback, we know it's orders."

"Maybe from Washington himself," Abner added.

"Thee can be sure he'll have his hand in it," agreed Benjamin.

"It's different taking orders that come from the general. I wonder what's going on," Thomas mused as the rider came to a halt, the militia officers gathering around his horse. Thomas stopped and watched the impromptu conference. Talking ceased as men stood, gathered over their small circle of fire, some with cups of hot coffee or leftover soup, all trying to listen even as the gentle breezes dissolved the words into a moaning, soft as the morning, mottled as they floated, dancing across the open spaces, spreading out beyond.

Guess we'll have to wait," Benjamin whispered, not wanting to break the attention of the group. They stood apart as the sergeant and two corporals huddled with the other noncommissioned officers, ready to hear the new orders. Suddenly the officer gave a kick with his spurs to the horse and cantered off to another group farther on. Thomas and his tent mates stood, staring at their captain as he gesticulated to the sergeant.

"Going to just stand there and gawk?" Caleb jibbed adding some further sticks onto their brightly burning fire. "You'll not get anything hot in that pot if you just keep hoping for a fire." Caleb stuck his elbow into Joshua's ribs to elicit a laugh.

Thomas turned his head and stared at Caleb for a moment then turned his back and ignored the laughter.

"C'mon," he acknowledged to Benjamin and Abner, still facing their tormentors, "he's at least got a point. If we don't get a flame going, it'll be cold porridge for breakfast."

"I imagine we're in for some cold food for a while," Benjamin said.

"I'm for hot broth while its possible," Abner said. He left and headed for the woods, but away from the sound of axes where the regular army was getting their own firewood.

"I'll help," Benjamin said as he joined Abner, striding quickly towards a promising clump of brush and trees, staying clear of Caleb and his tent mates.

It wasn't long before the sergeant came back along the

line. He strode ahead of the two corporals, jostling the militia, encouraging their organization and layout.

"Get yourselves together," he called out. "There'll be formation shortly and I want those fires banked. You men, get ready to move out." He was more officious than ever.

"A different man than when we drilled at Chester," Thomas said quietly to Benjamin. "I guess having the British this close gives us all an incentive."

"Look smart there, Pratt. You too Darlington and Baldwin." The three of them straightened up, involuntarily. "This is no picnic we're on."

"That's telling 'em Sarge," Caleb said, with a smirk in his voice.

"You're on no picnic either," replied the sergeant, snapping back. "All of you," he called out louder. "Smarten up! Square away! We'll have work enough to do."

The bellowing called for formation. There was an expectation among the men as they hurried to the level space in front of the captain flanked by the sergeant, talking in low tones, sporadically, looking over the other companies forming. Out of the woods came the Pennsylvania colonel, followed by a major of the Continental Army. The men stood taller, noise dying away, the Pennsylvania farmers and yeoman shifting unnoticed into ranks more evenly spaced. The colonel reigned in his horse as the company captains turned to face the mounted officers.

"Report!" ordered the adjutant.

The company sergeants sang out in a rolling cadence, some with more force than others. The men stood silently while officers saluted. The sun shone through the bare branches of the trees in the near hedgerow. The birds were silent. The countryside was quiet. Expectation hung over the army, regular and militia alike.

"Orders," the sergeant of Washington's Army sang out. The colonel started.

"General Washington has picked this place to make a stand," the colonel said. His blue and buff coat was brushed as finely as possible, the blue sash around his waist the primary indication of his rank. "The major of Washington's staff will continue." He turned to the young officer, who drew his horse up from behind, placed now alongside the colonel.

"You men of the Pennsylvania militia will support the men of General Sullivan's regiment. They're posted 200 yards to the north and stretching from General Greene's men to the west along the Brandywine to this point. Then General Lord Stirling's men will take position to their side to anchor our right flank. General Washington will use the meeting house at Birmingham as a hospital. It's far enough behind the lines and away from the Brandywine that it'll also act as a command post. You men act under the orders of General Sullivan through your own officers." The militia was silent. The officer's horse stomped the ground as if to emphasize the orders they'd just received.

"Does thee think we'll see any fighting?" Benjamin whispered.

"Don't think so," Thomas said.

"Quiet there," the sergeant hissed.

"The main part of the Continental Army will defend along the Brandywine." He paused and looked over the ranks of the militia, more or less straight. Men's heads tilted in all manner of curiosity, listening to the major, the first real army officer they had really heard. "You'll want to have your rifles primed and ready, your packs neat, ready to act like soldiers."

"What does he take us for," Caleb said, louder than a

whisper. This time the sergeant said nothing. "We're here because we're ready to fight," he added, spitting out on to the ground in front of him as big a lunger as he was able to develop, making a loud splat.

"We've never been tried in actual battle," Thomas said quietly. The major moved his horse closer to the Edgmont ranks, stopped and stared down at the lines of the farmer soldiers, some little older than boys, a few graying at the temple, most in dirty and patched shirts and pants, and black or brown hats, sweat lined at the brow, several turned up at the sides to form a tricorn. Most of the remaining hats were broad-brimmed that shielded the eyes from the major as much as from the sun. The major waited. The line shifted uneasily.

"Do your duty and we'll do ours and your country will be grateful." He swung his horse around and trotted back towards the forming ranks of the regular army.

"All right men," called out the Edgmont captain, in as much of a military a voice as he could muster. At age 25, he was not much older than most. "You heard the major." He turned to the sergeant, older by 10 years, whose face was lined from the outdoors as much as from his previous military experience under the British. "Form the men into a skirmish line. Let them find whatever cover they can. They can rest in place, but be ready to move. No fires. They can have water and biscuit only for midday." The captain strode off, headed towards the Continental Army line to inspect its formation and satisfy his own curiosity.

"Form along this ridge," the sergeant called out, "use the trees in the hedgerow to sight along and to provide cover." The militia moved ahead to adjust.

"I bet you want the biggest tree," Caleb challenged

Thomas as Benjamin and Abner staked a position by an old oak tree.

"If thee wants our place, we'll find another," Thomas replied with a bravura he didn't totally feel.

"You keep it," Caleb yelled back so that others could hear. "You need it more than we do."

"Let him be," Benjamin advised as Thomas walked over.

"We're fine," Abner agreed. "This tree's big around, but there're others."

"Yes, and I see Caleb has already found another tree as big." He forced a smile, annoyed that Caleb's jibes still bothered him.

The militia worked into their individual positions, some close by one another, others separated by an open space. The captain came back and waved the sergeant towards him.

"The army ahead is doing just like us," he said by way of confirmation in their own formation.

As the sun rose higher, the birds remained quiet, squirrels retreated to safer woods leaving only the locusts to keep up their vibrations, their sound undulating in waves.

Thomas sat with his back to a smaller tree, careful to avoid the poison ivy, facing forward as Benjamin and Abner sat against the large oak. Thomas chewed on a dry biscuit. He heard a far away rumble working through the distant woods and across the open fields. He stopped chewing. The sound echoed again. "What's that?" he asked, looking to the west.

"Maybe thunder, a storm perhaps," Abner guessed.

"And maybe cannon fire," Benjamin suggested. They

waited. Another rumble sounded, louder and more insistent.

"It's started," Thomas said with a quiet certainty. He continued to chew, putting the remainder of the biscuit into his pack. He ran his hands over the rifle, feeling the lock to assure himself that the flint was still secure as he kept his eyes focused to the far sound. Others heard too, some stood and reached out as if additional height would make the cannon fire more distinct.

"Someone's getting it," Thomas said.

"Better there than here," Abner said hopefully.

"Makes me a little nervous," Benjamin admitted.

"Anyone who ignores the sound is foolish," Thomas said. He turned to Benjamin. "Makes me a little nervous also," he admitted to his cousin, not loud enough for any others to hear.

The sergeant came down the line. "Far away lads," he comforted them. "But stay alert, be ready," he called as he made his way along the hedgerow where men stood with their rifles cradled in their arms.

Thomas looked around. The men gathered in small groups, two, three, or four. Their voices sounded soft, with none of the exuberance they had exhibited while drilling safely in their own villages. With each rumble of cannon, heads turned to the noise as if expecting a projectile to come careening through the trees to skip across the corn field and head for their protected stand. They shifted a bit to give some relief from the more insistent booming, the low thud of the heavy artillery accenting the lighter tone of the smaller guns with shells just as deadly. Men unknowingly fidgeted with their rifles as they automatically caressed the stock and trigger housing. They parted to look over towards the Continental Army, lying steady on the far side of the field. The conversation began again.

"I wonder where the British are?" Abner asked nervously.

Thomas twisted his mouth. "Over by the sound of cannon, I reckon, at least, some of them."

"Does thee think others are closer?" Benjamin asked with a certain apprehension.

"General Howe is known for spreading out his troops," Thomas said.

"So thee thinks the British might be closer than ever?" Abner took off his hat and wiped his brow.

"I'm sure they're not all standing on the backside of a battery of artillery having tea," he answered with a grim smile.

"What happens if they move up the Brandywine and attack just to our west?" Benjamin gave a quick shudder he hoped no one else would see.

"Then the Continental regulars will have something to do over there." Thomas tried to remain calm. "Thee sees them up ahead. They don't look concerned." He tossed his head towards them. "They're still lined up, easy as thee pleases, their officers standing by them. The colonel on horseback just keeps looking out towards the west. They're not afraid."

"Well, that's their business," Abner added, "but for us, it's the first time and I can't be so unconcerned." He used his sleeve to wipe some more sweat off his face.

Benjamin turned to Thomas. He spoke as softly as he could. "Thee's my cousin and my best friend." He looked Thomas straight in the eye. "I'm afraid."

Thomas interrupted quickly but with more force. "We all are."

"I know, but I keep getting this feeling. I don't know why. I think about home, my family, Mother always around, helping, working, encouraging, a warm hand for a hurt, kind of that steady place of safety on the farm. She is, like, always the place of comfort. Wherever she is, it's fine there." His eyes drifted off into the early afternoon light. He added very quietly, "I miss her."

"I miss my family too," Thomas admitted.

"Promise me?" Benjamin asked.

"Sure. Anything. What?"

"If anything happens to me, will thee take care of me, that my family will know, Father and mostly Mother."

"Nothing's going to happen." Thomas put it as lightly as he could. "We have all those soldiers ahead of us and we've got militia either side of us. No. Nothing's going to happen." He motioned towards Abner just coming back from a tree, buttoning up his front. "See, even Abner's easy."

Abner heard the last. "Sure, maybe on the outside, but not on the inside, else I wouldn't have to constantly head for a little spot away."

"Even Caleb over there seems to be talking a lot."

"Yeah, with hands flying." Benjamin laughed from an emotional release. "Maybe not always too smart."

"But brave," admitted Thomas.

"Sure, as long as he has Joshua by his side."

"Who really isn't too smart," Abner said.

"Being brave is useful," Thomas said, "but I'll always add a good measure of smarts. It's good to run, but it's better to know where to run."

"Thee means away from the British?" Abner asked.

"Sometimes for help, sometimes towards the enemy."

"And sometimes away," Benjamin said.

"If necessary, but never blindly." Thomas felt better for the conversation.

"So thee'll do what I say," Benjamin persisted.

"To do what?" Abner interrupted.

"Of course," Thomas agreed, ignoring Abner. "Thee knows I will." He gave a light punch on Benjamin's chest. Benjamin replied with a return punch, just as soft and slow.

"Hey you," Caleb yelled towards them startling the three out of their discussion. "The sergeant's waving us forward towards the regulars. Don't you see?" he dug in with the comment.

"We see," Thomas replied. They hadn't, but he was not going to let Caleb know. The Edgmont militia edged forward out from the tree line towards the Continentals who themselves were moving forward towards another hedgerow and woods beyond. The slope was down, the high trees keeping any underbrush from growing except at the woods' edge. The militia walked, slowly, then more quickly, then at a gentle lope. Cannon fire sounded closer, off to the west. Suddenly, a boom reverberated ahead of them, the retort of the explosion in the barrel racing along faster than the cannonball to follow. There was a crackling amidst a second thud which spread from the west. Cracks of rifles firing in a sporadic sequence drifted over towards them. All at once, an intense series of firing in a regular cadence came from directly in front of the Edgmont militia, the noise muffled by the trees, followed by an intermittent snapping of rifles from the Continental Army, interspersed with the regular cadence of seasoned troops firing on command.

Thomas looked to his left. Caleb and Joshua were closest, running towards the sound, the militia being urged by the sergeant and corporals waving the line on, in among the trees, across thin creeks, the cool of the woods in marked contrast to the heat and drifting smoke of rifles firing up ahead.

All at once, they reached the edge of the woods. There, in front of them, at the bottom of the incline, abreast the rutted Duke of Marlborough's Street, running towards the Brandywine Creek, stood the British Army. Their red tunics were a brilliant contrast to the green and brown of the countryside. The bluff and blues of the Continental Army fired back as the men crouched against any cover from a tree, fence, or rock outcropping. The British formations positioned straight across, the front kneeling with trained precision, poured a relentless rain of lead shot against the surprised army. The British artillery fired. Smoke signaled another cannonball coming, with its sound and final whistle as the steel pushed aside the air to land with a thud, beyond the army and before the militia. Thomas fell to his knees as the militia line, surprised, slowly came to a halt. He lifted his rifle to his shoulder, sighting along the barrel as a blur of blue dissolved into the black powder smoke. Another volley was loosed with the realization that the figure blocking his shot was a Continental soldier moving across his line of sight. *I can't shoot yet,* he thought to himself. He lowered his rifle to take in the whole scene as another line of white smoke erupted from the British line. Suddenly, one of the figures that had blocked his view shifted slightly then dropped from sight. *Maybe now,* he reasoned, raising his rifle again. He carefully moved to the left away from other figures in front. Suddenly, the smoke cleared and there stood a line of the British Army, the rear rank loading as the front kneeled again preparing to fire. Thomas shook, wondering whether he ought to pull the trigger. There was a simultaneous crack as the line fired. Thomas dropped flat onto the stalks of corn, his rifle laid out alongside. The whistle of several musket balls whispered overhead. He rolled over towards his rifle to see Benjamin lying as flat as he. *I've lost my chance,* Thomas figured, then realized he had not even loaded his gun. There was no bullet in the barrel, the powder still in his horn slung around his chest. He raised his head slightly, watching the redcoats work with precision, the Continentals firing unevenly, sometimes several shots at once, sometimes a long pause between the crack of powder in the pan igniting the charge in the barrel. The soldiers of Washington's Army were kneeling, then running to new positions in sharp contrast to the relentless regularity of the British troops. Thomas lay down again, wondering what to do.

"C'mon lads," he heard the bellow of their sergeant. "Up and fight."

Thomas hesitated, then rose to his knees. *I'm no good lying down with an unloaded rifle,* he thought. He looked left and right at his neighbors, most were up now, at least partially, some standing, others running towards some cover given by a few near trees. *I guess a loaded rifle is better than just carrying it around like an empty stick.* He worked quickly, ignoring those around him. He dropped to his knee and sighted again, playing the barrel of the rifle back and forth until he found a clear target through the drifting smoke without any figures before him. He took aim, pulled the flintlock back, and then squeezed the trigger as his rifle erupted into noise, the pressure familiar against his shoulder. He dropped down low, and then pulled himself up onto his elbows to see what effect he might have had. Smoke drifted across the area he had fired into. The redcoats fired again, the regular crack of the British muskets sounded across the field, no less than before, their ranks on either side still complete. Thomas took a deep breath. *I fired at another,* he said to himself and closed his eyes, flat again on the ground. He could hear shooting from either side of him, not frequent; it came intermittently with a lighter, higher pitch than the British muskets.

"Let's help the regulars!" yelled the sergeant. "Get up! Move!" he commanded. Thomas watched Caleb jump to his feet followed more slowly by Joshua, without enthusiasm. Others began to move. Suddenly, Benjamin stood.

"We're going to do it," he said, looking first at Thomas, then Abner.

"Here we go," Thomas agreed.

"I'm with you," Abner added. "Don't want to be left behind."

The militia moved forward by ones and twos. The sergeant was now 50 yards away from the Continental line.

Thomas started to run, jogging back and forth *to confuse any redcoat,* he figured. As he watched the British line maneuver, he stopped jogging. *If I go to the left maybe I'll just walk into a slug. There's no real safety except down and out of sight.* He came to a crouch, acting on his own analysis. The Continental line moved forward but hesitated, then stopped as the British regulars reacted to the beat of their drums, the colors riffling in the breeze as the forward line stood up. With the sun glinting on fixed bayonets, they started a slow march across the road and up the incline towards the waiting men of Washington's Army. The cadence was drummed out, the procession of troops steady, cannon shot whistling over their heads to land among the American soldiers loading and firing as quickly as possible, now with an increased urgency. The British firing almost ceased, the artillery now louder and more frequent.

Thomas watched as one shell landed between two men, exploded, leaving a space where they had been, familiar shapes disappearing. The Continental line fell slowly back into the mix of the militia who remained in place, transfixed with the enormity of the situation. They were fighting a battle for the first time, men trying to wound or kill, the smoke of gunfire growing thicker, eyes blinking from the acrid fumes with the noise of yelling and drums and explosions working in a crescendo until finally, Thomas couldn't hear it anymore. The scene of battle blotted out his normal senses, his fear mixed with determination, and his pride mixed with curiosity. He loaded his rifle again. Benjamin came up to him.

"Stay by me," he implored. "I don't want to be alone in this." He pushed his ramrod down on to the ball to set firmly in his barrel, the movement quick and practiced and deliberate.

"Where's Abner?" Thomas asked. He looked over but the confusion was growing, regulars mixing between the militia groups, hesitating about their next move.

Thomas and Benjamin shifted back, off to the side of the regulars. Suddenly, Caleb came up to them.

"Haven't run yet?"

"Not 'till we see thee leave," Thomas replied.

"No chance," Caleb said.

"I don't think we want to be in between the regulars and the British though," Benjamin cautioned.

"Well, that's one thought I can agree with," Caleb offered, a bit more kindly. He yanked his head towards the oncoming phalanx of red uniforms proceeding in a steady march. "Wish we had some cannon over here," he added. "It's hot work to keep those redcoats from coming on. They have their artillery ranging in on us." He grabbed his rifle by the barrel and stepped back to let some of the militia pass by.

"Getting close," Benjamin observed.

"Too close," Caleb said.

After thee," Thomas said, bowing.

"Makes good sense," Caleb said with as much bravado as he could muster. The battle became more intense.

Thomas turned to fire, this time keeping his eyes open for the red uniform he had targeted, watching as nothing seemed to happen. He stood transfixed as suddenly out of the far woods to his right came another formation of British soldiers, its officer on horseback, riding along the line behind the marching column. Caleb aimed and fired.

"Hit anything?" Thomas asked as he reloaded.

"Too hard to tell." He squinted. "I'll tell you one thing though, they're coming on faster and with more of them."

"We need to move," Abner shouted, running up to them.

"I see the sergeant moving back," Caleb observed as he loaded and prepared another shot. A cannon ball whistled overhead, landing just behind them to skip twice landing at a tree, cutting the trunk half apart.

"Let's shift," Thomas called, jogging up the slope, staying ahead of the retreating Continental Army, slowly moving back under the increased pressure of greater numbers.

Caleb stood up and fired, then turned and ran back to them. Joshua was already far back up the hill.

"Thy support?" Thomas asked.

"Getting a better position," Caleb answered, sounding annoyed.

"Well, at least he's picked out a position we can all use," Benjamin said.

"We'll not last long if we don't get some more men up here. We don't have enough firepower to stop those lines coming towards us." Thomas stood around, finished loading, and took a quick aim and fired.

"Anyone?" Abner asked.

"Maybe. Don't know. Too much smoke."

Does thee want to hit someone?" Benjamin asked.

"Yeah, Pratt," Caleb growled, getting off another round. "Are you just as happy to shoot into the air?"

"I hope he hits someone," Joshua finally jibbed. "They are getting closer all the time."

"And we're not holding them," Benjamin said.

"It's strange trying to shoot at someone," Thomas said to no one in particular. "Even as we are shot at."

"You better shoot back," Caleb yelled, " 'cause they're trying to shoot you and kill you if they can."

Soldiers were running back towards the woods, trampling the corn underfoot as they pulled back. Companies were still collected, holding together. As Thomas and the others shifted back, sometimes jogging, then walking, turning to fire when the breeze cleared the smoke away for a brief time to offer a fair target, some of the Continental soldiers ran past them into the relative safety of the woods.

Benjamin headed for the tree line. A shell burst off to the side. A regular soldier screamed. Thomas stopped to look. The man had lost his arm at the shoulder; blood spilled down across his chest. His rifle dropped to the ground as he grabbed the jagged stump with his remaining hand, flesh oozing from between his fingers. He gave another scream that dissolved into a loud moan as he slumped to his knees. Men ran by him. Thomas hesitated.

"C'mon," Benjamin yelled from behind a tree.

"Fool," Caleb added. "Get back here or you'll be next."

Thomas turned away and ran, twisting between retreating soldiers, militia and regular alike, into the shadowed canopy of the woods with its great trees.

"We need some help," gasped Thomas, out of breath, heart pounding as much from running as from the sight of the massed British regiments marching steadily up the slope.

"Where did they all come from?" Abner asked in a rising panic. "They were all supposed to be to the west, along the Brandywine."

"Well, they're not now," Caleb, said. He scowled from behind another tree.

"I can figure that one out," Thomas said, trying to calm himself.

"The Continentals aren't holding them back," Benjamin added.

"I think they're hoping for our help," Thomas said.

"Well, they're not getting any from us standing here." Caleb forced a certain confidence.

"Then let's turn around and do our part." Thomas headed for the edge of the woods. "Coming?" he asked over his shoulder.

"I'm not letting a farm boy like Thomas be the big soldier," Caleb said, even louder. "C'mon Joshua! Let's save the army." He sprinted up alongside several men of the regular army, loading and shooting as quickly as they could. Caleb could see groups of men falling back towards their position. Thomas stepped from behind a tree at the wood's edge and fired.

"Aim for one of those redcoats that has gold on him," advised the soldier, not unkindly, kneeling, loosening another round. "They make the best targets," he added calmly.

Suddenly, a whistling of several musket balls shattered into the wood's edge close by them.

"That was close." Thomas motioned to Benjamin, standing alongside him. "It hit just above in the tree."

Benjamin looked up and then over to where there had been four soldiers firing. Now there were only three. He looked down into the scrub on the edge of the field. One was lying on his back, blood seeping from below into his shirt, widening in a creeping red stain. Benjamin tried to look away. Thomas was standing stock-still. He moved over to him as they both saw the man, twitching slightly, then with one jerk of his legs, stretch out, and suddenly collapse, empty of life.

"C'mon," Thomas urged. "We can't help him now, and from the shouting over there, sounds like the British are getting close." Thomas looked back as the three Continentals ducked back into the woods. He saw the back of Caleb's shirt with Joshua close behind.

A cannon boomed. Shortly thereafter the ball ripped into the branches overhead, showering leaves and branches down where they had just been standing.

"C'mon," Thomas yelled to Benjamin, louder than he would have wished. They both ducked and ran farther into the woods. Men scattered about them, all shifting back, higher up the slope. Thomas kept going, reaching the other side of the stand of trees and looked at the open space of a fallow field in front, rising up to the stone wall of the burial ground. He could see an American cannon being wheeled into place, then an officer on horseback urging new troops out from behind the protection of the wall. They came down towards them but shifted suddenly off to the side. Thomas looked over to the east to see more British redcoats come from around the far edge of the woods.

"We got to get up to the top by the meeting house," Thomas said to Benjamin.

"Let's go."

"Where's Abner?"

"Over there, but he's heading up on his own."

"I suppose Caleb for all his talk has already retreated," Thomas said with a thinly veiled sarcasm.

"I think thee's right." Benjamin smiled as the two of them watched Caleb, followed closely by Joshua, running and dodging rock piles, following slower soldiers up the slope.

"Well, if he's gone, I guess it's all right for us to get up the hill. When we get to the meeting house, we can back up the regular army, and if they have cannon, it's a better place for defense." He pushed Benjamin on his back as they both started running towards the reserves coming down from behind the stonewalls. Regular soldiers stopped, waiting for the others to join.

A fresh barrage came from the new British position. Shells exploded among the few men still holding on at the bottom of the slope. The confusion increased as the first redcoats came out of the woods.

"Run faster," Thomas gasped as they both used all their strength to run, trailing their rifles at their side. More shells fell behind them. They heard the cracking of the British muskets as the new troops formed their line at the far side of the stand of trees where Thomas and Benjamin had emerged minutes before. The sound was muted in their ears by the pulsing of their hearts, rasping breath, and sweat rolling down from their brows. It was the change of air pressure as a bullet flew close by Thomas' head that kept him running towards the stone wall, not far away. He looked up towards the crest of the hill and saw rifles pointing out, heads of soldiers pop up and fire, the smoke from the discharge locating each round, then the heads disappearing.

Suddenly, a cannon ahead fired. The ball swooshed overhead towards the redcoats marching in a quick step around the near side of the woods forming a third thrust of the British. More soldiers laid their rifles across the stone wall, shooting in an even sequence.

"C'mon," Thomas shouted to Benjamin as they headed for a break in the wall. Smoke drifted down towards them, obscuring the ground in front. Another shell was fired from the British artillery now wheeled around in front of the far woods, aiming for the soldiers scrabbling up the slope towards the two American cannons. One cannonball hit the ground and skipped along, bouncing waist high to take another bounce. It hit a rock and careened off to the side, taking the head off a Continental soldier. The body took another step then fell forward. There was no sound, it had all been so quick. Thomas sprinted toward the gap in the wall. He heard the scream of a cannonball, felt the air compress as it passed close by exploding in a shrinking parting of the iron casing, pieces thudding into the ground, a few rattling off the stone wall just ahead.

"That was close," Thomas gasped to Benjamin, running several yards away. He looked at the gap at several soldiers squeezing through, amidst the pop of gunfire. "We're almost there," Thomas said, looking over for Benjamin. The space where he had been was empty. Thomas slowed and turned back. Benjamin was kneeling on the ground some paces behind. His head was down, looking at his belly. He was quiet. Thomas slowed, then stopped. Benjamin had an uncomprehending look in his eyes. Thomas bent over and ran back to him. Seeing him, he recoiled, a cold wash of horror surging into his stomach, his heart missing its usual beat as his eyes glazed over in a mist of tears. Benjamin slowly looked up at Thomas who kneeled beside his best friend.

"Look," Benjamin said in a quavering voice, a sob working its way up his throat. "Look," he said again, more of a plea than a demand.

Thomas forced himself to look. Benjamin was holding a mass of gut in his two hands as he nervously tried to push the intestines back into his body. A sharp fragment of the shell had shredded his shirt, slicing open his belly, spilling blood, liquid, and his insides onto his pants, his flesh falling in a great lumpy mass, some separated from its neighbor, more kept together by muscle and tissue. Benjamin pushed some of the gut back. Another section slid out. With a jerky motion of his hands, he kept squeezing his insides back together.

"Help me, Thomas!" he said weakly, crying silently.

"Oh, Benjamin," Thomas cried, putting his arm around his cousin's shoulder.

The sergeant came up. More bullets flew by. Smoke became thicker. The British were advancing up the slope, the sound of their muskets louder.

"I'll take your guns. Get him up behind the wall." The sergeant picked up the rifles and was gone.

"I'll take care of thee, Benjamin," Thomas croaked.

"Will thee?" Benjamin implored.

"Of course," Thomas responded, softly, "I'm with thee."

"I knew thee would," Benjamin replied. "I always knew

it." He squeezed harder against his middle not daring to look down.

Thomas went to his knees and carefully curled his arms under Benjamin's legs, clasping his hands tightly around him as he moved close, his head against Benjamin. He carefully lifted him slightly off the ground, and then brought him towards him. Blood and mucus seeped on to his chest. He squeezed harder and with his legs taut and straining, lifted Benjamin, his head curled down on to Thomas' chest, his soft curled red hair, long, fitting under Thomas' chin, moaning from the pain welling up from the massive wound. Thomas didn't hear the shells exploding, the bullets whizzing past, the yelling or crying, the popping of muskets, orders shouted by captains, relayed by sergeants. All he felt were the tears, which coursed down his cheeks as he cradled Benjamin in his arms, loose but steady, stumbling, mist in his eyes, clouded by smoke, stepping by instinct towards the cemetery wall. Men parted as he came through, then squeezed together again firing down upon the rapidly advancing British.

"Hold on, men!" the colonel called on horseback. "Let them have it," he ordered.

A cannon fired. No one cheered.

"Watch your right," a sergeant yelled.

"Keep firing into their formation!" the captain shouted.

More regular troops came up from the road. They streamed without orders off towards the right flank. Sullivan's brigade shifted from the west, the Brandywine no longer the center of action.

Thomas looked around, searching for help. No one paid attention. Other wounded waited as a strip of linen was wound around a bleeding arm, a splint attached to a leg broken by a musket ball, another with a mouth that brought up blood with every breath. They were taken to the meeting house, the only place out of the line of fire. Bullets pinged off the stone walls.

Thomas stumbled over others as he headed for the open door. As he started in, an orderly stood in the way.

"I need to see a doctor," he said desperately.

"So do all the others," the young man replied, not unkindly, himself covered with splotches of blood. He waved his hand around. "There's no more room inside."

"But my friend is hurt," Thomas persisted.

"Let's see," the orderly replied. He pulled Thomas' arms apart to look down at Benjamin's front, one look sufficing. "Over there," he ordered, pointing to a tree by the corner of the meeting house.

"Will a doctor see him?" Thomas asked with increasing desperation. Benjamin was breathing more quickly, shallow heaves, spasms racking him as he cried out, the pain surging through him in waves.

"Don't leave me, Thomas," he begged.

"I won't," Thomas promised. He sat down on the grass, still cradling Benjamin in his arms.

The sergeant came up to him. "Here's your rifle and that of your cousin."

"I don't need it now," Thomas said through his tears.

"Yes you do!" the sergeant snapped. "Get back on that wall yonder."

Thomas looked down at Benjamin, pulling his arms apart off his wound. He recoiled, then let Benjamin's hands curl again onto his stomach still pushing out, blood spurting in a slow, steady stream.

The sergeant watched. "You can't do anything more for him," he said in a brusque but kindly manner.

"I've got to stay here." Thomas held Benjamin tighter.

"If you stay here, you're both going to be dead." The sergeant jabbed the stock of Thomas' rifle against his arm. "Take it!"

Thomas hesitated, then loosened one hand and grabbed the barrel of the rifle.

"Oh, Thomas," Benjamin groaned.

"Don't worry," said Thomas, "I'm here."

"Get moving!" the sergeant ordered.

Thomas hesitated as an orderly passed by. "Can thee take care of my cousin?" Thomas implored.

"Sure. Sure," he replied, hurrying by to another who had just been carried to the meeting house.

"Thee'll tell my mother?" Benjamin asked. "I didn't mean for this. I'm sorry I disobeyed her." He choked on his words.

"Thee can tell her thyself," Thomas said with the dread of an untruth. "She'll know."

"If thee tells her, she'll understand." Benjamin's head slumped further down on to Thomas' lap. He raised his head up and with an effort and looked into Thomas' eyes. "Tell her I love her and I'll be home by the by."

"C'mon, Pratt!" the sergeant ordered with an urgency. "We need you. And now."

Thomas hesitated. The firing was more intense, coming from both sides of the meeting house, the sound of British muskets closer. Men were yelling, cannons booming, shells exploding in the field leading up to the meeting house. Trees absorbed bullets, cracked, then broke under repeated shelling.

"I'll be back Benjamin," Thomas whispered as he unfolded his arms, laying Benjamin on the grass to his side, bringing his legs up tight as his head bent forward as if to pressure his hands to keep his wound from spilling more of his insides out onto the ground. "Hold on," Thomas begged, trying to cover the sound of his tears. "I'll be back," he promised again, burying his head against Benjamin's neck, now cold and clammy, twitching, his hair matted from the cold sweat which no longer mattered, "and don't worry about thy mother." His lips were close to his ear.

"I can see her now," Benjamin replied. "She's coming for me," he said. There was a thin smile on his face.

"Pratt!" ordered the sergeant. Thomas slowly raised himself up. He ran his fingers through Benjamin's hair, untangling the knots at the hands.

"I'll be back," he said a last time.

"I know thee will," Benjamin replied softly.

Thomas got up and with a last look, ran after the sergeant towards the far end of the burial ground, his powder horn bouncing against his side as they headed for the gathering of the few in the Edgmont militia still fighting. Caleb walked out as he reloaded his rifle, face streaked with black of the powder exploding in his pan, his shirt torn.

"Back to fight are you?"

Thomas ignored him, looking for Abner. Joshua turned around and leaned over the last few stones at the end of the shallow wall. "Where's Abner?" Thomas called out over the noise of the fighting.

Caleb fired again then turned and answered, "Figured when you left from fighting, he'd had enough himself." Caleb stood back from a tree as he once more loaded, the motions automatic.

"I don't see him," Thomas complained, inwardly blaming Caleb for Abner's absence.

"Down farther," Joshua finally answered. "Mixed up with the regulars."

Thomas made to run past the open space to his friend.

"Better stay here," Caleb yelled, "safer than crossing, and we need you. Those redcoats are getting closer." He fired again.

"I'm running out of powder," Joshua yelled.

"Takes some of Thomas'," Caleb replied. "He's got to have extra."

Thomas loaded and, putting his head above the wall, fired at a red shape coming out of the smoke and haze closer than he could have imagined. The shape buckled and slid down below the layer of white smoke to remain still on the flattened field just beyond. *Did I hit him?* Thomas shuddered. *I wonder if he's killed?* He stared at the shape, now level with the contour of the land. He saw redcoats surround one of the cannons. The American soldiers firing the artillery piece tried to load one last time, the rammer with his back to the rush of British troops looking over his shoulder just as a bayonet was pushed into his back. He hung on to the rammer, then fell over it like a wet piece of laundry. Two others put up their hands, one too late as he was shot dead on by a redcoat coming through the drifting smoke. The other stood paralyzed as the remaining crews scattered in all directions heading back towards where Thomas watched, unbelieving, as the boredom of marching turned more quickly into terror and a race for survival. Suddenly, Caleb yelled to no one in particular. "God damn," and dropping his rifle, grabbed his leg. Joshua turned and saw a British soldier at the far end of the wall, aligned and firing towards them. He shifted his rifle to the side and carefully sighting, fired. The shot missed. The redcoat started to move forward, down the line, others forming behind him. Joshua said nothing. He bolted and ran with several others, militia and regulars alike, heading for a stand of trees, dodging in and around not waiting to reload. The British soldiers, bayonets fixed, marched deliberately towards the Continentals still in position. Suddenly realizing their danger, the Americans turned and leapt over a snake fence of chestnut rails and ran with the others.

Thomas went over to Caleb. "You've got to help me," Caleb implored as he grasped his wounded leg, blood spreading quickly through his pants.

"Broken?" asked Thomas.

"God damn!" was Caleb's only answer as both his hands tightened on his thigh.

"Let me see," Thomas demanded, and without waiting for an answer, tore away the cloth that had been rent by the bullet and looked for the wound in the blood. He ripped the pant's leg off and parting two strips, created a wad, using the other strip to hold it in place, pulling it tight around Caleb's thigh. The blood stopped flowing, easing around the edges of the patch, beginning to dry and cake.

"Is it broken?" Thomas asked again, feeling gently around the wound. "Move your foot," he ordered.

Caleb flexed his ankle. "Is it?"

"I don't think so."

"It hurts like hell," he growled. "Don't leave me Thomas," he said again through his pain.

"I need to go back to see Benjamin," Thomas said glancing around.

"No you don't. Besides, he'll be dead by now, and if you don't get me up on your back, we're going to be dead ourselves, or at least prisoners." The British soldiers were beginning to trot down the line, scattering the Americans away as they came, fewer firing in their direction. The regulars began to run.

"C'mon, damn it!" shouted Caleb, "you've got to do it."

Thomas looked back beyond the field towards the meeting house and burial ground where a confused mass of men began to panic and run. He couldn't see where he had left Benjamin. There were too many in the way. There was shouting well off as he saw the British flag beyond the corner of the stone work of the meeting house. Thomas swallowed to get rid of the knot in his stomach surging up in his throat, his eyes blinking with tears for Benjamin mixed with an acrid smoke now beginning to sting.

"Hold our rifles!" he commanded Caleb. He placed his in Caleb's arm and stooping down hauled Caleb onto his back, arms and rifles hanging over his shoulders.

"Damn!" Caleb moaned, gritting his teeth with no further complaint.

"Hang on!" Thomas said as he began to walk, then jog, mixing in with the remaining soldiers as they gave up their positions defending the artillery and meeting house. A British sergeant began to yell to regain formation, the redcoat lines reappearing and beginning with a practiced regularity to press forward. Thomas ran as best he could around fallen trees, seeking a break in the far fence and into more woods. There was sporadic firing as the British relied more on bayonets chasing after the remnants of Washington's Army as it dispersed along the country lanes, through woods, down coursing streams, splashing through seeping marshes, sodden and dank. Thomas went through the fence where it had been knocked down. A stray bullet whizzed by him to stop suddenly into a tree off to the right. He was tiring, sweat covering his chest and arms. Caleb said nothing but Thomas could hear his labored breathing, teeth grinding together with every hard step and bounce. Thomas stopped in the shelter of a tree and adjusted Caleb higher as the wounded man grunted. As he took a better hold on Caleb's thigh, he could feel the warm stickiness on his right hand. Caleb held his breath for an instant saving it to counter the pain, then breathing out as he settled higher on Thomas' back.

"Sorry," Thomas apologized. "We'll go farther into the woods then stop for a moment or so."

"Go on," Caleb grunted as they both listened to the sounds of firing and occasional shouts as the British pressed on. They headed deeper into the woods, others dodging in parallel courses towards the safety of distance. The snapping of twigs came more from men retreating than from shots fired. Thomas slowed to a plodding walk as he carefully worked his way through the trees, following a path already cut until he came across a large tree fallen by the path.

"We'll stop here," he said to Caleb who remained silent, breathing hard, his eyes closed from the pain. Thomas lowered Caleb onto the trunk of the tree and carefully moved away, holding onto one arm to keep him from falling backwards. Caleb opened his eyes.

"How is thee doing?" Thomas asked.

"I've been better," replied Caleb with a thin, pain-racked smile. "Damn," he repeated in an effort to ease the pain.

"Thee will still have that slug in thy leg, but at least it doesn't seem to be broken."

"Thank God," Caleb mumbled.

Thomas sank down on the ground beside him and drew his knees up, wrapping his arms around them. He let his head sink down onto his knees, closing his eyes, the tight of his stomach draining his emotion into an empty space to be swallowed up. *Benjamin,* he thought to himself and repeated, "Benjamin," he said softly.

Caleb was silent then offered with more compassion than Thomas had ever heard from him, "You did what you could." He waited, as Thomas said nothing. "You couldn't do any more." They were quiet, listening to the sounds of other soldiers retreating through the woods, safe from the regular thump of organized troops. "You had to leave him," he added.

Thomas raised his head, looking around at Caleb. "I wanted to be with him. He was my best friend and he was hurting and I said I would stay and I didn't. I said I would," he repeated. He hung his head again.

"You could have stayed," Caleb said between spasms, "then you would have been a prisoner, maybe killed on purpose, or by mistake, maybe only wounded, then to die. No, Benjamin understood."

Thomas took a deep breath to try for new air. Without raising his head, Thomas mumbled, between his legs, "He did say, 'my mother is coming.'"

"Then she took your place."

Thomas raised his head again and repeated, "I said I'd stay with him." Tears started to flow.

"Yes, and then with a leg shot up, I would have been target practice for a redcoat. No, you got me and yourself out at the same time, more than I can say for Joshua who skittered like a confused rabbit." Caleb debated whether to say *thanks,* but thought better of it, still jealous of Annie Green's attentions towards Thomas.

"Well, we're not out of this yet," Thomas said. "We better keep on going, find out where the regulars are." He slowly got up. "Ready?"

"Doesn't do me any good to sit here on a tree trunk all day."

Thomas stooped down and helped Caleb onto his back

as he readjusted the rifles over his shoulder. The backpacks were long gone, leaving only the powder horn and shot bag hanging from straps and digging into Thomas' side.

Caleb grunted as Thomas slid his hand under his thigh above the wound. "Damn," he said, as the pain shot through his leg.

Thomas walked purposefully on, coming to a crossroad leading from the Brandywine as regular soldiers moved along, headed east towards Dilworthtown. All were dirty, stained, shorn of their packs, marching with no pattern away from the lessening sound of cannon and rifle fire. A horseman came riding by, slowing down, calling out, "Assemble at the next crossroads," and then trotted along to spread the latest orders. Thomas joined the group, keeping a steady pace, his arms beginning to ache from the unnatural position. His thoughts swirled as he tried to make sense of the day. *Was there any reason why I was in a fight today? Was it a battle? What about the rest of Washington's troops along the Brandywine? Where are they now? Where is Benjamin now? Is he still alive? What do I do without him? Are we still an army? Is there any Edgmont militia left? What about Abner? And Joshua?* Thomas grunted, remembering Joshua jumping up and running.

Caleb grabbed tighter around Thomas' chest, pulling himself up to release the pressure on his thigh. Thomas stopped trying to make sense of the day. Coming around a bend in the road, he could see the roofline of a barn, then a house up ahead at the small collection of buildings at Dilworthtown surrounding a confusing mass of men. Officers were working to restore order. Thomas could see men jammed into the back of some wagons already drawn up with covers over the hoops, others bare, and still empty.

"We're coming where there is help," Thomas said over his shoulder to Caleb.

There was no reply. He kept on walking, men now parting to let him through, conscious of the wounded man on his back.

"Over here," an orderly in charge called out. Thomas walked slowly over to a wagon beginning to fill up, other wounded being lifted into place, crowded onto the bed of the wagon. Only a thin layer of straw softened the rough planks of the bottom.

"Set him down," another man said. He was older, sensitive to the pinched expressions on the men who were hurting, exhausted, and fearful. Thomas eased Caleb off his back to lean against the wagon resting on his good leg, the other bent, bare and bloody. Soldiers stopped, glanced, and shook their heads as sergeants in uniform worked to rally the gathering troops. Officers on horseback encouraged the reassembled formations from separate commands.

"Set them off, Sergeant," called out one major, "down the road to Concordville. We'll get further orders there."

Men kept straggling in, dirty and apprehensive. More wounded were lifted into the wagons. When full, the driver cracked his whip and started the bumpy journey towards increasing safety and care. Moans came from the back, an occasional scream from the delirious mind as the wagon headed down the narrow road.

"Keep moving," shouted another major. "Those redcoats can't be far behind." He turned his horse and cantered back up the road to report to the general's staff.

Thomas waited by Caleb holding onto his shoulder, offering support. Caleb was silent. He kept looking around at others who were wounded or fit, dirty, discouraged, angry, or defeated. He didn't turn to Thomas who stood there quietly. Finally, as Thomas saw others from the Edgmont militia coming down the road, he turned to Caleb.

"You'll be taken care of now." He slowly removed his arm from around Caleb's shoulder, afraid that Caleb might fall over. Caleb remained stock still, then slowly turned to Thomas, musing what to say. Finally, he looked Thomas square in the eye.

"I owe you my life." He hesitated. "Thanks," he said, and slowly held out his hand. Thomas took it as Caleb squeezed more powerfully than he ever had before. He kept looking at Thomas without changing his expression. Thomas returned the look.

"I'm glad we made it," he said, squeezing Caleb's hand in return. "Thee was getting heavy."

"I'm grateful," said Caleb quietly in a steady voice. "Now, get going," he added in a stronger voice with feeling. "You'll not do me any more good and I think the other fellows there can use you. Probably even General Washington will appreciate your continued attention to duty." He looked at Thomas, his gray eyes red rimmed and bloodshot, open, hopeful, the remainder of his thoughts no longer spoken, pulling away from Thomas ever so slightly. Thomas blinked, then turned away and headed over to the Edgmont boys coming in.

Chapter Thirteen

The loose form of the Continental Army formations marched with a sporadic regularity. Thomas marched alongside several others from Edgmont.

"Has thee seen Abner?" he asked.

"Not since that last charge at Birmingham," was the sullen response.

"When those redcoats began to come around the meeting house, it was time to get going," said another.

"We were all together," said the first, "and then those bayonets came flickering through the smoke and there was no stopping them."

"I saw Abner earlier," the other offered, "then no more."

"But I know he made it to the woods," another confirmed, "along with the corporal. Hell to pay," he emphasized.

They trudged on silently listening for any sudden gunfire. The sun hung low against the horizon, and shadows lengthened, black against the trees. It was dark by time they arrived at Concord Friends Meeting House that dominated the small collection of houses and shops at the crossroads. A major sitting on his horse watched the scattered remnants of the army reassemble. Orders were barked out. The supply wagons had escaped before the attack at Chad's Ford and were stationed in surrounding fields. Tents had been set up, and small fires were already burning as exhausted men fell to the ground, eating some gruel, shortly to fall asleep. Sentries were set out, picket posts were in place, and a discouraged calm pervaded the gathering army. Thomas went over to a militia sergeant standing near a command post, faces flickering in the dancing flames of a campfire.

"Where's Edgmont?" he asked.

"You mean, what's left of the militia?" he answered.

"Are there any around?"

"Oh sure, some came in and are still here. Others, no idea, home I guess." He shrugged his shoulders.

"Can thee tell me?"

"Go down past the meeting house, off to the left. That's where they've been ordered to reform." There was a tired resignation in his voice.

Thomas went back to the others standing in a cluster waiting for orders.

"I've got information," he announced.

"Yes," said one.

"The militia has a place."

"Well, I'd rather go there and be with our own than wait here in the dark for some Continental to tell us to do something no one knows what." The others nodded and with no further word started a shuffling march to camp.

Farther down the hill, some tents had been set up. Guards were posted.

"Who's there?" one militiaman commanded.

"Edgmont," replied Thomas.

"Good," came the answer.

"Any others?"

"By that line of tents. To the right, next to that line of trees." They kept on walking, coming at last to the first little fire.

"Abner?" Thomas called out hoping it was a familiar figure.

"Thomas!" Abner came running up, throwing his arms

around his cousin, "I'm mighty happy to see thee," he exclaimed.

"And thee," Thomas said, returning the hug.

"Benjamin?" Abner asked.

"Back at Birmingham," Thomas answered, reluctant to say the inevitable.

"I saw thee carrying him," Abner confessed. "Hurt?"

"Bad," Thomas said.

"What does thee think?"

"I don't think he made it. It was a terrible wound and he was sinking, going down." Thomas couldn't help the tears.

"I wanted to come," Abner offered, "but then some redcoats came up and we had to move, fast and away from the meeting house." He stopped, then added, "I was scared that a bayonet was going to get me. They were all lined up and I could see the determination in their eyes and they kept coming on," he said, his voice wavering, "so I took a glance at thee getting up from Benjamin and then I ran."

"We all did," Thomas admitted. "We had no choice." He sat down by the tent in front of the fire, his eyes watching the curls of flame from the few sticks charring and burning.

"Have this," Abner offered. "It's all we have, but thee needs something."

"It's all I've had all day," Thomas admitted. "Thanks."

"I think it's all any of us have had," Abner replied, "not much, but better than nothing, and I guess, under the circumstances, it's like a feast." He handed Thomas his cup filled with the warm liquid, bits of dried beef floating on the surface, softening.

"I didn't stay by Benjamin," Thomas confessed to Abner. "He is our cousin and I left him." Thomas kept staring at the fire.

"Those redcoats where intent," Abner soothed.

"I wanted to stay."

"And I guess the British wanted thee to stay and then there would be one less soldier they would have to fight."

"Maybe there'll be one less soldier anyway," Thomas said.

"Is thee thinking of quitting?" Abner was quizzical.

"After today? I think so." Thomas spoke in a monotone.

"Think about it tomorrow."

"Will anything change?"

"One day." Abner didn't persist.

"If there are more days like today?" Thomas said to himself.

"Not likely, not the same, maybe similar."

"Without Benjamin, it can't be the same." The tears started again.

"But we're together again. Still." Abner stooped down alongside Thomas.

"Yes, I don't know what I'd do it if thee wasn't here."

He looked over at Abner. "Thee's a good friend and cousin, but we'll miss Benjamin. He was one of us, the third." He sank back.

"Is thee sure he didn't make it?"

Thomas hesitated then said what he had been afraid to confirm. "No way, not a chance. He wanted to live and I tried to will him well so that he would live, but it was not possible, and when he said he knew his mother was coming, then I knew he was going to die. There was nothing more I could do. His mother was there to take Benjamin into her arms and I left because the sergeant ordered it, and because it was hopeless, and I couldn't do any more." Tears streamed down his face. He didn't try to wipe them or hide them. They were tears for his best friend, cousin, the one person he could truly confide in. Through his tears, he said to Abner, "I'm glad to find thee. I was hoping." He sagged down on to the ground. "I need to rest."

Abner guided him gently into the tent and put a blanket over him, a sack under his head. The stars came out as the fire died away.

Chapter Fourteen

The camp awoke before dawn. Washington ordered the Continental Army to Chester.

"Does thee think the British will attack us again today?" Thomas asked of the Edgmont sergeant who finally found the remnants of the militia.

"I don't know, Pratt, but if they do, we'll not be here for them." He scratched the stubble on his chin and rubbed his eyes, tired from lack of sleep. "The General is going to put some distance between us and the redcoats."

"What about our wounded?"

"We'll find them a place. They're out of the war. No one's going after them. Just you worry about yourself. You're what the British are looking for." He put his cup out and poured himself some of the hot broth.

"Did Edgmont lose many yesterday?"

"You mean, other than Benjamin?"

"Yes."

"Well. I heard we lost another. Most made it back here, but some are still missing. Don't know if they walked off and are still looking for us." He looked up and tried to see the other tents in the pre-dawn light. He brightened up. "Don't worry, Pratt, we'll reform and be ready for another go." He walked off with no further word.

Thomas ducked back into the tent, stepping over the others to get to Abner. He shook him.

"We're moving out."

"Already?" Abner asked in a groggy voice.

"Right soon," Thomas replied in an undercurrent of urgency.

Abner sat up, blinked in the dark, and crawled out onto the field, wet with the early morning dew. The horses were already being hitched, the rattle of chains sounding across the fields, reverberating against the far trees.

"Form up," the sergeant cried out.

Thomas grabbed his rifle and nudged Abner into place. There was little talking from the exhausted soldiers worried about the next move of both armies. Tents were folded, packs not lost were added to the wagon load as a distant drum began to beat the cadence for the advance troops to head for Chester and the Delaware River.

"Is thee going to stay in the militia?" Abner asked wearily.

"For now," Thomas said. "To leave like some of the others would mean that Benjamin's death was for no good purpose." He turned to Abner. "I can't walk away. Maybe later, but the British are now on our land and we three didn't join to just let them tramp all over us, at least not without a fight." He lowered his voice. "Just that having Benjamin gone was not part of the plan."

"If only the redcoats had held to Washington's plan."

"And maybe, if he had known of Howe's plans he would have changed the Army around, not depending on us as militia to fight British regulars." Thomas stared out into the darkness. "It's unfair that there were so few regulars at Birmingham. It's not fair that Benjamin was hurt. It shouldn't have been."

"So what are we going to do?" Abner waited for Thomas to answer.

"We have to make sure that Benjamin didn't die for nothing," he said quietly. Then in a stronger voice, he said,

"It's got to mean something and we're still part of the Army. We did our part yesterday with others, and I don't want to be known as someone to turn and run at the first shot when others are depending on me." His words were biting as he talked, working out his feelings to Abner, the only other one in the militia with whom he could share his real feelings.

"I want to go home," Abner admitted. "I don't like fighting anymore."

"Did thee ever like it?"

"Only in talking about it with thee and Benjamin and pretending when out hunting."

"I guess we all played that game," Thomas said. He was grim. "It's all so easy when we see a company of soldiers parade by or officers in dress uniform on a horse."

The orders came to move out. They trailed behind the sergeant, the ranks closer together, but with empty spaces where familiar faces were missing.

"It seemed so simple," Abner said. "Others were going. We needed to be with them."

"Yes," Thomas replied slowly, "but remember, we also talked about the real reasons. Reading that copy of the Declaration of Independence gave us purpose and pride in Pennsylvania and the other colonies, knowing we had a part to play, and not to let others do our work if we truly believed in our land, our country."

"I know we were afraid to ask our families," Abner smiled. He marched with a lighter spring to his step.

"We were afraid our families would say 'No. Thee can't.'"

"If they had said 'No,' would thee have gone anyway?" Abner asked.

Thomas thought again as he had numerous times

before. He finally said, "Yes. I think I would have, because I believe I had to." They marched on silently.

"What are we going to say to our families?" Abner asked.

"Worse, what are we going to say to Benjamin's family?"

"Thee'll know at the time," Abner comforted.

They marched on.

***

Small groups of people were silent watching the retreating army as it marched through Chester. It was only the drum that gave a spirit to the ranks of soldiers. In contrast to the citizens of Chester, the men were dirty, unshaven, downcast, afraid to look squarely at the civilians in front of their shops and homes, knowing that while the Army had failed them, they had done their best.

Rumors were rife as to Washington's next move. The fear of the British aroused mixed sympathies as the taverns became the source of most information, some accurate, much false. Newspapers were printed as quickly as possible purporting to have significant news, but no one knew for sure of the Continental Army. Washington was deciding, as soldiers and townspeople alike waited. The couriers between headquarters and the Continental Congress in Philadelphia galloped back and forth, with members of the new government anxious and nervous for their own safety.

Washington determined to march to Philadelphia and circle to the west in the Great Valley. It had become obvious the British were not following the Americans to the river. Lord Cornwallis had taken his troops as far as Aston and Village Green and no farther.

Chapter Fifteen

Two days later, the Continental Army marched westward along the Lancaster Road by Merion Meeting heading on to Radnor Meeting, the Edgmont militia following along in the rear of the regular troops.

"Where are we going?" Abner asked. Thomas didn't reply as they kept a steady pace in a loose formation. Their captain trotted back occasionally on his horse to see if his troops were still following. The men were tired, and exhausted by the forced marches. The Army had retreated to Chester and Darby, then across the Schuylkill River to Philadelphia and finally back across the river again to head west towards the Great Valley. Thomas kept his place in line with the regular pace of the men of the militia. Abner looked at Thomas for encouragement. Thomas finally looked back and shook his head.

"I don't know, but we seem to be headed back from where we started." He turned around, keeping the steady foot fall, maintaining his place in the constant surge of silent men, tired but afraid to stop.

"I recognize the sign of the tavern ahead," he finally softened in response.

"Which one?" Abner asked, never before out from Edgmont.

"The one by Merion if I remember rightly," Thomas replied. "Father said that the meeting houses marked the Lancaster Road. Merion, Haverford, Radnor, and if we go by the one, we'll probably pass by the others and find ourselves precious close to where we started. Seems like a great big circle, fighting the British, having them chase us, and now we're out trying to chase them." He spoke with a regular cadence in time with their marching.

"And then what?" Abner asked. "I don't like this. I'd rather be home," he admitted.

"So would I," Thomas agreed, "but our time's not up and we agreed to serve and not desert unlike others."

"But so many have," Abner said.

"But not most and I don't want to be shown as a person who can't keep his word. Besides, we only have a short time to go."

"But at least then we're marching back closer to home," Abner said in a quiet voice, not to let any of the others hear of his hope.

"And we're seeing places we've never been to," Thomas added with a forced humor.

"Yeah, but I didn't think I'd be doing it with a gun over my shoulder," Abner answered, "and I can't forget Benjamin."

Thomas lowered his head. "I know." He marched on, then added, "I keep thinking of him." He took more steps. "Couldn't do anything for him. I was there and he suddenly wasn't. I tried to help. He asked for it and I couldn't do anything. He didn't understand what happened and I had to hold him until he said his mother was coming."

"We had to get out of there," Abner explained, once again.

"I know, but I feel like I left Benjamin when he really needed me."

"Except that thee would have been the next to be skewered by the British if thee hadn't got up and escaped."

Thomas was silent. The captain rode on forward towards

the head of the column with no encouraging words. Men mumbled occasionally.

"What do I say to Benjamin's mother?" Thomas wondered aloud to Abner. He turned and looked at him with deep sunken eyes, red and dark from lack of sleep. "What can I say?" he asked again.

"Not the whole truth," Abner offered. "Only the good part, about being with us and in the wrong place by chance." He paused. "But then thee can say, 'he died at a Quaker meeting house.' That might help." Even Abner didn't smile.

"I guess if I run out of words I can say so," Thomas agreed, but not totally comfortable with the idea. "What if his mother asks questions?"

"Don't answer anything more than necessary, nothing that would hurt. Couch the truth in easy words, soft, meaningful, without blood."

"Is that really then the truth?"

"Don't lay the whole truth on her at once. Let it be kind. Come out with it later if need be when there's strength to receive. Don't let it hurt any more than thee ought."

Abner marched closer to Thomas. He needed the support as they plodded along in a thoughtful pace.

"I miss him too," Abner said quietly to Thomas. "We were three together." He was searching for his own comfort.

"And now we're two together," Thomas replied, realizing he was not alone in the loss of Benjamin.

The road was dry but rutted from the tramp of feet, the wheels of the artillery, and the Army's supply wagons. Thomas kept his eyes on the uneven surface. Men shuffled in a monotonous step placing one foot in front of another. Their shoes and boots were scuffed and thin, with holes in the soles. Their feet chafed against threadbare stockings. By mid-afternoon, the column halted. The militia fell out of formation to stand against the trees out of the sun. Some of the men slumped down with their backs against a tree, resting their heads on their knees. Thomas took off his hat and mopped his forehead. Dirt and sweat mixed on his sleeve as he rubbed his hand against his trousers.

"I'm tired," Abner moaned, sinking to the ground at Thomas' feet. "I'm tired of marching around and tired of trying to find some British to fight." He paused and looked up at Thomas. "I want to go home. I don't want to be here anymore." He looked down and plucked a stalk of the tall grass and put it in his mouth, chewing the end slowly and thoughtfully. "We've done our part," he continued. "We've been there, we've done it. We fired our rifles and we still watched the British come on. We watched men get hit and bleed then die." He waited for an answer.

Thomas squatted down alongside Abner. He snapped off his own stalk and placed it between his front teeth.

"I'm tired too," he finally said. "I'm tired of thinking about Benjamin, of his blood on my hands, of the pleading in his eyes, of my helplessness. I wonder, did it make any difference? Did his death solve anything? Would everything be the same if he were alive? Would it make any difference if the two of us were killed? Would things be better? Would the British say, 'Fine, we got them killed, and we have made our point. The Americans now understand. They'll pay their taxes and we'll go back to England and it'll be the same as before.' Is that the way it would be now if we had gotten killed?"

Thomas chewed the end of the stalk. He looked around at the other soldiers, some talking, most lost in a quiet reverie. The sun beat down between the trees, the air was still, the birds were resting from their early morning chirping calls.

"I'm scared," said Thomas. "Before Brandywine, we knew of war, and of fighting, but we didn't know what a bullet could do to a man. We didn't even know what blood looked like coming from a man or what an unnatural death was all about. Now we're marching towards the British Army just waiting to try to kill us. Now we know what real fighting is and the more I think about it, the more I don't want to fight. I don't want to get killed. I don't want to be like Benjamin, with my blood draining out of me, sinking towards death." Thomas looked at Abner. "I get this pit that hardens in the bottom of my stomach and I know I'm thinking too much, so I try not to think. I just keep on marching and try to forget. But I can't. Brandywine keeps coming back to me, and Benjamin, with his insides hanging outside his belt." He lowered his head between his knees and mumbled. "Are we the only ones who are scared? No one else says anything. Are they so brave?"

Abner had a crooked smile. "Maybe they're scared too, only they don't want to admit it or to let anyone else know. Maybe they don't want to admit to anyone else that they don't want to be killed or worse, to be torn apart to die slowly. Maybe they don't want to think they're cowards." He snorted half a laugh, the other half a nervous cough. "No one's talking over there, so they got to be thinking."

"Like us?"

"Like us."

They became silent.

"C'mon, you men of Pennsylvania, we're not going anyplace sitting here," the major from the Continental Army called out as he came trotting back on his chestnut gelding followed by the Edgmont captain. "We have a piece to travel before nightfall and work to do." His voice faded as he kept on towards the rear of the column scattered in behind. Their captain reined up at the middle of the militia companies, calling for the sergeants to report on the quick.

"What's going on?" Abner asked.

"If we're quiet, maybe we'll overhear." The rest of the men reformed in the roadway, ready for the impending information. They quieted, straining to hear the new orders. The captain addressed the non-commissioned officers, his voice rising and falling as he turned back and forth.

"We'll march off towards Radnor. Camp there for the night. Then…" and his voice faded away. They heard the last, "so let's do it," he ordered with an emboldened authority.

"Then what?" Abner whispered.

"Then I couldn't hear either," Thomas said.

The buzz from the men increased as they all waited for their own sergeant to return.

"Form up!" came the order. Thomas slung his rifle over his shoulder. "Face west!" came next, a more effective order to the farmers and yeoman who knew where the sun was in the afternoon. The major cantered by, kicking up dust and clods of the drying earth as he headed back towards the head of the long column. Thomas could see formations ahead starting to move. Finally, it was their turn.

"March!" was the only order. They knew enough to step out keeping the familiar steady pace as the militia worked to keep a sense of order, particularly as they passed groups of houses at crossroads. Children gathered by the fences staring at the army, their parents standing back, women in the doorways, men by their sheds not to show their own curiosity getting the better of their usual reserve. Quaker bystanders didn't want to have to answer probing questions or accusations of too much interest or curiosity about the army at meeting for worship the next First Day. Thomas kept looking, seeing for the first time villages he had heard about. Children waved at the soldiers whose heads turned, a few smiling in return, some with an occasional concealed wave of the hand. Soldiering was serious business for those who survived the Battle of Brandywine. Thomas marched on with an increasing dread of what might lie ahead.

It's so peaceful here, he thought, looking at the walnut trees loosening their grip on the delicate leaves, falling in a sprinkling to earth, the walnuts left in stark outline on the bare branches. The sassafras were coloring to a brilliant orange and red and yellow, while the ash and poplar trees remained green with a tarnishing of brown. They all formed a backdrop against the sky to give a border to the road and surrounding fields.

The column slowed as the lead troops came in sight of the open fields. Newly harvested wheat and corn stood in shocks waiting for a time to be threshed and picked in spite of the war. Thomas was tired. His shoulder ached from the straps of his sack and the tug of his rifle against his collarbone.

"Can thee see ahead?" he called out to Abner, marching alongside the road on the higher, grassy edges. "Are they pulling up?"

Abner kept the pace, the sergeant ahead keeping the cadence only occasionally looking back, little concerned with a tight formation.

"I see a line of tents already set up yonder, even a few fires, some smoke from them."

"Then we're close," Thomas replied with relief. "If the regulars found their places, we'll get our chance." He spoke too loudly.

"If you don't keep your opinions to yourself, Pratt," snapped the sergeant, "you'll land us all to camp next to a swamp, farthest from good water and no dry wood to be had."

Thomas opened his mouth to reply, looked at Abner who pursed his lips together as advice, then thought better of it and remained silent.

The captain came trotting on his mare and pointed to each sergeant in turn selecting the area for the militia. Thomas and Abner followed the company to the edge of a field and, leaving enough space from the men ahead, sat down with six others waiting for the wagons to come up with the tents and cooking pots. Thomas pulled his legs to his chest, his sack acting as a back rest, with his rifle resting across his knees, and looked out across the fields towards the Quaker meeting house at Radnor. It was built just below a slight ridge, the fieldstone walls blending into the softening fall colors and brown of the fields.

"What is thee thinking about?" Abner asked, crouched beside him.

"Wondering what the Quakers who sit in that meeting house would say if they knew that we're here from Willistown Meeting and carrying guns to fight with."

"Yeah, and I wonder why I am here carrying a gun to fight with." Abner glanced over as Thomas continued to stare across the fields. "Others have gone home and the captain hasn't said much and the sergeant only swore a little."

"But we did give our word," Thomas replied. "They called us into the militia and we said we'd go without the approval of Meeting because we felt we had to. Maybe it wasn't wise, but we knew what we were doing. This is our country, not England's, and we needed to do something about it. We gave our word and that means something. It means we can be counted on, that our word is our bond, not by swearing on the Bible, no oath, no signing a paper that binds us. No, our word, freely given." He drew a deep breath. "Our honor, sacred if thee will."

"But others are leaving, just drifting away."

"I know, I see, but until we drive the British out of Chester County or at least until we lead them out, with the redcoats chasing us if necessary, then we need to do our part. I'm not sure whether Father would be more upset by me deserting against my word or by continuing to place myself in danger."

"I don't want to get killed," Abner said in a soft voice so no one else could hear.

"I don't plan on it," Thomas replied. "I watched the British come on at Brandywine, up the hill, through the woods, around us. We kept firing, but more and more men appeared out of the woods and along the road. There was nothing more we could have done. Now we know. General Washington is going to need more men around to keep us fighting." Thomas looked around at the others stretched out waiting for the wagons coming around the last bend of the road into the clearing. No one jumped up to wave them on.

"Let the sergeant do it," said one.

"It's his job," said another.

Thomas watched as the teamsters repeated the routine, bringing the horses to a stop by the command post of the captain. Abner and several others strode to the wagon and waited for the tents to be handed down.

Is it so useless? Thomas wondered, getting to his feet, ready to erect a tent as he had over the days, his thoughts interrupted by the clanging of their cooking pots. He and another from their group headed into the trees for firewood.

"If we want hot stew, it'll not heat on its own," Thomas said as they broke off dry twigs and picked up fallen branches.

Rumors floated through the campground as the fires burned more softly into red coals, the ash already darkening.

"The redcoats are coming here."

"Washington's going to chase them back towards their ships in the Chesapeake."

"Well, I'm tired looking for them."

"Careful, they might be looking for you."

Thomas listened, the shell of bravado covering the core of fear and worry. *I wonder if the redcoats came to our farm, not so far away from the fighting?*

***

The light faded and the camp became quiet. Thomas got up and walked to the edge of the line of tents and looked back at the last few campfires dancing with a red glow, slowly collapsing onto their ashes. It was peaceful. The screech of an owl sounded across the field. He suddenly felt tired and sick of the militia and officers crying out orders, marching without knowing where, to what end, not sure of the result, only fearing more blood, of soldiers coming out from the woods again, trying to kill. He shuddered involuntarily as he thought of his mother and their warm and snug house, of being safe. Then of his father following the cycle of ages gone, preparing, planting, growing, reaping, tending family and animals. Of the peace of First Day meeting where all gathered in the sight of God. To worship in a simple, deep fashion open to the truth as the silence stripped away layers of reserve. The opportunity for an insight to be offered. An inspiration to be shared. The silence to return, surrounding the thought as it melded into the fabric of the vibrant but quiet gathering. Thomas missed the familiar certainty of his well-ordered life. *But would it be the same in the future?* he wondered. *Will the British impose their will again?* He stared into the darkness. *Or will the new American spirit prevail and overcome and succeed in separation from England? Then what? Will a new government be fairer? Can we sell our wheat for more money? Will our taxes be less?* Questions came faster than he could absorb them until his mind became a jumble and he was exhausted. He walked back to their tent and squeezed in through the flap and found a narrow space to lie down, with men on either side, already breathing deep and steady. He closed his eyes and let the thoughts drift away as he joined the others in sleep.

***

In the dark of the new dawn and the jostle of bodies, noises penetrated into the tent, sleep was over, and the only reward from the end of another day would be to rest again. Men shoved and pushed slowly with grunts and sighs, stretching aching muscles, restoring the coursing of blood through the legs down to their feet. Thomas came out into the pale early morning. As the sergeant came striding down the line of tents of the Edgmont militia, the camp was coming quickly alive.

"Where're we going today?" Thomas asked as the sergeant got closer. Others stopped their activity and waited for the answer.

"West," was the reply, "towards the Great Valley."
"And then?"
"Then it's up to the British."

"You mean, we're headed for another fight?"

"That's what this Army's all about, it's not just for a parade." The sergeant moved off, annoyed by the simplicity of the question but sympathetic with the seriousness of his answer.

The porridge was heated, and the rough, dry bread, was cut into chunks. The men squatted, filling their bellies with stuff to keep the pangs of emptiness away for the day. The taste was as plain as the look of the same food they ate yesterday and the day before that.

The tent was struck, folded into a tight square, and carried back to the wagon. The pots were scrubbed clean with gravel from the narrow creek running by the field. Its water was muddy from others doing the same upstream. The order to march was brisk, the step quick, a renewed urgency that Thomas could only suspect. The day was fair as they fell into their place in the long column stretched out as before. Morning passed into noon. After a short pause to drink from their canteens, or for the lucky few from springs or local wells with a cool, crisp taste, they pushed on at the pace of the morning. They marched faster than yesterday, which offered an increased certainty of purpose and hope in the confidence of any plan General Washington might have. By the Paoli tavern they came over the crest of the South Valley Hills and down the gentle decline into the broad valley defined by the southernmost ridges of the real mountains further north. The columns halted as the wagons moved among them on the sure level of the Lancaster Road. The guns ahead moved to make space for the supplies and equipment handy to each company and formation. It was different from yesterday. Thomas could hear the shouts and commands ahead. They moved forward, coming up to regular troops of the Continental Army. The militia had disappeared into the trees along the side of the turnpike. Thomas looked at the weather-beaten men of the regular army. Some were in uniform. Officers wore regulation coats with tricorn hats. The soldiers resting easy on their rifles, were used to marching, stopping, standing at ease, or braced up smartly if need be. But now, there was no need. Thomas was surprised as he watched their reaction to the militia marching by. The men of the Continental Army seemed older but as he looked more carefully, many were as young as he was. It was only that they carried themselves with a familiar purpose. The order came for the Edgmont militia to halt. The captain listened to a colonel coming down the line. A major left his side and trotted over to their captain to call him into conference. Shortly the sergeants were involved, and finally the orders came. They moved on past the battalions of the Continental Army towards the White Horse tavern. By late afternoon the skies had clouded over and the wind was picking up from the east. They moved onto the surrounding fields as the wagons drew up. Camp was immediate with the quick experience of the past several days and the example of the regular army close by. Rations were passed out, but with few fires permitted. The hard bread, brittle cheese, and dried meat was slow to chew. The buzz of the troops talking added to an increased apprehension for the following day. Thomas for all his hunger found it difficult to eat. His tongue felt so dry that even sloshing his mouth with water from his canteen was not enough to loosen the firm, tough strings of meat to meld them with the bread. He chewed mechanically, watching Abner sitting on a log, concentrating on his own meal. Thomas moved over to sit beside him.

"Ready?"

"For what?"

"Tomorrow."

"Why tomorrow?"

"Something." He looked at the tents of the regular army just beyond, the Pennsylvania brigade closest. "They don't put militia in among regulars unless the general has a plan in mind."

"You think?"

"I'm sure. It's not by chance that for the first time we're put next to the Pennsylvania line."

Abner was quiet, then looked over. "It's hard to eat."

"Yes, it is for me too," Thomas replied. "I feel as though I'm keeping all my juices hidden away in my stomach, none for my mouth."

"Is this what the body does when the mind is fearful?"

"I guess. I have a sinking feeling and I suppose my body knows more than I do."

"I wish we were home."

"Soon enough."

"I mean alive, and I want to leave this fighting to those who want to, who get paid for it, who signed on by their own choice."

"We did."

"Yes, but then we thought it would be an adventure and patriotic. We believed."

Thomas considered what Abner had said. "We still believe. What we didn't know was the honor of watching men die. We figured we had a duty, that we couldn't let others fulfill our responsibilities."

"Have we filled our responsibilities now?"

"Probably, pretty close."

"I think of Caleb. He gets wounded. Thee saves him. He's done with fighting, taking credit, going for glory, and we're still out here."

"Only for now."
They lapsed into silence.

* * *

Thomas tossed as sleep came deep then shallow, with dreams of guns firing, and bayonets pointed at him. No matter whichever way he turned, his only escape was to wake up, shudder, and turn on his other side, the sore shoulder aching under his weight. The smoke of battle came again, this time with Benjamin's head cradled in his lap, screaming silently from his open mouth, warm blood, sticky on hand, holding Benjamin's hands, clutching his ebbing life. He cried and woke up crying, no longer embarrassed by the tears streaking off his cheek in the dark.

He was relieved by the lightening of the dawn. It was a release from his mind to let the body take control.

"Up! Up!" Called the sergeant. "Tents down!" Others were calling out. "Cold breakfast only."

"Means we're onto something."

"Fighting," Abner suggested.

"A battle," Thomas agreed.

"Big?"

"Hard to tell, but the Pennsylvania brigade over there looks serious. They're already in formation." The other companies of the militia following the example of the regular army had broken camp with a newfound purpose.

"Fall in behind the brigade over there!" ordered their captain, giving general orders for the first time. "Line up. Keep pace." He strode around with an unusual energy.

Soon the Pennsylvania brigade under Anthony Wayne started for the Chester Road, working up the slope of the South Valley hill towards Goshen Meeting. The day was gray and humid, the weather close with the wind twisting the trees in a circular motion, gusting first from the southwest then the northeast.

"Looks bad," Thomas said as they watched the clouds scudding overhead outside their regular pattern from the west. Abner didn't answer as they picked their way up the steep road, slanting to the left then right, cut into the grade, making it possible for wagons to make the ascent. The trees began to whip back and forth with a sporadic intensity. They reached the crest and halted. Thomas could see General Wayne on his horse up ahead on a rise overlooking both the road and surrounding woods and fields, cantering out of sight only to reappear some minutes later. Officers gathered around in conference. With a wave of the hand by Anthony Wayne, they quickly dispersed. Their captain came towards them, summoning the sergeants and corporals to him near a grove of trees, the group visible to the militia. The sergeant came back. The men stood straight.

"Here are our orders." The militia was silent. "We're to take the left flank of the main body of the Continental Army. The Pennsylvania brigade will stand to our right and behind. We'll approach from just above Goshen Meeting to keep the British from turning our left flank. The Chester Road is their only way here. The British main army will be by the sign of the Boot on the road coming from the Turk's Head and General Washington plans to force an action here to prevent them from entering the Great Valley."

"At least now we know," Thomas said quietly to Abner.

"But if the British under Lord Cornwallis are coming up from Edgmont, they've been on our farms."

"Maybe so," Thomas agreed, "which is why we joined in the first place," he added.

"I'm going to let them have it," growled Abner with a newly found anger.

"The men of the Edgmont militia will be part of the Pennsylvania Militia protecting the whole of the army," the sergeant emphasized.

The captain came up. "The general is depending on us," he announced, "said, we're the men for the job." He swelled slightly with pride as he repeated the words, but without a total confidence.

"We're in for it," Thomas mumbled.

"I hope my family is safe," Abner added, thinking aloud, not listening to Thomas.

Thomas, listening, replied. "If the British Army is coming up here, whatever happened in Edgmont has already occurred. We'll find out soon enough, I expect."

"Gives us a reason to fight."

"As long as we don't get killed," Thomas answered.

"Move out!" came the order. They marched on, reaching the top of the incline as the rough fields with gray stones gave way to the softer brown of collected earth on the gentle southward slope. The farms became larger, the houses more substantial, the bounty of the land more abundant. Goshen Meeting was central to the area. Thomas could see the stonework and walls surrounding the burial ground as the road twisted towards the crossroads far ahead.

"Into woods here," the sergeant called. The other companies took up positions in the line facing south, the woods offering protection from the open fields and simple hedgerow between. "Get your cover. Place your line. Set your sights," he commanded with a firm voice based on little experience.

"Over here," Abner called. "I've got some trees and these big rocks." Thomas moved closer.

"We need to move closer to the edge of the woods if we're going to have a clear line of fire."

"But there's little protection there." Abner was reluctant to move.

"We're not much good here," Thomas countered.

"Safer," Abner retorted.

"Only until the British come upon us," Thomas said. "If we're to protect our part of the line, we need be where our rifles can make a difference." He stood firm.

"All right, thee select a good place," Abner replied, upset.

"Over here by this old tree. It'll do." Thomas started to arrange the branches to shield the spot. Abner came over and stood there, looking first at the tree and then at the open field in front. Others were working in among the trees and rock piles at the field's edge. Thomas stood back with a forced admiration for his work.

"Is thee satisfied?"

"Only if thee is," Abner replied sarcastically. He took another look. "There's precious little to save us from a British musket ball."

"And not much in the way for a good firing position."

Abner edged back, looking for a stout tree trunk with a clear vision. "I'll set up here," he decided. "I'll cover thee from the side if the redcoats don't follow our plan and come another way." Abner bit off his words.

"Fine," Thomas answered, "I'll depend on another to cover my other side where thee can't see, much less fire a rifle." Thomas showed his exasperation as he turned his back on Abner and stacked some more branches in the space between the several trees.

"Work in!" called out the sergeant. "Close by one

another. Have a sight!" Other sergeants were calling out their orders up and down the line.

Thomas stood and paced out in front of the tree line, looking left then right, pondering the other activity. He could see in the distance on the other side of the Chester Road an officer in the blue and buff of the Continental Army riding his horse up and down the line. He watched as the rider reined in, waved his arm with a quickness that surprised Thomas. He dropped his arm and rode rapidly away, pulling up shortly down the line.

"What does thee see?" Abner called out.

"A general working the Pennsylvania brigades into position. Must be Anthony Wayne. He's known for action, making it happen."

"Well, that does offer us some comfort."

"As long as the British determine to attack the regulars and not us, they'll have a more interesting time of it." Thomas continued to watch. Abner came out from the woods and stood alongside.

"Thee's right, the Pennsylvania line is a much better place to have a battle." The jest was serious.

"But just in case, we need some of those rocks there to build up a little protection."

"I'd prefer a stone wall," Abner continued, "with firing ports."

"Without some effort, we'll not have anything ready," Thomas said, annoyed as he heaved a large rock between some branches.

Abner watched, then grudgingly picked up a small rock and tossed it into the growing barricade. "There," he snorted.

Thomas ignored him.

The clouds darkened as the wind picked up and whipped the branches of the taller trees back and forth.

"Check your powder," ordered the sergeant stopping by, examining the defensive position they prepared. "Keep it dry," he added, looking at the heavy clouds in mottled grays and blacks. Finished as best they could, Thomas and Abner hunkered down, hidden behind their little barricade, thin and brittle except for the piling of rocks at their feet.

"Does thee have enough cheese to go with that bread?" Thomas asked in a more kindly voice.

Abner shook his head. "Ate it yesterday." He didn't want to ask for any. He knew the rules. "Carry your own. Save something for the next day."

"Here," Thomas offered, carving off a piece and handing it to Abner with a slight smile.

Abner took it silently, not looking directly at Thomas. He waited then looked up. "Thanks," he said quietly with as little emotion as he could muster, knowing it was a genuine gift. He turned it over in his hand but not yet daring to eat it.

"It's for thee," Thomas said. "Go ahead. Bread always tastes better with a little cheese." He put a piece into his own mouth.

"Thanks," Abner said again with greater meaning. He bit off a small piece of cheese to make it last longer.

"What does thee think will happen?" Abner asked between his chewing. "Will the redcoats really come up here?" He looked out across the fields, Goshen Meeting standing silhouetted against the gray sky, small and lonely by the road as it narrowed in passing.

"I don't know," Thomas answered, "but I don't see any troops behind us, so we're here alone, just our militia."

"I don't like it," Abner confessed. "It's too quiet, just

waiting. I wish someone would come by and say, 'There's no fighting today.' Then I could breathe again. Now I'm all tight, my stomach is knotted, my insides are pinching against each other." He dropped his head. "Do the others feel this way? Does thee feel the same?" The words came from the deep.

Thomas took a gulp of air shaking loose his own insides, then a long, slow breath.

"I don't know what will happen, but this I do know. We can't stand against a solid line coming towards us like at Brandywine. I've seen what happens. I feel more and more like a farmer, less and less like a soldier. I'm doing my part, but I don't want to die doing it." He looked over at Abner. "We already lost one of us. We're the cousins that still survive in this militia and we need to keep it that way. I look at the meeting house down the road and think of the peace and serenity within its walls. It's different there against all of us sitting up here with our rifles ready to shoot at those who are shooting at us. Before Brandywine, I didn't think much about it, didn't figure any of us would be wounded, much less killed. Now I know better and I'm afraid." He breathed out.

"I am too," Abner admitted. "So thee'll stay by me?" It was a plea to his taller, more resolute cousin.

"I'll not leave thee. We'll stay together." Thomas gave a soft punch on Abner's arm. "Together."

They fell into silence. Abner put the last of the cheese into his mouth.

Rain spit out of the clouds in a sporadic sprinkle, blown away by the next rush of wind. The militia hunkered down trying to stretch, keeping their legs from stiffening in the unnatural positions.

"Easy men," the sergeant called out quietly, snapping twigs as he came through the underbrush behind them.

"Anything?" Thomas asked.

There was no answer. Thomas strained to look down the road and across the fields and woods and hedgerows.

"Did thee hear something?" he asked Abner, straining his neck, pushing his ears as far forward as possible without moving his seat.

"No," Abner said.

"Listen," Thomas said quietly. A faint cracking came from far to their right. It was intermittent. It stopped, then sounded again, louder this time carrying towards them by the deep stillness of air and lowering heaviness of clouds overhead. Other cracks replied, different pitch, less frequent, but consistent.

"I hear," Abner said.

Thomas' heart thumped faster. His armpits became moist; his hands lost their warmth. He looked back from the right and straight ahead. The meeting house was shrouded in gray, a little contrast of color. Suddenly, a spot of red showed. He blinked and wiped his eyes and looked again. The red had gotten larger and still it came, more into focus. Faces assumed outlines in the midst of the color, a horse emerging from behind the far clump of trees, the gold on the red showing an officer. Thomas watched transfixed as the column kept coming. He struggled to keep his eyes on the enlarging display of the British Army coming forward. He quickly looked left, then right. Startled, he looked left again at a thin line of red running up to the farther tree line, not stopping as they ran through the field to the nearer hedgerow. The column broke apart, flattening into a wide swath of red, more men on horses, gold and silver braid mixing with the brown leather of harness and reins.

"What are we going to do?" Abner asked, terror choking in his throut.

"Get ready to fire," Thomas replied as calmly as he could, his heart now racing, the palms of his hands cold and sweaty. He jumped, surprised by the crashing of feet on leaves and sticks as others of the militia followed the sergeant into the copse of trees surrounding Thomas and Abner and men of their company of the Edgmont militia.

"Steady men," called out the sergeant with a wavering confidence. Splatters of raindrops fell, whipped by a gust of wind. Thomas could hear others adjusting their seat, the rasp of ramrods thumping against the slug lodged in the barrel of their rifles. The line of red came closer, the advance skirmishers dashing from tree to tree, always closer. Thomas could now see the shine on the bayonets of the British, their ordered ranks working with a discipline giving precision as he heard the muffled order to lower muskets with now the point of the blade and aim of the musket pointing straight towards the waiting militia. A rifle fired from one of the Americans to his left. Another and another fired and still the British came on.

"Hold 'til you have a clear shot," yelled the sergeant. "Wait!"

More firing sounded. Thomas raised his rifle. The approaching ranks seemed larger as he sighted along the barrel. He licked his dry lips. A branch got in his way as he moved his rifle slightly left towards the closer redcoats. Abner was steady, following Thomas' example.

"Pick your shot!" called out the sergeant.

Thomas squinted, steadied his rifle, blinked to clear his eye and sighting on a soldier in the nearer rank, squeezed the trigger. Smoke boiled up to his face. He closed his eyes to avoid the stinging. The wind pushed the white away. The

British line was firm, coming constantly on. More rifles fired from the militia. Thomas heard Abner shoot. He quickly up ended his rifle and standing sideways behind the near tree, reloaded. All of a sudden, the order was given.

"Fire!" in a large, husky voice, a different accent, powerful. Bullets whizzed by his ears, branches snapping, a cry of surprise beyond. There was a shriek of pain muffled by the volleys coming into the woods, pinging off the rock piles, plunging into trees with a thud of whistling through the woods to drop harmlessly to the ground having done nothing more than instill a greater fear. Thomas gave a last tap to firmly seat the bullet, replaced the ramrod, and raised his rifle again. Fewer sounds came from the militia. He fired again, the faces clearer now, closer still as a violent volley from the British crashed into the scattered formation of the militia.

"Let's get out of here," Abner cried.

Thomas looked around. It seemed that they were alone except for the redcoats coming on with a never-ending courage and confidence. He couldn't see any breaks in the British line. The firing from the militia had stopped.

"Come on then," Thomas answered. They lowered their heads, turning back, trailing their rifles, grabbing their small packs, and ducked into the deeper woods. They kept away from the woods' edge, running and darting around the larger trees, scrambling through the tumble of briars and bushes. Thomas looked ahead at the backs of the militia moving in and out of sight. More bullets whistled overhead, chasing them, their speed slower now, more able to wound for a slower death. Raindrops began to fall, fitfully then frequently until the rain became steady. The noise of the firing diminished as they ran towards an open field at the back of the woods. Thomas could see men scattering in every direction, always north towards the Great Valley.

"I got to stop for a minute," Abner cried. "I need to get my breath."

Thomas ran towards the largest tree ahead and waited, his arm braced against the rough trunk for support. Abner came up, his chest heaving.

"What are we going to do?" The rain came heavier. Thomas shook his hat as water spilled from the upturned brim. His throat rasped from the wild run, his face scratched from the briars and twigs that had slapped against them. He wiped his hand across his face, surprised to see lines of blood in the palm. The rain came in sheets, water in the field ahead quickly puddling in the little hollows, the grasses flattening from the weight of water constantly pounding down, the sound of rain drowning out any noise of fighting.

"Let's go off to our right. There's a row of trees at the far side, give us cover and we can figure it out." Abner didn't wait. He picked up his rifle and started in a steady jog across the field, quickly becoming slippery from the wet and new mud. Thomas followed. He could see some of the militia ahead, small groups dodging this way and that, mostly individuals making their own decisions. Abner got to the tree line first. He turned around to watch Thomas come up. There were no others coming. The rain had seemingly dissolved the militia as effectively as a cone of sugar standing in a waterfall.

"I'm tired," Abner said with a solemn resignation.

"Yes," Thomas agreed. "I'm tired too and sick of fighting and trying to kill."

"Shall we go home?" Abner asked.

"There's no more fighting to be done here," Thomas

observed, wet to the bone. "Let's follow the tree line until we come to a path that will lead us towards Paoli and when we find Sugartown Road we can take it and head for Edgmont."

"Will there be any redcoats on the way, does thee think?"

"We need to watch, but if they had a full column on the Chester Road and then we heard firing to the west, I think we're safe." Thomas heaved his sack onto his back, adjusting the straps. "What we need now is a dry barn to hide in until tomorrow. We'll not make it home today. It'll be dark soon and nothing's going to move in this rain and mud." He looked at Abner with a smile. Abner replied with a softening of his dirt-streaked face, rain pelting his cheeks.

"I'm ready," Abner said with a nod of relief. They looked over their shoulders to make sure of the emptiness of the field behind and set off wet, exhausted, and uncomfortable. They walked silently, only the noise of the shaking rain and groaning of trees against the wind interrupted their thoughts. In the distance a shed loomed out of the darkening light. A farmhouse further on showed. Both were dark.

"What does thee think? Abner asked.

Thomas wiped the rain from his eyes and stared. "The shed looks dry, safe. Don't know about people hereabouts. Quaker, they'll turn us out of meeting for fighting. Tory, they'll want to turn us over to the British. Patriot, they'll want to turn us over to the authorities for leaving. They'll call it deserting."

"We call it enough," Abner replied with a renewed confidence, "let's head for the shed."

They slogged on looking carefully for any other signs of life. Around the corner, hidden from the farmhouse, they were startled by a bleating. A flush of surprise, then panic stood them in place, tense. The baaing came again and they relaxed.

"Sheep," Thomas said.

"Warm and dry," Abner offered, hopefully.

"Whatever," Thomas said. "I think it's our home for the night." He found a latch to the rough door and carefully pushing in, stood out of the rain, his eyes adjusting to the dim interior. Abner pushed in alongside. The sheep cried out in their own surprise. Thomas and Abner waited as the little flock settled again, one against another. Thomas pushed the door shut, the rain sheeting hard against the boarded sides of the shed, rivulets working in through unprotected spaces. The floor was dry with scattered straw mixed with the round pellets of fresh sheep manure. It was humid inside from the heat of the sheep, the smell of wet wool, lanolin softening the muskiness. Thomas leaned his rifle against a dry wall and dropped his sack to the ground. He sank to his knees and pulled out his canteen. He was thirsty, realizing suddenly it had been hours since they had first seen a glimpse of red from the distance. He tumbled back against the wall and closed his eyes. His energy drained away from him.

"Is thee alright?" he asked Abner. There was no reply. He leaned over to the lump of Abner's body up against a sheep, his breathing heavy but regular. Thomas smiled to himself and pushing himself away from the wall, wedged himself in between several sheep that shifted in annoyance as he let the warmth of their bodies seep into his.

***

Morning came early. It was still raining, the nor'easter not yet blown through as Thomas turned, the sheep working to stand, his head now at their feet, the damp warmth laying heavily on him. He scratched his temple, knocking off several pellets of sheep droppings.

"Ugh," he moaned. "Uff," he added in disgust, brushing his face to remove anything else. He nudged Abner, turning over and stretching his legs. The sheep began to move about.

"We better get going," he said.

"No hurry," Abner replied, his eyes still closed, "it's still raining."

"Yes, but that won't stop the farmer of these sheep from coming to check on them, and we don't want to be seen. Besides, I want to get home." He stood and pulled the door ajar. Water was everywhere, the field flooded and sodden. The gray rain clouds blanketed the land with a steady force as the storm moved on. "We're going to get wet all over again," he confirmed.

"Better wet than dead," Abner said, as a matter of fact getting to his feet, shaking himself loose of the packed straw and droppings. The sheep began to baa, anticipating some grain from the two of them. This they understood.

"Sheep are all alike," Abner muttered, "always wanting something."

"They have the right idea though," Thomas said. "Here, let's finish this cheese," he said, pulling the last chunk out of his sack, followed by the sodden bread. "It'll get us home." They were silent as they ate the last of their provisions.

Thomas adjusted his coat. "It's light enough now, and I think we'll come across the Sugartown Road shortly. It'll lead us south. Shouldn't be any troops on it."

"And no one else if they have any sense," Abner added, peering out into the rain.

Pulling the door ajar, they stepped out into the cold

rain, Thomas using his foot to keep an anxious sheep from following him. He looked quickly around toward the far farmhouse. It was quiet, no movement to be seen. He waved to Abner.

"Come on!"

They hurried across the field, heading for another stand of trees. The roadway beyond was rutted, deep with mud, but it ran in a straight line. They hesitated, looking for any activity. There was none.

"Let's make for it," Abner said as he started a slow walk hoping for the least slippery step. Thomas followed. They sloshed and sucked as they reached the roadway, the slurry of mud pulling at their boots, working in and around their legs and back down inside their boots filling with water and grit. They kept their hats down close on their foreheads to prevent the rain from coming directly at them into their eyes. They plodded along, silently, steadily, looking up frequently, watching for any other person. The little village of Sugartown showed ahead, the small collection of farmhouses and shops looming out of the morning gloom.

"Think we ought to bypass the village?" Abner asked as they got closer.

Thomas watched ahead. They walked on. "Let's chance it," Thomas said, pulling Abner over to the side among the trees. "Even if we skirt around, we might be seen and appear more suspicious traipsing through someone's field with rifles than just going straight." He wiped the rain from his face.

"I'm for it," Abner agreed. They stepped back into the cartway and, adjusting their sacks and carrying their rifles lower, continued on. Little wafts of smoke appeared from the chimneys of several of the homes. Thomas kept looking, Abner right behind. Suddenly, a man appeared from behind the nearest house, his head down. Thomas and Abner kept walking. The man raised his head, seeing them and halted in his tracks, remaining frozen to the spot. The farmer wasn't sure whether to slosh quickly back where he'd come from, but curiosity got the better of him, seeing only two and not in any uniform. He waited. As they got closer, he finally put his hand up. Thomas kept on towards him and then slowed to face the older man.

"Thee's out in a poor weather," said the villager to Thomas in a neutral tone.

"Raining a bit," agreed Thomas as evenly as he could still some paces away.

"Going far?" asked the other.

"Not far," Thomas replied. Abner came up along side. There was silence. Finally the older man determined to satisfy himself.

"Has thee and thy friend been with the fighting?" Thomas recognized the man for a Quaker.

"Has there been any here?" Thomas answered with a question.

"No," The man hesitated, "but soldiers came and took off with some of our feed and steers and foodstuffs," he continued.

"British?"

"If soldiers in red coats make them English, then yes."

"Any damage?"

"To our pocketbooks, yes. To our persons, no."

"Did anyone resist?"

"Only by riding the horses out into the woods when those farthest away saw the soldiers coming." He smiled a grim smile. "When one has a musket, it's difficult to reason with them much less argue." He looked closer at two of them.

"You two have rifles. Use them?"

Thomas pulled his up closer to him. "A bit."

"With the Army?"

He nodded, then confirmed. "Yes."

"And what happened?"

"It rained."

"And then?"

"Then, we're going home." Thomas shook the wet off his hat. "Are there any soldiers, British or American, here about?"

"No Friend, thee and thy companion are safe. The war's gone by with much of our livestock, but it's a small price to pay to let us live in peace."

"Thank thee, Friend," Thomas said, finally admitting to being a Quaker. As the man stood there in the rain, Thomas strode away with a high step, secure now of their safety. Abner ran to catch up, splashing about.

"Will he do anything?"

"No," Thomas said. "He was just as happy to see us move south as he was for the redcoats to move north." They walked on, side-by-side, slipping occasionally. As they passed by the last house, they saw no one else. "We'll be home soon," he said to Abner. "Where we belong."

"Does thee think our families will be all right?"

"Probably. As that man back there said, all the British want from our Quaker farms are provisions. They know Quakers don't fight."

"Most Quakers," Abner corrected.

"Most," Thomas agreed, "and now, even us."

Chapter Sixteen

They came over the brow of the hill. The rain slackened and Thomas could see the peak of the barn at the top of the small rise, close by the solid stone farmhouse of home.

"What does thee think thy mother will say when she sees thee?" Abner was becoming excited at their return, anxious about his own welcome some miles farther on.

"I guess I don't fret about my mother. It's my father that I don't know."

"He knew thee was going away with the militia, with the Army."

"Yes, and he was none too pleased about it." Thomas glanced over at Abner. "So, what do we say about Benjamin? Blurt it out. Or wait for someone to ask?"

"If thee wants advice, let it come easy, no details, not at first," Abner said in a quiet, low voice, thinking again of Brandywine.

"I wish the three of us were coming down into the clearing." He stopped short. "What if our aunt and uncle are there, Benjamin's parents, what then?" There was fear in his questions.

"Let's hope they're not," Abner replied.

"Don't leave me until we're sure," Thomas pleaded. "I couldn't face that alone."

"Don't worry, I won't," Abner said. They started to walk again along the familiar path where the trees were sure and strong, dripping the last of the storm even as the clouds scudded faster overhead, a lighter gray, and higher.

"We're going to have to face them some time," Thomas

said, "not today, but soon, at their farm. Then we need to go together. It has to be the two of us."

"You held Benjamin, but I saw. So yes, I'll be there."

They came around the curve on the path towards the barn, the house showing beyond, and smoke lifting from the big chimney. Thomas walked faster down the wet, slippery flat stones laid against the rutting. A man came out from behind the barn. Startled, he backed a step, and then recognizing his son, came hurriedly forward, dropping his pitchfork and reaching for Thomas. Joseph Pratt said nothing as he grabbed Thomas within his arms and buried his face against his neck. Thomas shifted the rifle so he could get his arms around his father with a strong, felt squeeze, different from any he had ever given. Joseph gave the last little pump and drew away holding Thomas' arms in his hands to stare at his youngest son.

"Thee's home," he said simply.

"Yes, Father," Thomas said with more meaning than he had ever offered.

"And Abner," Joseph said, noticing him for the first time. "Good to see thee."

"And thee, Uncle." Abner took his hand, happy to be included.

"Come. Come. Thy mother will be mighty pleased to see thee," Joseph said as he led the way, not looking back. "Jane," Joseph called out. "Jane," he repeated, pushing open the door to the great kitchen where his wife was kneading dough for the weekly baking. Before Joseph could say further, Thomas appeared in the doorway. She dropped the flour mixture back into the dough board and came running the several steps to grab her son with an affection given mostly to babies in their cribs.

"Thomas, is thee all right?" she quickly asked, pulling away.

"Yes, Mother, I'm fine," he answered, "and Abner's here too."

"Oh, Thomas. I've been so worried," she cried through her smile. "I've thought about thee every day and prayed for thee. Thee doesn't know," and she hugged him again.

"It's good to be home," was the best Thomas could muster as his older brother and little sister came to see what the excitement was about.

"Hey, Thomas," William called out. "Thee's back," he said, oblivious to the obvious. "We're going to need thee here now that thee's done thy part for Washington."

"Is thee finished with the Army?" Jane asked anxiously. She searched for an answer with her eyes. Thomas turned towards her. The rest were suddenly quiet.

"Yes, Mother, Abner and I are done, finished with fighting." It was a somber reply.

His mother looked at Thomas, then Abner, and realized someone was missing. "Where's Benjamin?" she asked apprehensively.

Dread surged through Thomas as he knew it would. He looked to Abner for support, swallowing to wet the sudden dryness in his throat. The rest stood quietly waiting. "He's gone," Thomas said simply.

"Gone where?" asked his father.

"Away," Thomas answered and then added for clarity, "to God."

"Oh," Jane gasped, tears welling in the corners of her eyes.

"Killed?" Joseph asked, not satisfied with the ambiguity. "Where?" he pressed. "How?"

Thomas swallowed again and started. "At Brandywine.

We were together." He stopped to look around. They were all staring at him, waiting. Thomas took a deep breath and decided to get the truth out. "We were close to Birmingham Meeting and the British came from the direction we didn't expect, at least not in such great numbers, and we tried to hold them back. The regulars were there mostly, real soldiers of the Continental Army, but it was too much for us all and we were pulling back. The British fired a cannon and one hit Benjamin. Abner and I were there and we helped and cared and we did what we could, but it didn't make a difference." Thomas had a tear in his eye. "He died." Thomas looked around at the faces surrounding him, wondering if their expressions were of grief or condemnation. He lowered his head.

"Where is he now?" Joseph asked kindly.

"At Birmingham, I expect," Thomas replied. "Can't be sure for they were coming on and we had to run for our lives."

"If so, we'll go there." Joseph looked to Jane for concurrence.

"Of course we will, with his family, my brother and his wife. They'll need our support and thee also Abner and thine. We are all family together." She put her arm around Thomas' shoulder. "We are grateful for thy return," she said with a welling up of feeling from the depths of her being.

"You two are all wet," William observed to break the spell.

"Get out of those things," Joseph said, attempting to soften the emotion. Thomas complied. He was cold, wet, tired, and exhausted emotionally. He stood the rifle by the door, sloughed off his boots, and dropped his clothes to stand naked to the fire, his back to the family.

"We'll get thee clothes too, Abner. Thee'll get a chill

walking about damp and cold." Abner did the same, leaving his inner pants on, hoping the fire would dry them in place. The mustiness and sweat and sheep and dirt and smell of powder gave a pungency to the pile of clothes. Jane picked them up and put them outside.

"Abigail, come help me," Jane said now taking charge. "We need more hot water. William, get some wood for this fire and Joseph, if thee'll get the washtub, we'll get these boys—no men—warm and clean." She turned to talk to their backs still in place. "We'll get you some fresh food."

"Whatever they left us," William added.

"Did the British come here?" Thomas asked.

"Yes. A squad," his father answered, "and grubbed around our place."

"Even came into the house here," Jane said with indignation, "didn't ask, just barged in and went upstairs, took some blankets."

"But most of all," William added, "they took our steer and the pigs."

"I'm afraid it'll be a lean winter," Joseph said.

"Is there anything left?" Thomas asked, suddenly angry.

"Enough, not much. It could have been worse. They didn't have enough soldiers to carry everything, so we're left with what they didn't want."

"The horses were in the far field," William said. "They didn't see them and I guess they have enough horses. It's food they were really searching for."

"Here are some of thy things from thy chest," Abigail said, placing them on the bench behind Thomas and Abner. "Thee can dress with a certain modesty," she giggled, "as long as thee doesn't turn around to see what I've brought."

"Now shush," Jane said kindly. "I'll hand the clothes to

thee, Thomas. No need to turn around and the same for thee Abner."

"I'm obliged to thee, Aunt," Abner said. "I'll get whatever back to Thomas so this winter he won't be any more naked than he is now." He sniggered. The spell was off as they all began to talk at once.

***

Joseph sat opposite as Thomas and Abner hunkered low over the food placed before them, eating with a hurried intensity as though still on the march. "We need to let your aunt and uncle know about Benjamin." He waited for a reaction. Neither raised his head.

"It's not fair to keep them unknowing."

"When does thee think Father?"

"Not today certainly. Abner needs to get home, but tomorrow I would think."

"Would thee come with me Abner?" Thomas asked.

"Sure, it's not thy burden alone." He lowered his head for another bite then jerked it up. "What if Caleb has already gotten home and spread the word around?"

"More likely Joshua," Thomas muttered, "not hurt, running the fastest of any of us." He snorted. "The type to spread bad news first."

"Then thee needs to go tomorrow," Joseph said to his son. "Thee too Abner." He had said enough. "Visit thy parents of course, tell them, but come back here tomorrow and we can all go to the Darlington's. They'll wonder at the crowd, but better for whatever comfort we can offer."

"I just hope they have not heard already," Thomas added, "unless it be from a compassionate source." They sat quietly in their thoughts.

***

The following day, Abner returned, cleaned, in his own clothes, his rough misshapen hat dirty and discolored now exchanged for his broad brimmed go-to-meeting hat. He strode along with only a stick, harmless but comfortable.

"Did thee see anyone?" Thomas asked, getting to him first.

"Thee means Caleb or Joshua?"

"Well, yes."

"Maybe Annie Green?"

"Haven't thought," Thomas answered.

Abner opened his mouth to reply, thought better of it, shut it, and remained silent.

"We're ready for thee," called Jane from the doorway.

***

The carriage bounced over the cartway, muddy in the hollows, drying where the sun shone through. Thomas and Abner rode the two last horses as the carriage bounced around, creaking left and right as they headed the several miles to Benjamin's family. As they approached the lane, Joseph pulled up.

"I think it's best, Thomas, if thee goes first, perhaps with Abner, and search for Benjamin's father. Only thee can break the news. We'll come along in a bit."

Thomas became uncomfortable as he looked at his father, his eyes steady, hardly blinking, calm and serious. He could see no help for it, no other way. He gulped and guided the mare on ahead as Abner followed. Thomas worked the horse up the hill, stopping in front of the stone house, long in the front similar to the Pratt house, plain and comfortable. His heart was beating as he came down off the mare, tying her to the nearest rail hoping to see Benjamin's father first. He searched around the side towards their barn, the few animals sheltering in their pens under the slope of the upper levels. He listened to the bleating of goats, then headed in that direction. As he passed a back window, it opened and Benjamin's mother called out.

"Why Thomas, what is thee doing here?" His heart skipped a beat. He turned to see his aunt duck back inside and shortly come around the back of the house, drying her hands on a cloth. "And Abner, thee also," she smiled. Watching their solemn faces, she stopped, and bringing the cloth to her mouth, cried, "Oh, no." She came towards them. "Benjamin?"

Thomas swallowed hard, giving a little shake of his head.

"Where is he? What happened? How is he?" The questions tumbled out.

"He didn't make it," Thomas said, reluctant to pronounce the final word.

"Did he die?" his mother said, asking the inevitable.

Thomas slowly nodded, then answered. "Yes."

"How?" She continued with as much brave control as possible.

"He was wounded at Brandywine and we were there and I held his head and he called for thee and said he saw thee coming." Thomas quivered, and Abner shifted nervously on his feet.

Benjamin's mother's eyes filled with tears. They didn't stop, flowing down her face onto her hands as she grasped the cloth held fast at her bosom. Thomas felt helpless. He stood there, uncomfortable, wondering what he could do.

"I'm sorry," he said at last, "we didn't mean for it to be that way."

"We tried," Abner added, struggling to find something to say.

Susan Darlington came to Thomas and Abner. "I know you care. You are—or were—Benjamin's best friends. It's just that when you all went away, against our pleading, we hoped and prayed that you'd all be safe and be back home. I'm grateful for you two coming," she said, pausing as the tears came again, "but I do so miss my Benjamin, a good boy who didn't deserve to die so young." She saw the wagon with the Pratts coming up the way. She stood there wiping her eyes, red and puffy, embarrassed for her lack of control. Jane Pratt was the first down off the carriage running to her.

"We needed to come Susan," she offered, bringing her close.

Jared Darlington came up from the barn, hearing voices above the bleating. "Joseph. Jane. Family," he announced counting them off. "Thomas. Abner," he noticed with a question to his voice. "What's this?" he asked.

"It's Benjamin," replied his wife.

"He's not here?"

"He won't be," she sobbed.

"Where?" he asked directly.

"He was killed at Brandywine," she blurted out.

Stunned, Jared Darlington held on to a fence post. His breath left him, as he seemed to deflate it in front of them, his ruddy, full face suddenly ashen, his hands fumbling, trying to grasp on to the lost life of his son.

"I told him not to go!" he mumbled.

"And so did we to Thomas," Joseph said, "and I know the same for Abner, but it was not to be. They were of a mind and set in it and determined. Could we have chained them to the farm?" Thomas felt more uncomfortable, ready to be blamed for Benjamin's death. It was Susan Darlington who spoke.

"Yes, he was grown up, just like thy Thomas and Abner here. It is their life to live and die when God sees fit to take that which was given." Her tears were drying as she clung to her faith in that great, all encompassing spirit that occasionally burst forth with an inner light in a meeting well gathered. "Come in now," she offered, working to regain her composure. She took Jane by the arm and led her in. Jared looked at Joseph then changed his mind and went to Thomas.

"Come, thee too Abner, we'll go in." He followed them in to sit in the front parlor in a small circle, silently as a meeting for worship, each with his own thoughts. It was Jane who broke the stillness and quiet of the room.

"We thank God for Benjamin's life and trust in the Lord that his death brings a peace not only to our son but this country." Birds twittered outside, the sporadic deep breathing inside rising and falling in and on even cadence.

Jared raised his head. "You've come a distance. We're grateful for that and the courage of thee Thomas and thee Abner to come here to us. We'll visit Birmingham Meeting in due course, on a First Day and find for ourselves, feel and seek Benjamin's place after we've had a chance to understand." He looked at his wife. "Have we any apple cider to offer?"

"Yes, of course," she replied quietly.

They slowly got up to the back room, somber, drawn together, deep within.

Chapter Seventeen

"Did other farms get raided by the British?" Thomas asked of his father. "Were we the only ones?"

"No, others lost provisions to the redcoats."

"Much?"

"I'm not sure. After the Army came through, not many were able to attend Meeting on First Day." They were out in the cornfield, cutting the stalks, bringing them together in a shock to dry the yellow kernels of corn to last the winter. "We'll have more corn than we need this year," Joseph said to his son. "Without a steer to feed and pigs gone, we have some to sell, maybe to buy a pig back if we can find one for sale."

"How about Phineas Massey? He always has pigs. Perhaps he'll sell us one, for a price of course."

Joseph stopped and gave a wry smile to Thomas. "Thee's got a good head on thy shoulders. We'll let this corn set a bit and take what we don't need towards Marple and the Masseys, work for a trade perhaps, at least an arrangement." Thomas thought of Hannah.

"Will I be able to go with thee?" He tried to be casual in the question.

Joseph laughed. "I'm sure Hannah would be happy to see thee," he agreed, aware of the flickering interest.

Thomas kept at the tall corn with full ears, bright yellow beneath the browning husks on the drying stalks. He thought of their neighbors, then of the Greens. *Were they pillaged also?* he wondered. *And what about Annie? And what about Hannah?* He turned to his father. "Would it be safe to go to Marple? Will the British come out that far?" Thomas was curious.

"I hear that Washington lost at Germantown and that the British are now in Philadelphia with the Continental Army encamped north of the city." Joseph kept on working. "We'll ask around, and at the same time help others where we can. We ought even to go over to the Darlington's and help in place of Benjamin."

"I'd like that," Thomas replied, still hurting about Benjamin, but he kept thinking about Annie Green. Finally he decided to ask. "Does thee think the Greens need any help?" He didn't look at his father as he asked the question.

Joseph faced his son with a quizzical stare, tossing the question around. "If thee feels neighborly towards the Greens, then thee should follow thy leadings." He had his suspicions about the real reason, but was content to let them be.

"Perhaps I will," Thomas answered. They kept at the corn.

***

"I'll be at the Greens," Thomas announced some days later.

"Give them our greetings," his mother said with an innocent lilt.

"Take care," Joseph said.

"See if Annie is safe?" his brother asked.

Thomas colored, determined that a quick departure was the safer course. He made his way out onto the cartway and then by the path along the fields, close by the creek bottom and skirting the woods. The hour passed quickly. Thomas hummed a tune from the militia to himself, striding by the familiar fields, already harvested, the hay mostly in, a serenity about the farms, well off the main roads.

"Hello Abel Green," Thomas called out as he came in sight of their neighbor.

"Welcome Thomas. You're right sprightly having survived that fighting at Brandywine."

"Lucky," he replied. He came closer. "It was fierce. Nothing ever like it." He shook his hand.

"I hear tell. Joshua told us all about it and I see Caleb's quite a hero, wounded in the process, but a mighty help to the militia and Washington's Army." He was satisfied with the knowledge.

"Did he tell you all?" Thomas asked.

"Only that wounded, he was still able to get away."

"How?"

"He didn't say."

"I carried him away from the battle," Thomas said, his anger rising. "I'd left Benjamin Darlington dying so I could get Caleb away. Did he say that?"

"Not that I heard. Maybe Annie knows better. He talked to her."

"May I see Annie then?" Thomas asked, sensing an opening he wasn't sure how to broach.

"Surely Thomas. Caleb has been limping around here a lot lately." He nodded towards the house. "She's there likely, although it's more and more difficult to keep track of her."

"Thanks," Thomas replied, still smarting from Caleb's bravado. He walked purposefully toward the house but turned as he saw Annie in the barn, tending to the rabbits and chickens. "Is that thee?" he inquired.

"If you mean me, then it's me," she answered with a laugh. "Come here," she waved, "while I finish." He went into the cool dark of the lower level, smells of various animals mingling with the fresh perfume of the newly cut hay.

"Did the English come here? Take thy food, animals, blankets, harness?" He was curious.

"No, none came. Maybe we're too far off the main road, not going anyplace."

"Then thee and thy family are fortunate. We were visited while I was away with the army," he felt emboldened to emphasize.

"Oh Thomas, I know, Caleb said you were there."

"Where?"

"At Brandywine."

"Did he say anything else?"

"Only that he was wounded and they let him come home for it."

"And how did he get away?"

"On a wagon, he did mention." She put the eggs into a basket and stood up. "Why do you ask? Weren't you there?"

"Yes, and I carried him away from the battle." He was upset.

"Joshua didn't say anything about you either."

"They have both been here?"

"To make a call on Father."

"And that's all?"

"Well, on me too," she giggled, "and are you making a call on Father or on me?"

He laughed. "On him and then on thee. To be polite, of course."

"Well then we can visit if you're finished with Father."

"Here?"

"In the hayloft," she teased, but started up the ladder

nevertheless. He looked at her strong legs down below her skirt, hefted up for the climb. She reached the top, went over the edge, and disappeared into the hay. Thomas grabbed the rungs of the ladder and made his way up, careful not to slip with the new hay hanging about. He pushed the harder stalks aside and rolled over into the springy softness of the newly raked grasses, cracks between the rough board siding allowing a dim light to filter in. Thomas waited a minute, letting his eyes adjust.

"Over here," Annie said, teasing, rustling in the depression formed in the hay. Thomas crawled over, sinking down alongside her.

"Are you happy to see me?" she asked with an apprehension.

"Of course." He felt for her arm.

"It's been a long time. When I heard of the British Army marching towards Philadelphia coming through Chester County I feared for you."

"Me alone?"

"I knew the Edgmont militia was off to join the army."

"And?"

"And that you were part of it and Caleb and all the rest."

"We were all together."

"Was it hard?"

"Not at first. We just drilled and rested, then some marching."

"Where?"

"After Chester, when we heard that the British were coming up from the Chesapeake, we marched, following Washington to the Brandywine." He shifted his position.

"I hear it was fierce fighting."

"From whom?"

"Those who returned."

"Caleb?"

"Yes." She hesitated. "He said it was intense, fighting all around, men getting hit, why, even he was wounded, said he was in the middle of the charge of the redcoats. One got to him, but he was lucky. He was able to escape and regroup and then get taken to Chester with help from a doctor." She reported what she had been told without blandishment.

Thomas didn't respond.

"What are you thinking?"

Thomas turned over, his face to the rafters. He waited, and then replied, "Wondering what you see in Caleb?"

"Oh, silly," she chuckled, "we're Baptists together, go to the same church and he is amusing. Sure, I like him, but he's different from you. You're more serious. You talk less, but mean more." She laid her hand on his chest, bringing her face closer. Thomas didn't move, feeling the warmth of her hand, afraid to let it spread.

"Did Caleb tell thee that I was the one to carry him away from the battle at Brandywine?" He was talking to the rafters hoping Annie would hear.

"No," she replied defensively, "but he was wounded. He showed me his scar."

"And I saw his blood. I saw it on me when I finally got him to a gathering point where other wounded men were and where there were wagons to help them escape, not be captured, where the care would have been worse." He spoke with an angry urgency. She shifted her hand up towards his neck, feeling the pulsing of his artery, intense against the muscles pushing against his skin. She leaned over and kissed him on the cheek as softly as she could.

"I didn't know that," she confessed. "There was no way,

for it was only Caleb who related his experience. I couldn't question him."

"He's full of words and bluff," Thomas answered. "He's strong and determined and loud."

"But he's kind to me," she added, "and I do think he's a little bit jealous of you which is why he doesn't want to talk about you." She moved her hand around on to his cheek to turn his head towards her. She brought her face to him and softly laid her mouth on his. She moved her lips back and forth over his with a gentle pressure, moisture easing the dryness until finally he opened his mouth, letting her tongue wiggle in searching for his. He responded, his tongue pressing out, finding the underside, wrapping around as she curled her tongue against the undulating surface. He brought his body around to face her, his arms circling, one behind her head as he worked his mouth back and forth. She broke away, drawing in a deep breath and came close again, her hand dropping down, resting on his chest then down to his stomach. His muscles tightened involuntarily and relaxed. She slipped her hand under the belt and then lifted the shirt out, playing with a line of soft hair descending from his navel. He didn't move for fear of confusing her intent. He put his hand up to her breast, rubbing in a circular motion, lightly with an increasing pressure. She drew away to loosen her bodice. His hand dropped lower as though not to be noticed as she inched her skirt up. She loosened her shirt to draw her skirt apart. His hand worked down then up finding her soft, warm skin. She worked his belt loose and parting the pants, felt down. He was there, ready as he explored her. She thrust her hips up towards his hand, his fingers slipping against the encouraging hair, newly moist, searching for the source. She gently grabbed between his legs, stiffening as she pushed his pants down.

Their hands moved more quickly. Thomas rolled over and with an urgency thrust with a moan as she enveloped him. They were in unison, opposite, with a crescendo of rhythm. He stopped with a shudder, taking his lips off hers to grab a breath as she let out a guttural sigh. He collapsed onto her, fitting his face alongside hers. Their breathing slowed. He pulled apart, huddled close in the comfort of the tender hay. They remained for some minutes. Annie broke the spell.

"You're all man, even if you are a Quaker."

He couldn't help but laugh. "Don't let somber clothes fool you."

"I never did," she replied.

"I may not be as big or as strong as Caleb, but I can hold my own."

"Well, you can certainly hold me," she replied.

"Is Caleb ever been up here?" he asked, his curiosity taking hold of his sense.

"That's a forward question," she replied.

"Sorry," he answered, feeling guilty to pry.

"It's all right," she chuckled. "I like Caleb. We've known each other for a long time. We've grown up together. Yes. He's been up here." She was silent. "He's all right," she said defensively, "even if he didn't escape all on his own." She sat up pulling little strands of grass from her hair, retiring her top and shifting her skirt to its normal position.

"Now you better make yourself presentable as though we've been chasing about for eggs or Pa is going to be asking questions."

"Does he?" Thomas asked.

"Never had to," she replied with sprightliness.

"Well then, I'm not one to give reason," he said, standing up in the shifting hay, tucking his shirt in and adjusting his pants. She quickly made for the ladder and taking a look below, lowered herself to the barn floor.

"It's fine," she said to Thomas, ready to follow. He climbed down several rungs then jumped.

"Still have a little spring there," she teased, gathering up the basket with the eggs. "You head on away," she ordered, so I don't have answer too many questions with you standing around looking guilty or having to change my story." She didn't turn back as she left for the farmhouse, leaving Thomas to watch her confident step. He looked about and following her lead, not seeing her father, strode with an uncertain hope for the path back home.

Chapter Eighteen

Thomas was apprehensive. He had not been to First Day meeting for worship since he and Benjamin and Abner had joined the Edgmont militia.

"Thee needs to go," his mother encouraged. "Friends are still divided as to what action should be taken about thee and Abner. Of course, some will say that God's will has already been done with Benjamin's death."

"It would be well if thee were to come," his father echoed. "Friends will talk, but it's much harder when they see thee in person."

"I'm not sure I want to go if everyone is going to look at me and talk behind my back with a 'tut, tut'." He got up and stood by the door of the kitchen looking out at the fields and down by the creek, misting in the early autumn evening.

"It is only meeting for worship and thee has been away for a time. Many will be happy to see thee and I expect Abner will be there also."

"How does thee know?"

"I saw his mother," Jane replied. "In fact, she said Abner was asking the same questions."

Thomas laughed. "Well, if he is going to be there, I don't want him to have to face all the pinched faces alone."

"Thee has many friends," Joseph said, "and the question of thy joining the militia will not come up 'til monthly meeting, and if they see thee, it'll make it easier on those who can put the Army behind them, an expediency if thee will."

"So, we'll all go as a family again," his mother said with an optimism she hoped was not misplaced.

***

Thursday morning was bright, crisp, and clear, the smoke of battle long gone, the nor'easter having blown through leaving the countryside cleansed of both armies. Peace was returning to this small section of Chester County. As the armies maneuvered over by the Schuylkill River, families returned to their routine, assessing the losses to the Americans and British, wondering if the notes of promises to pay or paper money were of any value. That taken by force in haste was gone they knew. The empty space at the family table left an emotional scar as fathers searched the battlegrounds to find proof and they hoped, solace in their loss.

***

The Pratts arrived at Meeting early. The doors of the meeting house were open. There were a goodly number of carriages already present. Horses stood contentedly in the sheds, easy in the familiar routine. Thomas jumped down, staying by the hidden side, looking for Abner and trying to avoid any elder. Joseph helped his wife down and they walked side-by-side, hands to themselves, towards the group already gathered waiting to enter.

"Greetings, Friend."

"Good morn." The regular courtesies were offered.

"Is that thy son yonder?" asked one.

"Yes, it's Thomas," Joseph replied, waving his son over.

With a dread, he came, comfortable for the presence of his father close by.

"Welcome back," offered one kindly woman, her husband silent. Another came over.

"It's good to see thee again," one of the elders offered. "We've missed thee."

Thomas wasn't sure the older man was totally aware of the reason for his absence. He looked around. Some of his friends were there, but it was hard before Meeting to be very free and expressive. It was a time of increasing calm as they went into the meeting house to take their places on the plain, unpainted, wooden benches. Thomas hoped his father would lead them to a rear bench but was disappointed when Joseph paraded his mother and brother and sister to the front of the great room, taking seats close to the facing benches. Thomas knew he would be the object of curiosity not only to the elders facing him, but also to those behind. As he sat down, he could feel their stares boring into him. He wanted to turn around to see who was looking but he didn't dare. The Meeting settled into silence as the sun shone through the high windows above. The leaves of the treetops waved back and forth with the fresh breezes. The quiet seemed oppressive to Thomas.

They must all be thinking of me fighting and the testimony on peace. He would have someone speak. *I hope it's not on the Army or militia,* he said to himself, *for whatever the first message, it will guide the thoughts to follow.* There was a rustling. Thomas stiffened. A woman pushed her skirt even. A man coughed. *How many more minutes?* Thomas wondered. A man stood. He waited before speaking. Thomas shut his eyes to make the voice go away or at least to become disembodied.

"We are grateful," the message started, "for the blessings we have. God has shown us the way," Thomas relaxed, "that fighting and war are no answer towards the love of God shone through the life of Jesus for an everlasting peace."

Thomas stiffened again. The man sat down and Thomas tried to become smaller. Shuffling of feet sounded as an older member towards the side stood but facing most.

"It is God's will that we have a choice. The Bible and the teachings of Christ lead us towards a better life, one in which we can search for one's own way, knowing the example set before us but with the knowledge that there are many paths towards a more perfect society." He coughed for emphasis and sat down. Thomas was thankful that the messages were few as those assembled in meeting struggled for an understanding with compassion. Finally, the two weighty Friends sitting center on the facing bench shook hands and the meeting was over. People began to talk, softly, still in the meeting room not to disturb the calm of the silent worship before. Thomas looked at his father who nodded. He got up and left as quickly as possible, unnoticed he hoped, stepping outside to head for the sheds where he, Benjamin, and Abner always met, away from the curious, where privacy counted when their thoughts were personal. He came around the corner. Abner was standing there putting out his hand. Thomas grabbed it, thumping his cousin on the back.

"How'd thee get here?" he asked, pleased to see him.

"Sat in the back. Like thee, my parents got me to come, but we were the last in, so no one took notice. At least they didn't turn around so I could duck out quickly. Saw thee, figured."

"It's strange back here. It feels different, not like before."

"Not without Benjamin."

"What does thee think Meeting's going to do with us? Ask us to leave?"

"Maybe, but if I understand the messages at Meeting there won't be any unity. No consensus."

"So?"

"So, if the Meeting can't come to a conclusion, then there's no decision to read us out of meeting, which means it would be a decision not to do anything, which makes it a decision."

"Thee thinks?"

"Probably." Thomas bumped Abner on the shoulder. "What have thy parents said to thee?"

"They don't know what to say. They're happy to see me back, but they haven't asked much about Brandywine. They're afraid to know the truth, I guess." He shrugged. "Sometime, I'll tell them, when they're ready to hear." He looked over at Thomas. "Funny, we've done things they know nothing about and aren't sure they want to know, afraid it will do something about being a Quaker."

"I've been thinking," Thomas said. "We've seen, been there, know the blood and have been afraid."

"Thee can say that again," Abner agreed.

"Which gives us reasons to believe as Quakers, not everything, because I still think we need to be an independent country, free of Great Britain. It's the English who started this war with their soldiers and we need to stand up for our beliefs and this country is doing that."

"Mostly."

"Not all, sure, but enough to at least make a difference, give the British something to think about."

"What if they win this war?"

"The country will still be different, but look at the differences. The redcoats are all lined up, told to do so and they march in order. Our Army, not even the same uniforms, lines up, listens, heads for cover, adjusts, and is always thinking, following orders, but still with a personal belief in what they're doing. Fighting. Losing. Fighting again. They have a purpose." He shook his head towards the meeting house. "We know. We made individual decisions because we thought about it, not always lining up to suit someone else because we've been told to do so, but joining because we knew it was right for us. For others, they can make their own decisions." Thomas felt better for Willistown Meeting and Abner.

The younger boys of the meeting had gathered their courage and approached the two of them.

"Tell us about the battle at Brandywine," the tallest said as the rest gathered around to hear.

Chapter Nineteen

In December, in an irregular time, a sense of regularity returned to Chester County and Edgmont Township. British were now firmly in control of Philadelphia only given to sporadic forays out to collect information and provisions. The Americans settled into winter quarters at Valley Forge, less in control, but with a greater necessity for regular forays to the surrounding countryside for information and as desperately for provisions. Agents of the Congress and of Washington worked the area, seeking flour and corn and beef and blankets. Patriots accepted the Continental currency, Loyalists accepted only hard British coin, and Quakers accepted either none or some from either, by force of circumstance or belief.

"I've looked at our provisions," Joseph said to his sons. "We've corn aplenty, not useful to the British after Brandywine, but enough to sell. They didn't get all our wheat and we have an ample supply of potatoes and turnips and apples, all which was still in the ground or on the tree when they came through. Without our hogs and steer though, we're without much meat, just what was left from the summer."

"So what's to be?" William asked.

"I have in mind to load our wagon with our excess, corn especially, perhaps some potatoes, and make for a market."

"Will thee try Phineas Massey first?" Thomas asked. "He seemed to have a goodly yard full of stock when we passed by last spring." Thomas said it on a hopeful note.

"Thee's on to his Hannah?" William joshed.

"There's more than a single reason to visit," Joseph said, protecting his son. "Thomas is right. An honest man, Phineas, probably spared by the army coming through, and Hannah Massey is a right nice girl, comely to be sure." He smiled at Thomas. "Besides, with a heavy load, I'll need you both."

"When father?" Thomas asked.

"As soon as possible. Before traveling becomes too difficult."

"And It'll give thee a chance to forget that Baptist girl," William jibbed.

"I've not seen her for a time," Thomas said, defending himself.

"Let it be," Joseph said, aware, but not anxious to impose his own feelings. "Come with me to the barn. Let's see what we can spare. If we don't have a pig to care for or cattle to feed, we have enough to sell."

"Saving some for a new pig from Friend Massey?" Thomas was happy to be included in the discussion.

"To be sure. We'll set aside what we think will do and hope the provisioners won't find us to requisition what we have for either army."

"Doesn't thee think we need to offer some to Washington's Army?"

"Still thinking of thy experience?" William asked.

"If needs be," Thomas replied. "They're men too and need to eat to survive while they're fighting for us." Thomas was aroused, remembering the regular army, marching and fighting with a strength of character he had come to admire. "Father," he asked with a seriousness in his voice, "can't we spare some for Valley Forge? It's not like the British who are billeted in houses in Philadelphia. Washington's men are out in the open. Food will be short, and even if we only get paid in paper money, it's our money." He stood, imploring his father.

"Looks like we have a real patriot in this house," William exclaimed.

"Every dwelling needs one," Thomas snapped back.

"Let's see what we have," Joseph answered calmly, "and make our decision."

Thomas glowered at his brother who shrugged his shoulders. They made their way to the corncrib, sizing up the number of ears tumbled into the wooden slated crib alongside the small barn.

"Mice are working at those ears at the edge," Thomas said as they began to take stock.

"Rats and squirrels maybe," William added.

"We share whether we like it or not," Joseph said with a certain resignation.

"Our horses will be well fed," Thomas said. "Good thing they weren't taken."

"Fortunate," Joseph agreed.

"So here's for the two of them," William said, placing his hand on a slat.

"And here's for a pig," Thomas said, placing his hand on a further slat.

"And for us, a bit more," Joseph said, looking at the length of the crib, "which leaves us a goodly amount. Ought to give us some ability to trade or sell and buy." He nodded agreeably. "We're then agreed?" He looked at his two sons.

William nodded.

"When shall we start to load?" Thomas asked, indicating his satisfaction to have been asked.

"Later this week. We'll go to Marple and visit the Masseys on Sixth Day, cast about on Seventh Day, see if we can make arrangements. That leaves us First Day. I understand Quarterly Meeting will be held then at Springfield. We might go, visit, learn, and get all the latest news." Joseph had a look of satisfaction. It had been his plan all along.

Thomas stood there thinking. *'It'll mean taking along my good suit. After farm clothes, it will make a better impression,'* he figured, already looking forward to their visit and to Hannah.

***

The wagon was loaded, heavy now from the shelled corn and barrels of apples set in place. Canvas was lifted over the great wooden ribs covering the wagon, the front one leaning forward offering protection for the three of them on the seat. Thomas waited for his father to say goodbye to his mother, then went and gave her a light kiss on the cheek and followed his father up onto the seat. William snapped the reins. The horses leaned into the harness and with the wagon creaking from the new pressure, slowly moved out and up the cartway towards the Philadelphia Road and on to Marple. The day was crisp and the road solid. The stretching limbs of the trees were mostly bare of leaves as the wind blew in from the west behind them.

Thomas watched the horses as they kept a steady pace, mesmerizing in their cadence. *I wonder if Hannah will remember me? Or if she does, whether she'll even care?* He fretted, then brightened at the prospect.

Joseph sat, his body moving with the motion of the wagon, was comfortable to have his younger sons along to help. They passed few others on the road. The intense fighting between the armies had diminished as the troops moved into winter quarters. There were only sporadic clashes with forays from the city by the British and probing from the Americans at Valley Forge. Families withdrew to the safety of their own farms. Villages became muted in activity. Taverns felt the loss of business, keeping what little food available carefully hidden. Only beer and whiskey remained readily available. It was late in the day as they came to the familiar crossroad among the fields leading to the substantial holdings of Phineas Massey. The horses picked up speed as they anticipated feed and a warm barn. Coming alongside the barn, William pulled the horses to a stop. Joseph jumped off the wagon as Phineas put down his pitchfork and came towards him, his arms wide with enthusiasm.

"Thee and thine are always welcome," he said to Joseph with a hearty handshake to each. "Nice to see thee William," he offered pleasantly, "and good to see thee, Thomas," he said heartily out from a broad smile circling his mouth.

"And thee Friend Massey," Joseph offered. "May we visit, then ask thy advice on business?"

"Of course thee may. It gets lonesome as the cold comes on and now with the British occupying Philadelphia, people are afraid to venture too far from home, concerned for patrols on the roads even this far out. They're afraid that perhaps they'll lose the horse they're riding on and have to walk back home, more sore and poorer for it." He headed for his house, dusting off his pants from the dirt of the barn. Joseph followed. Thomas hesitated as he looked around. The chicken coop was empty, but he could see the cow was safely in the barn, methodically chewing her cud. The pigs grunted from their corner, contented, unaware of their upcoming fate.

"Looking for someone?" William teased out of hearing of Phineas Massey.

"Just looking," Thomas replied.

"Then perhaps we'd better look inside," William said. "I'll help thee."

Thomas wasn't sure that he either needed or wanted the help, but there was no reason to stand outside waiting for something that wasn't going to happen. He turned and walked with William into the farmhouse. The kitchen was warm. His father was already seated on a bench next to Phineas as they began to exchange the news. Suzanne Massey was tending the pot hanging over the close-set fire. As Thomas came in, he saw Hannah standing by the table, her hands working beans. She stopped, waiting. He couldn't help but look at her with a smile that came on its own. She dropped the beans into the bowl, mixing the shelled with the unshelled, brushing back her hair and stroked her apron so that it lay flat. Her flaxen hair, uncovered by any bonnet, fell by her ears, light and loose, framing regular features, her green eyes bright. She slowly smiled in return, happy to see Thomas again. He had difficulty taking his eyes off her. It was Suzanne Massey who straightened and came over.

"How is thee Thomas, and I see thee brought thy older brother, William."

"For protection," William said.

"From whom," she teased. "From us to Thomas? Or for us to be careful of thy younger brother who has learned all his lessons from thee?" She laughed. "Perhaps to keep Hannah from his blandishments." Hannah blushed.

"As I observed," William replied. "There's no danger there, except maybe to warn her that Thomas was at the battle at Brandywine with tales to tell, experiences to recount."

It was Thomas' turn to redden. He wished the greeting had not been so public. Suzanne Massey had suspected and now eased the situation. "Thomas, thee take Hannah and tell her what thee will and I think thy brother can pick up the beans and finish what Hannah started." There was no help for it as William took her place and began with uncertain fingers to push the beans from the pod. Thomas didn't know where to go. It was Hannah who decided as she put on her cape and bonnet and sideling by her mother, grateful for the suggestion, pushed open the door and went out followed closely by Thomas as happy as she for the respite. They walked side by side out towards the fence at the edge of the field. She stopped and turned towards him.

"Was thee in the Army?" she asked troubled.

"Yes, but only the militia, from Edgmont."

"And was thee at Brandywine?"

"Yes." He waited, not sure she wanted more.

"Was it terrible? I've heard reports that it was fierce, that many were wounded, many killed." It was her turn to wait.

"The militia was there, close by Birmingham meeting, but only to help Washington's Army, and then the British out flanked us, coming from a direction we didn't expect, and we were directly in front of them, not expecting a real fight. There was nothing to do but stand alongside the Continental Army and support them."

"Did thee fire thy rifle?"

"Yes."

"Did thee try to kill someone?"

He swallowed, not sure how she would understand the answer. "Yes."

"And did thee?"

"I don't know," he answered truthfully. "In a battle, it's very confusing."

"So what happened?"

"The British pushed us back."

"And men were wounded?"

"And killed," he added. "It was a hard battle, but because we were forced from the field, we escaped. The British were left to plunder the countryside, taking food and supplies from the farms as they passed through headed to Goshen going by our farm. They took our livestock and the Continental Army couldn't stop them even at Goshen, just as it began to rain." He poured out his feelings more freely as Hannah listened sympathetically. She did not interrupt, her eyes showing concern.

"Thee came through safely!" It was a statement.

He nodded. "But my cousin and best friend was hit by a cannonball and died in my arms." His eyes glistened at the memory. As she put her hand into his, he wrapped his fingers tighter around hers. They were warm and soft against his hardened, cracked, and chaffed hands.

"I'm sorry," she said.

"I had to join," he replied, "but now I don't have to. I've done my part in the fighting, even at Goshen as the rains dispersed the militia, including us." She moved closer to him.

"I'm happy thee's no longer in the militia. It's for others, not for thee."

"Are there others in thy Meeting who joined?"

"Several, but most did not and some are still there, but one came back. It's a concern that will be brought up at Quarterly Meeting, this First Day."

"Perhaps we'll be there," Thomas said hopefully.

"I'd like that," Hannah agreed. "Then thee can hear of the discussion back and forth." They stood there looking out at the trees along the far hedgerow beyond the snake fence. Thomas carefully and hesitantly put his arm around

Hannah. She did not resist but moved closer against him, content to be there listening to the breathing as his chest moved up and down.

***

"What's thee want for all thy corn?" asked Phineas of Joseph. "It's a goodly load."

"What thee might spare, something in fair value, preferably breathing," he laughed. "The redcoats came and took most of our livestock, especially the pigs, so I know the British will eat well of our pork, even of the steer which was close ready for market."

"Well, Friend, I haven't a steer to spare but perhaps a pig or two. We had a good litter, grown well. I think one for breeding and I suggest one for the pot." He guided Joseph to the pigpen. The large pigs came towards Phineas ready for another feeding even if out of the regular schedule. "See that one over there, shy, but pretty as a sow can be, and she'll be ready to breed in the spring. She's thine if thee likes, and that big old porker over there might keep thee in food for a year."

"Right nicely. I thank thee."

"I wouldn't want to see thy youngest son waste away," he chuckled.

"Thee has a concern?"

"For Hannah."

"Thee thinks?"

"I think she has an interest in thy Thomas. Now I don't know, but I do listen to Suzanne and then I watch." He smiled with an appreciation.

"I've wondered. Ever since Thomas has come back, he's changed, more serious, more purpose, grown up."

"After Brandywine, I've no doubt. It would do it to

any of us." They left the pigpen and walked towards the springhouse. "Thee and I have had a fine space of years to settle in."

***

Thomas led Hannah back around the barn, looking in on their cow chewing her cud contentedly. They didn't talk as Thomas kept his arm around her waist, watching the cow in its regularity, the horses just beyond, a young heifer off to the side in its own pen. There was order to the barn, all was in place and Thomas felt at ease. He finally broke the silence.

"Is thee planning on Quarterly Meeting come First Day?"

"I don't like to go. It's only old people talking and discussing issues they have debated many times before."

"Would thee go if I go?" He looked at her expectantly.

"If thee goes and stays with me, then it won't be boring. That would be fine." She pulled away and grabbed his hand. "Come. I want to show thee what Father just bought." Thomas was unsure about the change of subject as she led him out of the barn and towards the shed at the rear, pulling open the door to look in. Standing there was a new carriage, shiny, handsome, and black with brass knobs to hold the leather side curtains. "This is what father wants to drive to meeting tomorrow. Mother thinks it a bit too fine, ostentatious, but Father wants to drive it anyway, so I think he'll have his way. Would thee come in this with me?" He felt a pleasant surge in his head.

"Sure, fine, absolutely, if that will get thee to come." His words tumbled out.

"I do think Father would like passengers in the back. It looks better."

"I'd be happy to sit there and I did bring my meeting suit." He brought her close and looked down at her. She looked up directly and raised her chin ever so slightly. Without thinking, driven by impulse, he bent down and kissed her. She did not flinch. She was steady. He applied a little pressure then drew away. He was unsure of his approach and remained silent. She smiled a soft, appreciative smile, and he relaxed and gave her another kiss, longer, gentle, warm and tingly, nerve endings dancing through his chest as he stopped worrying, exhilarated with the result. He drew back, took her hand, and smiled broadly, *a little silly,* he thought, but he could not help himself.

"We'd best be in," she said. Thomas nodded. They left the shed after one more admiring glance and headed for the house, hand in hand.

***

Thomas woke early the following morning, First Day. He was anxious, full of hope to be with Hannah, apprehensive about the business affairs to come after meeting for worship. He slipped off the straw pallet and put on his work trousers and boots and went outside. No one was around. It was quiet, cold. Frost was on the ground, and the frozen overnight moisture silvered the trees. The sun reached to break the tree line and soften the harsh coming of winter. He made do, then walked to the shed, opening the door and looked in at the proud carriage, ready for its first public showing. A shiver came over Thomas, more from the anticipation than the chill swirling about. *Am I foolish to go this way?* he wondered, *but it's with Hannah,* he rationalized, *and I don't think Father will mind!* The chill seeped against his bare chest and he was suddenly cold. He walked quickly back to the house hoping no one would be up. He pushed open the door into the kitchen looking for the warmth of the few embers, bright and red under the layer of protective ash from the night before. He poked, then added a few shavings and twigs to bring the glow to a flame, watching the ashes scuttle way from the burst of fire, spreading heat slowly from the hearth, moving closer to capture the rising warmth. He was surprised as Hannah came into the kitchen, her feet silent on the smooth wood-planked floor.

"I wondered if thee might be up," she said.

"Couldn't sleep any longer," he answered, embarrassed without his shirt.

"It's my job to get the fire going, make it ready for breakfast, usually hot porridge." Thomas noticed as she tried to hide her feet beneath the bench.

"Thee will have cold feet standing over there," he motioned for her. She hesitated and then came towards the warming hearth.

"And thee without a shirt," she said almost too quietly to hear. Thomas noticed her eyes drop to look at his chest, his muscles showing with only a small clustering of light hair.

"I should have dressed," he apologized. She came close and put her arm around his waist, feeling his strength, smelling of a steady sleep, hair falling naturally before combing. Thomas was afraid to move. She was shorter without her shoes, firm in her quick dress. He felt again the surge of pleasure as he looked down at her feet, arched and strong, her toes regular and ordered.

"Thee plans to come still? In the carriage?"

"Yes, though I haven't told Father, but as soon as he's up, I will."

"What's this?" came the question from the near room, loud, but not unkindly.

"Father!" Thomas said, surprised. Joseph was already dressed, his meeting suit on, brushed and neat.

"What should I know?"

Thomas started. "Uh."

"Go on," Joseph urged with interest.

"I'd like to ride with Hannah to meeting, in Friend Phineas' new carriage," he said by way of explanation.

"Is it the carriage or Hannah?" he asked with a bright smile.

Thomas flushed, then answered, "Both, I guess."

"Thomas!" Hannah exclaimed.

"Oh, mostly thee," Thomas recovered.

"I would think so," answered Joseph for him, "and I hope so," he said in a further encouragement. "No matter, William and I will come in the wagon and hope that those pigs won't keep on squealing." Thomas now felt out of place, half dressed. He shifted away from Hannah and headed up the steps by his father and disappeared. Joseph came down and sat on the bench opposite Hannah.

"I think I'd better go also," she said, "now that the fire is going well," she explained.

"I'll watch it for thee," Joseph said. "It'll be safe enough." He gave a small wave of his hand that allowed Hannah to scoot by. She was gone in a whisper leaving Joseph to muse alone about Thomas. *He's grown a lot of late,* he thought, rubbing his chin, newly shaven but only in cold water. *A man now.*

***

It wasn't long before Suzanne came down followed by Phineas, dressed for meeting in their finest.

"It looks like you'll have a passenger," Joseph said as they came down into the kitchen.

"Oh?" Phineas replied. "If it's Thomas, that explains the look I got from Hannah as she dashed by me. She did have a purpose." He smiled. "Well, good for the company. Thee doesn't mind?"

"William and I will make do without Thomas, for it's obvious he'll not miss us."

***

Phineas Massey guided the horses into the meeting house grounds towards the carriage sheds, a little faster than normal, his team stepping smartly almost conscious of the new equipment. Phineas slowed then stopped by the stepping-stone, a reason on its own but well in view of the others as they gathered from various meetings.

"Now, don't be too proud," whispered Suzanne to her husband, well aware of the little show. "This will be just fine." She turned around. "Thomas, thee'll help us alight?"

Thomas jumped down and held out his hand for Suzanne Massey as she stepped carefully down, unsure of the new carriage. Hannah waited, then took Thomas' hand and with a light jump, ended down beside him. He held her hand just a bit longer than acceptable, the stares of some older women a silent criticism. Thomas didn't wait for his father and brother as they drove the wagon out back of the sheds, some distance from the meeting house. He followed Hannah in, hoping they would select a bench off to the side, away from the facing benches and the gaze of the elders. Joseph and William entered from the far door and settled, looking across at Thomas who appeared unsure and nervous. Silence layered over the settling meeting, but it wasn't long before the first to speak arose.

"Our testimony for peace is more vital to us than ever before. With two armies on either side of us, waiting out the winter, but ready like angry cats to spring upon one another, may our example of peace offer an example of the love of Jesus for all and the evils of war."

Another spoke from a sitting position. "May we forgive those who participate in war."

Thomas' throat constricted. *I wonder if they know about me? Was that directed to me?* He tried to lower himself to hide behind those on the bench ahead. It was silent again. Finally another spoke.

"We respond to God's message in various ways. Let us not condemn those who lose the path, rather offer the way in love and peace."

Meeting continued. Others spoke, but Thomas didn't hear. *Do I dare look at Hannah even to look down at her knees alongside mine? I joined the militia from a belief. If I feel that we must fight for our freedom then I couldn't let others do it for me, but the killing, agony, blood. There must be a better way. The Quaker peace testimony? When will I see Hannah again after today? Will Father stay awhile for the business meeting? What will the meeting say about the battle at Brandywine, the British taking our cattle without paying, the damage to our fences. Do we remain quiet and passive and let it happen or do we stand for our rights? What does Hannah think about it? I hope she doesn't know about Annie Green!*

Suddenly there was a rustling and a voice, then many. Meeting was over and Thomas relaxed, looking over at his father talking to another. William eased himself away. Thomas looked for the shortest way out with the fewest number between him and the freedom of the outdoors. He gave a little smile to Hannah and nodded towards the door. She gave a quick nod of approval and they left. Younger members gathered by the side towards the burial ground, young enough that the thoughts of imminent death were absent. Only Thomas who glanced at the small headstones beyond the cemetery wall thought of it.

"What is thee thinking?" Hannah asked.

"About Benjamin, and whether he has a separate grave or all together with others, and is there a marker, a headstone, even if with no name. Will his father ever find where Benjamin is buried and leave him at Brandywine or bring him back to Willistown?"

"Thee still misses him doesn't thee?"

He nodded in agreement. "Yes, it seems so long ago, but it wasn't. He was my best friend." His voice trailed off. Hannah remained silent as William came up.

"Greetings. How's that new carriage?"

"Nice fittings," Thomas replied, "and a good ride."

"Father is pleased," Hannah offered pleasantly.

"Maybe it'll keep some minds off the British or the Continental Army."

"I hope so," Thomas said grimly.

"I want to go in," Hannah said.

"Might as well," Thomas agreed. "It'll be warmer in there."

"Maybe even hot," William said, "if they get going on this war."

"I don't want thee to say anything," Thomas pleaded.

"What does thee say, Hannah?" William asked.

"As Thomas says, silence," she answered with serenity.

"You win Thomas," William agreed. "Of course, if they become too direct, perhaps Father will become exercised. He's not one for a narrow point of view."

***

The business meeting was long and intense. Friends were involved, the issues keenly felt, the considerations close at hand, too close for most. At the end, there was not a unity regarding those Quakers of the Quarter who joined the army to fight, who broke from the peace testimony, whether they be removed from membership and 'read out at meeting.'

"I objected," smiled Phineas in recounting this sequence of events, "and others stood with me," he added, "so thee can go back to thy meeting at Willistown with the knowledge that at least at this Quarterly Meeting, there was no general agreement, only that war is bad, but not what to do about it." Phineas exuded a feeling of satisfaction.

***

Thomas was not sure how to say goodbye to Hannah. Others were offering the final pleasantries as Thomas finally took Hannah by the hand and drew her aside.

"I'd like to see thee again," he confessed, nervous for a response. It was quick in coming.

"I'd like that also," she said. Thomas breathed out in relief and hope. He wanted to kiss her but not in front of her father, especially not at a meeting house filled with concerned Friends. *I guess if they didn't toss me out for fighting, they probably wouldn't remove me for kissing, but I'm not going to take a chance. They might add the two actions together, however, and feel I should be read out of meeting!* He took Hannah by the arm and led his hand across her wrist before feeling for the warmth of her hand. He was reluctant to let go.

"See thee Phineas," Joseph announced, indicating their departure. Thomas followed his father towards their wagon, turning just once to wave goodbye to Hannah. They rumbled out of the meeting grounds, the pigs squealing from the hard bouncing.

Chapter Twenty

The snow lay thin between waving drifts in the woods as Thomas worked the sled off the cart way towards the fallen dead tree, ready to be cut for firewood. The horse breathed white smoke of heaving lungs into the cold, crisp air. The sky was pure blue and still. William stood alongside his younger brother, holding onto the stanchion of the front set of runners, as Thomas let the horse take deliberate foot falls where the snow had blown clear leaving icy leaves on the hardened ground.

"This will do," William said.

"I can see," Thomas replied, miffed from the unnecessary instructions. "I don't want to carry wood any farther than thee," he added. The sled bumped over a frozen rut as Thomas pulled the gelding to a stop. They unloaded the great crosscut saw and trudged over to the tree, knocking the snow off the upper length showing out from the deeper woods.

"Here?" Thomas suggested.

"Might as well," William replied. They adjusted their heavy coats and rawhide gloves and carefully pulled the saw across the wood, the first cut easy and straight, through the bark of the sapwood, long dried. Carefully, they pulled the saw back and forth cutting deeper and deeper, maintaining a steady pace until finally the upper trunk bent away from its own weight as the cut became sawed through. Thomas, warm sweat forming under his shirt from the work, held onto the wooden handle to keep the saw from dropping, looking at the length of the trunk and the work yet to come. William was happy for the respite. Thomas looked beyond William towards the cartway where a horse was picking its way carefully towards their farm.

"We've got company," Thomas said as William turned around.

"Who can that be?"

"We'll know soon enough," Thomas said. They stood there waiting, watching as the rider came closer. He looked up and saw the two of them standing dark against the white snow, blending into the shadows of the woods beyond. The rider abruptly turned his horse and carefully came towards them in the same path they had trod. Thomas put down the saw as he recognized Abel Green, his horse coming to a halt. Abel did not dismount.

Hello neighbor," William offered.

"I've come to see Thomas."

"And so thee does now," William answered, nodding toward his brother." Thomas remained silent.

"I've come to say that my daughter would like to see you. You've been absent and she needs," Abel Green emphasized in spite of himself, "to talk."

"How is Annie?" Thomas asked, unsure of the conversation.

"Just fine," Abel replied with a bite, "but she'd be pleased for a visit," he added, softening his approach. "I know that winter is not an agreeable time of the year to go visiting, but I found the way tolerable," he said as an encouragement.

"I've got work to do here," Thomas said defensively, "with my brother here. Then Father."

"Yes, so I see, but I trust there might be a time, soon," he said, his voice rising a bit, "when you will come see Annie." The horse stomped the frozen snow with a thud as if for emphasis. Abel looked straight at Thomas not flinching.

Thomas shifted his eyes towards William, then returned the look to Abel.

"I'll ask Father. I think he'll free me for a visit."

"This Saturday?"

"Seventh Day. Saturday, yes. I'll see."

"We'll count on it," Abel said, indicating a family interest in the visit. Abel turned the horse around and made his way back and off down the road, a slow walk that kept him in sight for what seemed to Thomas as an interminable time.

"What's that all about?" William asked as Abel went out of hearing. Thomas didn't respond until he saw Abel disappear beyond the bend, never looking back.

"I'm not sure," Thomas finally replied.

"Must be something important."

"Hope not," Thomas said with a sinking suspicion. He picked up his end of the saw and waited for William to do the same. His brother hesitated, ready to ask further, then thought better of it and grabbing the other handle, set it in place for the next cut. They were silent as the rasp of the saw sounded a cadence into the stillness of the woods.

***

"Father, may I leave off my chores on Seventh Day?"

"Thee has some thoughts?"

"Yes, Father." He waited. His father waited longer. "To make a visit."

"To whom?"

Thomas knew he would have to say. "To the Greens," he answered as innocuously as possible.

"They need thy help?"

"No," Thomas confessed, then finally, "Annie Green. She said she'd like to see me." He lowered his voice in case his mother might overhear.

"Well, as thee will. Offer our respects to the Greens."

"Thank thee, Father."

"Take the mare," Joseph said. "It's cold and a long walk alone through the snow."

***

Thomas put on his second best pants, brushed off his boots, and took his heavy coat off the pegged rack adding a muffler and hat, close over his ears to keep the cold at bay. The mare was content to be saddled and let out of the barn. Thomas adjusted the stirrups and mounted, giving a gentle kick below the ribs, urging the horse on and out into the midday cold, the sun casting a gray light through the overlying clouds. Thomas had little to do in guiding the horse down the path on to the cart way and into the road, marked by wagon tracks through the soft snow. The horse kept a regular pace, slowing at the bottom of little creeks, then with an extra effort regaining the far side to resume the pace. Thomas let his mind wander, his body rocking in concert with the motion of the horse. *Benjamin would like this ride,* he dreamed. *He always did like being out, just us, in the snow and cold with no one else around.* A line of snow fell off a large limb with a whoosh. *I'd rather be going to his farm than the Greens.* The horse snorted. *I wonder if the whole family wants to talk.* He dreaded the thought. *Perhaps better than Annie alone.*

Their barn appeared, then the house. Smoke billowed from the chimney as he let the horse pick its way towards the door where the snow was packed down and the hitching post was handy. He swung his leg over and jumped down. The window showed the fire within, but there was no one to be seen. He walked to the stone step reluctant to knock, but there was no help for it. He grabbed the knocker and let it fall with a thud against the heavy wood of the door. There was silence then scraping as a chair was shifted inside. The latch was lifted and the door swung open. It was Abel Green.

"We were expecting you." Thomas didn't wait for an invitation but walked in. He didn't offer his hand to Abel who remained silent and sullen. Esther Green appeared from the further room with a civilized, careful smile.

"Will you come in?" It was a needless gesture since Thomas was standing there, his coat and muffler still on, hat in his gloved hand.

"Thank thee," replied Thomas.

"I expect you have come to see Annie," she determined.

"Yes ma'am."

"She is right here. Annie. Your Thomas has come," she called hopefully. Thomas remained silent. Esther Green gave an embarrassed cough, not sure what to say. She looked at Thomas then turned and went back into the other room. Abel Green stood there, silently watching. Thomas put his hands behind his back and tried to act as nonchalantly as possible as it became more uncomfortable. Abel didn't move. Thomas averted his eyes, looking around the room, watching the flicker of flame in the fireplace. The steps squeaked and Annie Green came into the kitchen, passed by Abel, and with a smile, gave her hand to Thomas.

"How are you?" she asked. "Well, I hope." Her hair was neatly brushed, tied behind and tucked beneath a fresh bonnet. She gave a tentative smile.

Thomas nodded, and then got enough moisture onto his lips to get out, "Fairly well."

"It's hard in the winter," she said lightly. She looked at

her father who shifted his head and went back to the other room, leaving the door open.

"Did you walk here?" she continued.

"No, Father let me ride the big mare."

"Is it in the barn?" she asked, concerned.

"No. Just at the hitching post."

"Then we must get it out of the cold. It's too much weather to stand out for long." She hurried over to slip on her heavy shoes and coat. "Come," she insisted. Thomas was relieved to be out of the house, warm in his greatcoat, not anxious to take it off to suggest a longer visit. Annie pulled open the door and let him out. The flanks of the mare began to shiver. Thomas rubbed his hands over the neck and nose of the horse, then took the reins and followed Annie to the barn.

"There's room enough by our two," she said. "Just in the middle there. Company for ours and warmer for yours." She was efficient as she shifted the Green's horses back against the stable area.

"Thanks," Thomas said. "It is better. The cold can bite."

"Are you well?" Annie asked carefully, coming from behind their gelding. "You haven't visited."

"I'm fine," Thomas answered, "but Father keeps me busy. I haven't had time." His breath was white in the cold of the barn. She remained by him, not touching.

"Do you like me? Do you love me? Do you care about me?" The questions suddenly flooded out. Her eyes glistened. The stream of words ended with a struggle of hope. He swallowed hard. He had not expected the questions so soon.

"I like you," he finally answered. "You're a nice girl." He stopped.

"Is that all?" she asked hesitantly.

He nodded.

"Do you care for me?" In the dark of the barn he could see her eyes as they reflected the pale light from outside. They were clear and staring.

"Yes," he answered more confidently.

"I need you," she said. "I need you very much," she continued in a plea.

"Why, when thee has thy family and I know Caleb cares for thee?" He shifted away slightly.

"I need you because I'm pregnant and you're the father of our unborn child." She said it in a practiced cadence, rehearsed in her mind over the past several weeks. Thomas was unmoving, his heart racing, a swirl of heat across his face that turned quickly cold. He was afraid to shift, fearing any movement would provoke Annie in a way he feared, but would not understand. "I'm going to have your baby," she added for emphasis.

"How did that happen?" he asked, groping for words, knowing the shallowness of the question. "It can't be," he continued denying the statement. "I don't believe it."

"You have to believe it. It's been two months gone by."

"Gone by what?"

"You know. When a person is pregnant."

"Was there Caleb?" He was trembling.

Tears came to her eyes.

"Caleb keeps talking about thee, keeping company with thee, for others to know that thee is his."

"What does he know. Boastful talk, muscles bulging, bravado. It's what he wants to believe. But you're different, full of life, optimism, with deep feelings. You were willing to save him at Brandywine, in danger to your own life."

"Who told you?"

"Not Caleb of course."

"Oh!"

"It was Joshua. He let me know." She was quiet, breathing deeply. "I love you," she said, "still, in a way perhaps you…"

"When?" Thomas asked, his mind racing to catch up with the wave of emotion surging over him.

"Late spring," she said with certainty. She turned up to Thomas. "Will you marry me?"

His stomach heaved, his breath stopped, his muscles tightened.

"I love you," she said tenderly and waited.

"I can't," he said. She said nothing, the answer explicit. "Thee's Baptist and I'm Quaker."

"I'm willing to change."

"It's not that simple." He searched for the way to the real truth. "I'm in love with another," he finally said, snapping the silent string of hope Annie held out.

"Not even your child could make a difference?" It was a question he had not considered. Then the vision of Hannah came and the choice for Thomas became clear.

"No."

"What will people say if I have a child and I'm not married?" She wanted to cry.

"Thee'll not be the first and Caleb would be happy for the chance to marry thee."

"And have him raise your child?"

"If need be." Thomas became more resolute. The baby was unknown, but Annie was and so was Hannah.

"Will you come see me again?"

"Maybe, if work needs to be done."

"What will I do?" she pleaded again. Thomas wanted to get away. He didn't want to answer to Abel, or Annie's mother, or her sisters. He wanted to be gone, to escape.

Annie Green burst into tears. "I feel awful," she said. "I was so happy." She pushed her hands against her front, pressing down. "I don't know what to do," she said again.

"Thee will be fine," Thomas said helplessly. "Thee has family and will make Caleb a wonderful wife." Annie Green sobbed. Thomas was unsure what to do. He finally put his arms around her and she buried her face against his chest. Her heaving subsided, hands up in her front as if to brace herself. Thomas waited quietly, not saying anything. He released his hold on her, hesitated, then pulled away.

"I must go," he said, pushing open the barn door, backing his horse out into the late afternoon, the gray light of the winter sun filtering through the trees. He threw the reins over the head of the mare and with a quick lift was up into the saddle. He headed the horse for the path, then leaned back towards the barn. Annie was hidden inside. "I do care about thee," he called out, loud enough he hoped, then nudged the horse forward onto home.

Chapter Twenty-One

"William. Thomas. We've gotten a letter back from the Masseys. They will visit us week after next. Thy mother and I are pleased they accepted our invitation to come to Edgmont for several days."

"Will Hannah come with them?" Thomas asked.

"Yes. Their sleigh fits three nicely, so we'll need to have the two of you sleep in the loft. We'll give over your room to them." Joseph was expansive.

Thomas couldn't help himself. *'I wonder if Mother has another motive, or Father, or both of them?'*

"Thee's silent, Thomas," his father said.

"Just thinking," replied Thomas.

"Thy mother hopes thee's pleased," Joseph said, confirming Thomas' suspicion.

"Yes Father, very."

"Sounds too good to be true," William jibbed, not oblivious to his brother's interest in Hannah.

"Well then, thy mother needs thy help to clean and polish."

"So Hannah will be impressed," William said.

"Now, don't thee talk ill of that girl," Joseph said. "She's a right nice person."

'Thank thee, Father,' Thomas thought.

***

William preceded Thomas as they climbed the ladder to prepare the loft. His arms were full as he carried the linen sack filled with dried and scratchy wheat stalks to soften the hard boards onto which they were both to sleep. Thomas followed with two heavy wool blankets and linen sheets that would makeup the rest of the simple pallet.

"It's going to be cold sleeping up here," William said.

Thomas did not answer. He was quiet. He faced his brother. "William?" He hesitated.

William waited.

Thomas finally blurted out. "Annie Green is pregnant!"

"Yes?"

"She thinks I am the father."

William let out his breath and puckered his lips as he tried to find an answer.

"I'm not sure that I am," Thomas continued. "It might be Caleb's."

"So now I know why you were so anxious to go and help Abel Green." William was serious.

"I don't want to marry Annie. She's nice and all that but it's Hannah that I love and I want to marry her." He looked into William's eyes. "What shall I do?"

William thought for a minute. "Well, you're not the first to face this sort of situation, and I guess you won't be the last."

"What can I do?" Thomas implored his brother.

"If you don't love her, there's no sense in making yourself miserable and eventually Annie miserable by marrying her."

"What if I am the father?"

"Then there's going to be a child running around this area that may look something like you—boy or girl."

"I don't want to hurt Annie. She's a good girl."

"And you think she'll make Caleb a good wife?"

"Caleb thinks he owns her."

"Then hope that Caleb gets to marry her."

"What do I tell Father?"

"Nothing yet. But you owe it to him and Mother to let them know before long."

Thomas lowered his head and said softly, "Do I tell Hannah anything?"

"If you propose to Hannah and she agrees to marry you, then I think you need to say something. You don't want her to hear about Annie after you're married. Keep it simple. Not much detail. Just enough. You might be embarrassed but you'll get through it all." William grabbed Thomas by the shoulders. "You're growing up. Faster than perhaps you figured." His hands squeezed a bit then released. "You're a good brother."

"Thanks," Thomas replied with a weak smile. "I didn't mean to get into this trouble."

"Don't continue and make it worse," William said. "There's some pain now, but it will settle down, slowly perhaps." He turned towards the ladder. "We better get down out of this loft or Father is going to think we're changing everything around."

***

Light snow drifted across the cartway, leaving it white and cold with a bright sun shining over the fields and woods with only the frozen creek showing an even surface. Thomas was outside, replacing chestnut rails into the worm fence bordering the field along the way to their house. He worked carefully, listening for any sound. Only the caw of deep black crows flying from branch to branch broke the stillness. Thomas stood up, stretched, and looked up the lane. A slight jingle sounded. He waited, then heard the sound of sleigh bells across the hill. He dropped the rail and walked quickly back towards the shed where the sleigh would be kept, brushed the snow off his coat and put his gloves into the pocket, his hands bare in spite of the cold. At the last minute, he took off his hat and smoothed his hair. The sleigh came into sight and Phineas Massey urged the horse to a slow trot to make a show of their arrival. Thomas stood at the bottom of the slope as the horse found its footing in the snow. The black of the sleigh was accented by red stripes on the curve of the body, the bells on the shafts dancing a confused tune. The Masseys offered a festive air coming to a stop at the end of the lane. Thomas was happy to see Hannah with red cheeks and a bright smile beside her mother. Joseph heard and came out.

"Greetings Friend," he called to Phineas, "and thee too Suzanne, and of course thee too Hannah." He stepped around to help them down but Thomas got there first. He took hold of Hannah's hand as she stepped out. Phineas jumped on his own helping Suzanne.

"Welcome to Edgmont," Joseph said to the three. "Let's get you inside. It's right nippy out and Thomas will place thy sleigh and settle thy horse."

"William," Joseph called. He appeared around the corner of the springhouse. "Help thy brother here, before it's too late and thee will have to do it thyself." Thomas was deep in conversation with Hannah, ignoring the activity around.

"Here, let me help thee with thy case there," Joseph said to Phineas as they headed for the warmth of the house.

***

It wasn't until after supper when everyone removed into the large main room that Hannah and Thomas were alone in the kitchen, scrubbing the pots and carefully banking the fire for overnight.

"Its nice to see thee again," Thomas said.

"And thee." Hannah moved closer. They sat on the bench watching the fire. Thomas was full of things to say, not sure where to start. It was Hannah who spoke. Thomas listened, then they both talked faster in their exhilaration.

***

As the evening wore on, Joseph called out to his son from the other room.

"Thee needs to let Hannah find her bed now. They've had a journey."

"Yes, Father," Thomas answered. It was now his chance he figured. *'We're alone.'* He took Hannah's hand. It was comfortable as she molded hers into his. He smiled at her, hesitated, then as she looked up with an openness and anticipation, he said, "Hannah."

"Yes." She was helping.

"We get along with one another."

"Yes."

"And I like thee."

"I like thee very much. Thee's nice," and she squeezed his hand in encouragement.

He swallowed. "Will thee marry me?"

"Oh, yes," she answered immediately.

"I love thee," Thomas said softly, relieved that he had finally said it.

"I loved thee from the first time thee came to our place. I've known since then." He brought her to him and gave a long kiss. He didn't care if anyone saw them. It was now theirs to have.

***

The following morning, Thomas got up early, anxious to see Phineas Massey alone. Thomas worked the fire, then adjusted the large pot, filled with porridge, over the rising flame. Hearing nothing from upstairs, he took a pitcher in the gloom of the pre-dawn out to the springhouse and dipped some milk from the crock sitting in the cold but unfrozen water. He held back the cream to return again to the surface of the crock. He brought the milk back to the kitchen, setting the pitcher onto the great table. He was fidgety and nervous as he brought out bread, laying a large knife alongside ready for cutting. He lined up cheese, butter, and blackberry jam. The dawn was close. He listened and heard steps. His heart raced. *Is it father?* he wondered. *Or Phineas Massey?* He walked over to the doorway into the kitchen, then thought better of it, came back and, reaching for the lantern, took a wooden taper from the fire and set the wick ablaze with its little flame. Suddenly, the kitchen became more welcoming. The door opened and Phineas Massey stepped down.

"Thee's up early," he said to Thomas, "thought I'd be the first."

"I couldn't sleep longer," Thomas replied, sharing the truth.

"Well, I thought I'd go see after our horse, check out how she's gotten along in a new stall."

"I'll accompany thee," Thomas offered.

"Always happy for help," Phineas said. "Thy barn. Thee can make sure I don't miss a step." He put his arm out to go. Thomas opened the door and they made their way across the packed snow to the barn, pushing open the full door to let Phineas go in first. It was warm and musky from the horses, sheep, and pigs huddled together in their own enclosures. Phineas rubbed his hands alongside the horse's neck, then stroked its nose.

"She seems fit," he said.

"It's a tight barn," Thomas replied. "Father made sure of that."

"Well, then, shall we get back into that warm kitchen?"

"Yes." Thomas stood by the door holding the handle but not moving.

"Well?" Phineas asked perplexed.

Thomas hesitated then said, "I'd like to ask something of thee."

"Go on then," Phineas replied impatiently.

"Its about Hannah," Thomas said, building up his courage. Phineas was silent, less anxious. "I'd like to marry her," blurted out Thomas, happy for the shadows in the barn unsure of the reaction. The breathing of the horses and the seeping cold from the door ajar tumbled into his apprehension.

"So that's it," Phineas exclaimed in a comforting voice, "that's why thee is willing to help me on a frozen morning in the barn before we've had a bite to eat and a little warmth for our insides." He laughed, understanding Thomas' nervousness. "Well, Thomas, thee needs to satisfy Hannah more than me, but I do have a question or two." He pulled the door shut. "Does thee love Hannah?"

"Oh, yes, Friend—uh—sir." Thomas was not sure how to address his future of father-in-law.

"And does Hannah love thee?"

"She said so."

"If that be and thee will care for her, then thee will have our blessings and permission."

"Do I need to address thy wife?" he asked.

"No, Thomas, and thee would know that this

conversation is not a surprise. Suzanne surmised that there was more than one reason to come here and she suggested that thee is a right nice young fellow. No, we would be happy for thee as a son-in-law." Thomas relaxed, smiling in spite of himself.

"Thank thee" was all he could figure out to say in reply. Then, "I do love her," he added in confirmation.

"I'm happy for that," said Phineas, "but it's getting cold out here and I'd just as soon be back in the warmth of thy house." He allowed Thomas to lift the latch and push out into the lightening day. They walked alongside one another.

"Do thy parents know?" asked Phineas.

"I haven't talked to them because I only asked Hannah to marry me last night."

"Well, I won't say a thing, let thee do the talking, but I don't think it'll be a surprise to them," he said with a tight-lipped, squinting smile. "Besides, young Thomas, women always know these things before men folk." His smile became open.

The kitchen was filled with the scraping of iron on the hearth and talk from the night before that had not been completed.

"Oh, Thomas," Jane said. "Did thee bring in this milk and set the pot to heat?"

"Yes, Mother."

"Can I speak to thee and Father?" Thomas asked.

"Why certainly," Joseph replied. "Go ahead."

"Maybe in the next room?"

"Don't worry," Phineas insisted. "We'll go to the next room, then thee can have thy parents to thyself." He took his wife by the hand and pulled her away from the table and out from the kitchen.

"So, what is all this that thee needs to speak to us?" Joseph was interested. Jane stood back quietly setting the dishes in place, confident and serene.

"Well Father," Thomas said with excitement, "I've asked Hannah to marry me."

"That's nice."

"And she said yes."

"That's better!"

"And Phineas Massey gave me his permission."

"That explains his constant smile," Joseph said understanding, "and Jane, does thee know?"

"I suspected," she replied with a lively look to her. She put down the knives and came around to Thomas. "She's a fine girl," she said, giving him a hug.

"Thee has a good one," Joseph confirmed.

"So do I have your assent also?"

Joseph looked at his wife. She nodded. "Of course," he replied, thumping his son gently on the back. "We're very happy for thee." There was laughter in the next room.

"I guess that thy Hannah has just come down," Jane said. It was William who came into the kitchen next.

"What's all this talk? It's hard to stay abed with all this noise and commotion about."

"Thy brother is going to marry Hannah," Jane said.

"Oh, I thought it was something really important," William said as he grabbed Thomas' hand.

***

First Day worship was shortened to be followed by the monthly meeting for business. The meetinghouse was dank and chilly, the big central stove giving out the only heat, little smoldering brass charcoal pots taking the chill from the legs of people fortunate enough to have brought one. Thomas knew that his service in the militia would be a subject for consideration. He was happy to see Abner Baldwin there with his family. *At least I will not be the only target of the elders,* he thought. *I wonder what they'll say about Benjamin's death with his family here?*

The clerk called the meeting to order, and a moment of silence was observed. The concern for the Quaker response to war was brought up immediately. Those against fighting mumbled in approval as an older member exclaimed, "We must have nothing to do with either army."

"I agree," many quickly repeated.

"Fighting has no part in the quest for peace," said another. More undercurrent of approval.

Then Benjamin Darlington's father stood to speak. "Do we not give our young people the encouragement to come to their own decisions? Must we condemn all who disagree with us?" He spoke with a deeply felt passion, against his own beliefs, but in support of a son who felt differently and acted upon that belief and lost his life for it. "I cannot condemn my own son," he said, his voice breaking.

It was Joseph Pratt's turn. "I have struggled with our peace testimony. I believe in it. George Fox, our founder, let the concern out for all to consider. Not all can hold to it. Thomas here by right of independence of determination with our country in mind came to a different conclusion than most of us here in this meeting house who can avoid war for we're too old to fight." There was grumbling behind him. "But there is another consideration to come before this meeting." Friends looked up at him paying particular attention. "Thomas here has asked Hannah Massey, sitting beside him, to marry, and under the care of this Meeting." He let the words drop slowly and distinctly. The tension was broken as the Meeting knew that by reading Thomas and Abner out of the Meeting and the Society of Friends that they were criticizing and condemning one of their own killed in battle, a mark against the Darlington's, an action thus taken from which there could be no response from Benjamin. But the call of marriage to another Quaker girl, apart from war, was a welcome diversion. The Meeting struggled without agreement about those who fought, but by the end took the marriage under its care determining to consider further the Quaker peace testimony. It was awkward for the weighty elders, for to speak against Thomas was now to speak against Hannah and the Masseys. The Meeting was torn, and consensus evaporated. Thomas could hardly sit still as his future was debated. He was relieved that the marriage had overtaken the concern for his military service. The ride home in the Pratt family great sled was a relief. Thomas pressed close against Hannah. He was happy.

Chapter Twenty-Two

The British left Philadelphia for New York, leaving the city denuded, ransacked, but free. The Americans, reinvigorated, broke camp at Valley Forge and followed the British into New Jersey, Pennsylvania no longer the scene of war, of fighting, of spilled blood. The tension in Chester County was released as Quaker farmers could once again sell their product to merchants, either Patriot or silent Loyalists, the others having gone with the British. The challenge for the Quakers of Philadelphia and surrounding areas became less of statements and actions against war than for a return toward normalcy with everyday affairs. The armies in New Jersey seemed far away from the tranquility that returned to Chester County. Early summer brought with its softening weather, a renewed recognition for the abundance of the land and a spirit of hope for independence.

***

Phineas Massey promised a farm to Thomas and Hannah as they rode to Willistown Meeting to be married in the manner and after the fashion of Friends. Thomas held Hannah's hand tightly as the horse stepped lively on the dirt road to the meeting house. He was exhilarated. Hannah trembled with a becoming nervousness. The meeting grounds were filled with carriages, horses quietly nibbling any spare grass still standing, families entering into the meeting house. The day was bright, blue, and clear with steady wafting breezes blowing the heat of the summer away, a day of perfect comfort. The Meeting settled and after a time, Thomas glanced at Hannah for readiness. They stood, and facing each other repeated their vows. "In the presence of God and these our friends, I take thee Hannah to be my wife, promising with Divine Assistance to be unto thee a loving and faithful husband so long as we both shall live." Hannah repeated the same words to take Thomas to be her husband. The certificate was placed before them to sign, read to the gathering, and the marriage was accomplished. Meeting continued with messages of support and faith and joy for God's benevolence.

Chapter Twenty-Three

Thomas couldn't help from smiling as Meeting ended, the overseers shaking hands, the tension released. He and Hannah were married. It had happened. They stood as Phineas Massey came forward and held out his hand to Thomas. "Nice to have thee as a son," he said. Thomas felt different as he held out his hand, knowing he had become part of another family. They moved outside, others stepping aside giving the couple the chance to be first out, to be greeted by the small group of family and friends. Thomas had a feeling of exuberance placing his hand in Hannah's with a gentle squeeze.

"Are you two ready to go?" asked Abner. He had driven Thomas up from the Pratt's farm and was now to take Phineas' new carriage and best mare to drive the couple back to the farm for the anticipated great midday dinner, everyone bringing his own special offering. Abner stood, holding the horse while Thomas with a new solicitousness helped Hannah up into the rear bench. He followed quickly to sit along side his bride. Abner leaped up and with a flick of the reins, urged the horse towards the road to lead the light-hearted procession on. Thomas still with a broad smile looked at his new wife with admiration. She had a fresh, pure look about her, her best dress of silk in a muted soft brown, falling gracefully down to her new leather shoes well turned and supple in the same color. Abner urged the horse into a trot, feeling important for the task and pleased for Thomas' good fortune. As they came to the crossroad, standing there waiting were Caleb and Joshua.

Abner slowed to a walk as Caleb stepped forward holding up his hand.

"So you're now married?" he said.

"Yes, thank thee," Thomas replied, anticipating good wishes.

"Well that's all right I expect," Caleb added with a curl to his lips.

"Meet Hannah," Thomas offered, "my new wife."

"So you're the one who succeeded?" Caleb said with a hint of sarcasm. "Nice to meet you." He turned back to Thomas. Joshua came alongside Caleb. "Thought you'd like to know," Caleb said, "that Annie Green has given birth to a baby. A boy."

Thomas remained silent, the smile gone.

"That's nice," he finally said quietly.

"And guess what his name is?" Caleb continued, with Joshua chuckling, nudging the other.

Thomas didn't answer.

"Thomas," Caleb said in a direct loud voice. "That's right. A new baby boy by the name of Thomas. Thomas Pratt," he emphasized. Joshua burst out laughing.

Abner, stunned, watched as Caleb stared up at Thomas, then shifted his gaze to Hannah. Caleb's smile became a sneer. Thomas was embarrassed in front of his bride and shifted uncomfortably. He struggled for a retort.

"She's yours now," he snapped, staring down at Caleb.

Abner realized that there was no good to come from any further talking and snapped the reins. The carriage drew away with a shake. Caleb and Joshua burst into laughter, standing in the dirt of the road. Thomas reddened with a rising anger. Hannah held his hand tightly.

"It's no matter," she said. "We're married now."